Barbara Murphy worked in advertising and publishing before becoming a full-time writer. She currently lives in Southampton.

KATHLEEN

When orphaned Kathleen O'Connor receives an unexpected legacy, she fights against a working-class background and sexual discrimination to achieve her dream of becoming a barrister. It is expected that she and Desmond Marshall, a special-needs teacher, will eventually marry, but her loyalties to her career and the young man who shared her wartime childhood are to be tested. While defending photographer Paul West on a rape charge, Kathleen finds herself increasingly attracted to him and his glamorous lifestyle. Now Kathleen must face a trauma that seems destined to change her life forever.

Books by Barbara Murphy
Published by The House of Ulverscroft:

JANEY'S WAR
FIVEPENNY LANES
A RESTLESS PEACE
A GIFT OF TIME

BARBARA MURPHY

◆

KATHLEEN

Complete and Unabridged

ULVERSCROFT
Leicester

First published in Great Britain in 2004 by
Robert Hale Limited
London

First Large Print Edition
published 2005
by arrangement with
Robert Hale Limited
London

British Library CIP Data

Murphy, Barbara
 Kathleen.—Large print ed.—
 Ulverscroft large print series: general fiction
 1. Women lawyers—Fiction
 2. Large type books
 I. Title
 823.9′14 [F]

 ISBN 1–84395–887–2

Published by
F. A. Thorpe (Publishing)
Anstey, Leicestershire

Set by Words & Graphics Ltd.
Anstey, Leicestershire
Printed and bound in Great Britain by
T. J. International Ltd., Padstow, Cornwall

This book is printed on acid-free paper

For my god-daughter, Nancy, because I love her — and she had the good sense to fall in love with James

Acknowledgements

Legal procedures and terminology have changed considerably during the last fifty years, and I am deeply grateful to the following for their time, knowledge, and memories:

The Bar Council
Inner Temple
The Inns of Court and the Bar Educational Trust
David Hoad and Mike Haseldin (Winchester Crown & County Court)
Nancy and James MacNish-Porter
Patricia Lane
Paul MacDougall (CMC Coffee suppliers)

I also found that the autobiographies of John Mortimer and Geoffrey Robertson, and Henry Cecil's books, were invaluable aids to the essence of the period, as well as being hugely entertaining and interesting.

The staff at Exeter University were kind enough to send me details of the transformation from college to university status and details of the law courses.

A word of thanks also to Martin Taylor of Habitat, Sister Carol Biddlecombe, and the staff of Seadown Veterinary Hospital, Hythe, for answering my questions.

As ever, the staff at Hythe Library continue to help when I am struggling to find the reference book I need — with such nice smiles, too. And I shall always be grateful to my agent, Judith Murdoch, for her support.

1

The lilac taffeta dress rustled as Kathleen moved in front of the wardrobe mirror. Carefully, she placed the headdress on top of her dark curls. Auntie Nell had made it: two circles of flowers, held in place by a velvet Alice band. Now she only had to pull on her gloves, silvery-grey, like her shoes, with their impossibly high heels.

'You look lovely, Kathleen. Really lovely.' Jane smiled at her in the mirror.

'Thank you. But your guests will have eyes for no one but you.' She smiled back. 'Sandy will think he has died and gone to heaven.'

The door opened. 'Our car's here, Kathleen . . . ' Auntie Nell began, and then stopped, staring at the bride. Kathleen could have sworn she saw a glint of tears as Mrs Harrison murmured: 'Rose would have been proud of you, Janey,' and gently lifted the veil to cover her daughter's face. It was a wonderful moment.

Auntie Nell turned to Kathleen. 'You look very nice, too, dear.'

'Thank you. And isn't your hat absolutely gorgeous with that outfit.'

'It should be, the price I paid, but . . . '
Jane's mother peered into the mirror. 'You
know about these things, Janey. Is it too
young for me?'

Jane laughed. 'Of course not. The mother
of the bride should wear the smartest hat in
church. It couldn't be better.'

'Well, if you're sure. I don't want to show
you up in front of all your posh friends from
the magazine.' She adjusted the hatpin. 'And
you'll be the next bride Fred will give away,
Kathleen. Don't leave it too long, or this
outfit will be out of fashion.'

Kathleen didn't really want to pursue that
line of thought. But Auntie Nell was
persistent.

'Have you and Desmond fixed a date yet?'

'Oh, no. We haven't talked about it at all.
Not really. I've only just got my law degree.
There's no point in tying ourselves down with
anyone before we're both qualified.'

'With anyone? Who else would there be?'
Auntie Nell looked quite bemused. 'You've
been friends since you were children. Never
gone out with anyone else.' She shook her
head. 'I still can't believe that our
little Kathleen is going to be a solicitor,
and her intended will be a headmaster one
day.'

'Sometimes I have to pinch myself. Oh, my,

hasn't it been the most wonderful year, to be sure?'

'I know. Who would have thought that Janey would be asked to commentate on all those lovely gowns at the Coronation? And to cap it all, she's going to marry a surgeon.' Auntie Nell's mind went off at another tangent. 'Pity Sandy's best man couldn't make the rehearsal. Were they at medical school together?'

Jane nodded. 'And they both did their National Service together in Korea.' She glanced at Kathleen. 'You'll like him. He's great fun.'

Suddenly, Auntie Nell looked flustered. 'I don't know whether to wear the white gloves or the navy ones.'

'The navy ones,' said Jane, firmly. 'If you get the white ones grubby you'll fret all day.'

'Goodness, that would never do. Ah, here's Fred. Make sure she's on time, won't you?'

Uncle Fred laughed, but his eyes were fixed on Jane.

'I thought brides were supposed to be a little late,' he said. 'And I'd like just a moment with my daughter, if you two beautiful ladies don't mind.'

'Come on, Auntie Nell. You said the car was waiting.' Kathleen blew a kiss to Jane.

An hour ago, the house had throbbed with

chatter. Buttonholes were distributed, shoes shined, brushes and combs in constant use, and Jane's grandfather proudly showed everyone the new suit he had treated himself to from the Fifty-Shilling Tailors. Now they had all left for the church, after frantic last-minute visits to the bathroom, and the house was strangely quiet.

As always, the neighbours came to their doors to look and wave. Kathleen had asked Mrs Harrison to travel with her, as she would have felt rather self-conscious on her own in the huge limousine.

Both women were immersed in silent thoughts on the journey. Auntie Nell fingered the signet ring she wore on a chain around her neck, probably thinking of Rose, just as Kathleen was thinking: *If only Mam and Da' were here.*

As Kathleen followed Jane along the aisle, she noticed some of the aunts, uncles and cousins she had met from time to time, and some unfamiliar faces. A group of young women, impeccably dressed and made up, must be Jane's colleagues from the magazine, and the young men ogling them from the other side of the aisle were bound to be Sandy's doctor friends. They looked extremely well turned out in their hired morning-suits. As they drew level, Desmond turned, but his gaze was on the bridesmaid, not the bride. Slowly, he took off his glasses and cleaned them on his handkerchief, something he always did, even as a child, when he was anxious or excited. Kathleen hoped it was the latter, but found his intent expression rather disconcerting, and quickly glanced away. Sandy was looking at Jane with complete adoration and, by his side, his best man turned and looked directly at Kathleen. His fair hair was slightly longer than Desmond's neat cut, and curled slightly as it reached his collar, giving him the look of a grown-up cherub. But there was nothing cherubic about the wide grin that slowly spread across his face, nor his wink. Now she didn't know where to look and, feeling somewhat breathless, she didn't respond at first when Jane turned to face her. Then she remembered her duties, and took the sheaf of apricot tea-roses from the bride.

It seemed strange, hearing the service completely in English and not using the Latin language she was used to in her own church, but it was quite lovely and, in no time at all, they were guided through to a pleasant garden behind the church, for the photographs. Everyone seemed to have brought along a Brownie box-camera, and there were three official photographers, so there should be plenty of choice for the album.

There was little opportunity for Kathleen to speak to Desmond before the wedding-breakfast, but Tim Henshaw, the best man, was seated next to Kathleen at the top table, and she couldn't have had a more attentive companion. After he had made sure that everyone was in the right place and had read the grace, he told her about his parents' home in Hampshire, his years of training alongside Sandy, and their harrowing time in the field hospital. It didn't bother Kathleen throughout the soup and fish courses, but when the *coq au vin* was served, she laughingly suggested that they talk about something other than amputations and war wounds.

'Of course.' He didn't seem in the least perturbed by her request. 'Trouble with us doctors is that we're so used to all the gory details, we forget about those who haven't stood around the operating-table for hours on end, and then happily tucked into steak and chips afterwards.' Tim signalled to the waiter for a refill of their wine-glasses, before he went on: 'This must have cost a few bob. Are Jane's ma and pa loaded?'

Kathleen burst out laughing. 'Far from it, although they are loaded with kindness itself. The magazine is running a feature on the beauty editor's wedding, so they were quite generous, and I think Uncle Fred had taken out an insurance endowment when Jane and Rose were born, for such an occasion.'

'Ah, yes. I remember Sandy talking about Jane having a twin sister. Tough luck, though, the poor kid being blown to bits so close to the end of the war.'

Suddenly, Kathleen didn't feel hungry any more.

'Sorry.' Tim looked concerned. 'It can't have been much fun for any of you.' He finished his mouthful. 'We were lucky. Our village is miles away from Southampton so we didn't get the bombing.' He paused for a moment. 'My war came later, in Korea. That wasn't much fun, either, but it's not the same as losing your home, or your family.' He squeezed her hand. 'Sometimes I just open my big mouth without thinking. Didn't mean any harm. Sorry.'

As Kathleen turned to look at him, she was touched by the expression on his face. It was almost like that of a child who had just realized he had been naughty, but desperately wanted to be forgiven. She smiled, to show her forgiveness.

'Let's hope and pray that we never have another war,' she said.

'I'll say 'Amen' to that,' Tim replied. He pointed to a huge pile of greetings-cards and telegrams in front of his plate. 'I'm supposed

7

to read these out in a minute, but we'll be here all night if I do. Any suggestions?'

Kathleen could see his point. 'Well, all the telegrams should be read out.'

'What? Even the rude ones?'

'Surely there won't be any that are too rude?'

'You don't know our chums at King's. Perhaps I'd better vet them first.' He pushed some of the cards towards Kathleen. 'Do you think you could help me out by putting these in some sort of priority. You'll know whether Great-aunt Agatha is the one who might be leaving Jane some of her lolly, or whether she's the dear old soul who couldn't care less whether her loving wishes are aired or not.'

Kathleen certainly knew one or two aunts who would be very put out if their names were not mentioned. Lesser things had caused family feuds. By the time the coffee cups were produced, she had three neat piles prepared for Tim.

'Must read the first one, some of the second if there's time, but don't worry about the third.'

'Thanks. I knew you were a sweetie.' His smile was as engaging as it had been in church, and had the same effect on Kathleen, who used one of the cards to fan her cheeks.

She had wondered how Uncle Fred would

cope with making his speech, with so many of the guests being strangers to him. He was obviously nervous, and cleared his throat a few times, but his words were straight from the heart and warmly received. Auntie Nell looked quite proud as she patted him on the arm after he sat down.

Sandy's speech followed the tone of his father-in-law, leaving no doubt that both men loved Jane dearly. As he ended he handed a small package to Tim.

'This comes with our thanks, Tim. You've done an absolutely splendid job today — well, apart from putting two of the guests into the wrong car. I understand that they are now in Southend, tucking into a plate of jellied eels, and will be with us before the bar closes.'

'You lying so and so.' Tim laughed. 'I rescued them before the car reached the church gates.' He looked at the package. 'Can I open it now, or do I have to wait for Christmas Day?'

'Go on, then.'

The silver cuff-links were promptly used, and Tim's existing ones relegated to the box.

'Thanks, Sandy — and Jane.'

Sandy passed another small package along to Kathleen.

'I asked Jane to choose something nice, as I

don't have a clue.' There were one or two caustic remarks from his friends before he went on: 'It comes with love from both of us.'

The package contained a gold locket and chain, with a card, written by Jane, *To my nearly-sister, and very best friend Kathleen.*

The locket opened, to reveal two blank spaces for photographs. Kathleen knew she would be able to find a snapshot of her mam and da' that she could use.

'Thank you,' she whispered, knowing Jane would understand that she was perilously close to tears.

At last it was time for Tim to respond to Sandy's toast to the bridesmaid. For a long moment, he stared at Kathleen, again with that captivating grin.

'This is the fourth wedding I have attended this year,' he began, 'and I confess that I have frequently scoffed at the willingness to be shackled to one girl for life, until . . . ' he paused dramatically, 'until I saw the bridesmaids. There were some absolute beauties, and I'm a connoisseur.' He waited until the raucous laughter died down, and then went on: 'However, I can honestly say, hand on heart, as you can see, that never have I had the good fortune to behold such a stunning bridesmaid as the young lady at my side, and I couldn't be more grateful to Sandy for asking me to be his best man.' He looked around the room. 'Actually, I think the best part is still to come, when I lead Kathleen on to the dance floor.' He waited for the ripple of laughter to subside, and then picked up the first pile of telegrams.

Kathleen knew she was blushing, and there was nothing she could do about it. Although he had had wine with his meal, Tim was not drunk, and he had an excellent turn of phrase, which delighted the guests. Suddenly, Kathleen caught sight of Desmond, sitting next to his grandmother, who was laughing at one of Tim's comments. But Desmond wasn't laughing. He wasn't even smiling. Slowly and deliberately, he was polishing his spectacles, but the expression on his face as his eyes flitted from Kathleen to Tim was very strange. Oh, dear.

2

As the band set up their music-stands and hotel staff moved back some of the tables, Kathleen excused herself and searched for Desmond, but he was not sitting with his mother and grandmother. Then she spotted him, standing at the bar, drinking a large Scotch with a rather morose expression.

She pushed her way through the small group around the bar, and tapped him on the shoulder.

'Hello, Desmond,' she said, 'lovely meal, wasn't it?'

He turned and looked at her, before draining his glass and ordering another. Eventually he muttered: 'Hello.'

'I haven't had a chance to speak to you all day.'

Desmond shrugged his shoulders.

'With the best man giving you such devoted attention, why should you want to speak to me?'

'Because *we* are old friends, and I've only just met Tim Henshaw.' Kathleen tried to curb her growing frustration. 'I thought you would realize that etiquette demanded that the best man and bridesmaid would be together throughout the meal.'

'Being together for etiquette is one thing, drooling all over each other is quite different.'

'Oh, Desmond, for goodness' sake! Anyone would think you were jealous.'

'Jealous? Why should I be jealous? You have a perfect right to drool over anyone you like, without my permission.'

Kathleen knew it was the whisky talking, so she bit back the retort from the end of her tongue and softened her voice.

'I'm sorry if you misunderstood and thought I was drooling over Tim. I was only being polite.'

'Ha.' His laugh was short. 'I should have thought that telegrams and cards were a simple enough task for any best man to manage, but you obviously thought it necessary to sit with your heads touching, in a very intimate manner.'

'There were too many greetings to read out, so Tim asked my advice as to which ones he could safely leave out, as he doesn't know the family. There! Does that satisfy you, Mr Suspicious?'

'I suppose so,' he conceded, after a pause, 'but it looked like drooling from where I was sitting.' He picked up his glass and tossed the whisky down his throat.

'If anyone is drooling, it's you, right now. Will you look at the state of your jacket?'

He had drained the glass so quickly, half of it had tipped down his front.

'Oh, hell!' He dabbed at it with his handkerchief. 'Never mind, Moss Bros always clean the suits after each hiring. Would you like a drink?'

'Not just now, thanks. My head is already spinning from the wine.' As he ordered another whisky, she felt like adding, *And I should think you've had enough, too.* But it wasn't her business, and wouldn't help the uneasy truce, so she went on: 'Anyway, I came over to ask you whether we can perhaps fix that date to see *South Pacific* in a couple of weeks' time.'

Desmond's back was turned to her as he paid for his drink, and it seemed to stiffen, but he didn't answer. Perhaps he hadn't heard, with the hubbub around the bar.

'Would you still be wanting to see *South Pacific*?' she asked, watching his face as he turned towards her, not meeting her eyes.

'Actually . . . I've already seen it,' he said, staring into his glass.

'You've what? But didn't we agree that we would see it together?'

'That's what I thought, but you kept putting it off. It wasn't my fault.'

'Only because of the wedding, and my starting a new job on Monday. I thought you understood that I still wanted to see it, but just a bit later. Why should you want to go on your own?'

Desmond looked even more uncomfortable as he swirled his drink around his glass. 'I didn't go on my own. I went with Sylvia. She's taking the same course as me. I might have mentioned her once or twice.'

'More than once or twice, actually. And to think you had the nerve to question my behaviour with Tim.'

'It's not like that, Kathleen. But she already had the tickets, and her mother wasn't well, so Sylvia asked if I would like to go.'

'And you said yes, knowing that we'd already arranged to see it.'

'I thought maybe you'd gone off the idea.'

'The only person who went off the idea was you.' Her voice was cold.

Now he looked at her face. 'Please, Kathleen, don't be like that. We can see something else.'

'I don't want to see something else. I wanted to see *South Pacific* and you knew that.'

'Sorry. Didn't think it was that important.' His speech was beginning to react to the alcohol.

A ripple of applause interrupted their conversation as the band played the introduction to *Waltz of my Heart* and Sandy and Jane led the dancing. Kathleen noticed Tim making signals across the room.

'I think the best man wants to dance with the bridesmaid,' she said. 'If that's all right with you, that is.'

'Of course. Look, Kathleen, I'm sorry, but it all got a bit out of hand.' As she walked away, he called out: 'Will you save the last waltz for me — please?'

She stopped and looked back at him, already unsteady on his feet. 'I doubt whether you'll be able to walk, let alone dance, the state you're in,' she answered. 'Will you go and get some coffee, Desmond, before your mother notices.'

Back at the top table, Tim was holding her locket and chain.

'Lover's tiff?' he asked, nodding towards Desmond.

'We're certainly not lovers,' she said.

'Just good friends, as they say.'

'We've known each other a long time. But that doesn't give either of us the right to be . . . ' she paused, not wanting to go into details.

'Possessive?' he suggested.

'Exactly.' She looked at the jewellery in his

hand. 'Could you fasten the clasp for me, please. I'd like to wear it.'

'Thought you might.' His fingers were warm on the back of her neck. 'And I'm glad.'

'About what?'

'That I'm not treading on someone else's toes.' He led her out on to the dance floor.

'As long as you don't tread on my toes, I really don't mind.'

She needn't have worried. Tim was an excellent dancer, and they waltzed, quick-stepped and cha-cha-cha'd happily together for the next hour or so, until it was time for her to help Jane change.

After Sandy and Jane had been waved away to catch the night ferry to the Channel Islands, a huge sign telling everyone they were **JUST MARRIED**, and a collection of tin cans clattering at the back of the car, Desmond's mother sought out Kathleen.

'We're taking my son home,' she said. 'He really isn't used to drinking.'

Kathleen nodded.

Laura hesitated before she went on, 'I know it's none of my business, but did you and Desmond quarrel? He seems very upset about something.'

'He's not the only one.' Kathleen realized her voice was sharp, and she apologized. 'I'm sorry, Laura. Yes, we did — have words, but I'd rather not talk about it, if you don't mind.'

'Of course. There's only one thing, dear. How are you going to get home?'

'Tim has already offered to drive me back to the flat.'

'But won't he have to wait until the end, to pay the bills for Sandy and so on? It might be rather late.'

'That won't matter. I've promised Auntie Nell I'll help her with boxing up the cake, and gathering up presents and flowers and things, so I'll be here till the end, anyway.'

'I see.' Laura sounded as though she, too, was reading more into the situation than it warranted. 'Well, I'd better help Len get my son home and into bed. He'll probably have a sore head in the morning, which should teach him a lesson.' She leaned forward to kiss Kathleen's cheek. 'Good luck for Monday.'

'Thank you. I'm looking forward to it.'

'Good. And Kathleen . . .'

'Yes?'

'Don't worry too much. I'm sure it will all blow over. These things usually do.'

Kathleen knew she was referring to the quarrel with Desmond, so she just shrugged and watched Laura walk across to her son, who was sitting with his head in his hands, looking very sorry for himself. Jane's uncle looked up and waved goodbye to Kathleen as he helped Desmond to his feet. Kathleen wasn't sure that Desmond could have walked out unaided, but at least he hadn't disgraced himself too much.

It was quite late by the time Jane was tucked into Tim's little car. They didn't converse much, and when they arrived at her flat, he looked across at her.

'I suppose there's no chance of a cup of coffee?'

'Oh, Tim. It's been such a long day, and I'm very tired. Do you mind?'

'Of course not, silly.' He grinned cheerfully as he came round to help her out of the car. 'I'm feeling a bit whacked-out myself. All this responsibility isn't good for my health. But I'd like to give you a ring some time. Can I have the number?'

She hesitated only momentarily. It was unlikely that he would telephone. People never do, she thought. When he'd snapped his diary shut, he looked at her for a long moment, then said:

'Thank you, Kathleen O'Connor, for today.'

She looked surprised, but he just shook his head and held out his hand. 'I've really enjoyed meeting you.'

'So have I.' His handshake was warm. 'Tim — do you think you could help me with the flowers, please? I don't want to drop the key.'

He waited until she had unlocked the door of her flat, then handed her the two bouquets. Swiftly, he kissed her on the cheek.

'You're the nicest bridesmaid I've ever met,' he said, and then ran back down the stairs to the street.

Although tired, Kathleen could not sleep at first. Too many thoughts were racing around her mind. The wedding; the argument with Desmond; Tim's cheeky grin. Although she had sometimes gone to the pictures with fellow-students, she had never allowed herself to become too involved. Her studies were too important for complications, and there was always Desmond in the background. She had never contemplated being kissed by anyone other than Desmond, but she could not help wondering what it would have been like if Tim had kissed her on her mouth. Then her thoughts went to Sandy and Jane. They would be crossing the English Channel now, snug in their little cabin. She felt her body glow as she contemplated the thought. Her mam had told her once that there was something magical in the expression of love between man and wife, but she really couldn't imagine it, and felt she should stop her thoughts rambling along such a path, or she would not know how to confess to Father Donovan.

The telephone woke her the next morning before the alarm clock. It was Tim.

'Hi. I told you I'd ring you.'

'You didn't say seven o'clock in the morning.'

'Sorry. Did I wake you?'

'Well, you just about beat the alarm clock.'

'Good. I had you down for an early riser, not someone who lies in bed on a Sunday morning.'

'Actually, I usually go to early mass. Then I have the rest of the day clear for whatever.'

'You're a Catholic?'

'Yes. There are quite a few of us around.'

'Don't be so defensive.' He laughed. 'With a name like Kathleen O'Connor, I should have guessed. Anyway, when will you be back from church?'

'About nine.'

'And then you have breakfast?'

'Usually.'

'Can I gatecrash and share a crust of bread and cup of coffee with you?'

Kathleen had never entertained a young man at breakfast-time before.

'I suppose so,' she said, wondering why he wanted to come so early.

'Good. And I thought perhaps we could

21

have a run out to the country. It's a glorious day.'

'Is it? I haven't woken up enough yet to notice.' A furry head distracted her for a moment. 'Go and get your lead, Bridie. I'll be with you as soon as I'm dressed.'

'I didn't know you had a dog.'

'You didn't ask.'

'That's true. I don't know much about you at all. But we have a whole day ahead of us to rectify that.'

'Tim, I'd love to, but I have to go to the cemetery with the flowers. And Jane's mother might need some help.'

'We can go to the cemetery straight after breakfast. And I'm sure, if you phone Mrs Harrison, that she won't mind in the slightest. She told me that her family were not driving back to Devon until tomorrow, so she is surrounded by helpers. Now, take your four-legged friend for a walk before she leaks all over the place. I'll be with you at nine.'

Kathleen stared at the receiver, the dialling tone informing her that Tim had hung up. Then she laughed aloud.

'You really are incorrigible, Tim Henshaw, but I suppose I'd better do as you command.'

As she turned the corner of the road, just before nine o'clock, she saw the car parked outside the row of shops. It had been dark the night before, so she hadn't taken much notice of it, but now she was able to admire the sleekly polished bottle-green exterior — it was a Morgan, and very sporty, like its owner.

For a few moments, she was able to study Tim Henshaw without his knowing she was watching. His fair hair shone in the morning sunshine. With his tweed jacket, college scarf loosely around his neck, and sunglasses, he looked exactly right to be driving such an exclusive little car.

Suddenly he heard her footsteps and turned round to wave.

'Nice timing,' he called, as he tumbled out on to the pavement. He wasn't exceptionally tall, but most people were taller than Kathleen, so she always had to look up into their faces. Tim's face was a nice one to look up into, she decided.

'I've a couple of rashers in the larder,' she said, 'and might even be able to run to an egg on the plate as well.'

'Sounds good to me.'

Tim was quite useful in the kitchen, insisting on helping with everything, and making a great fuss of Bridie. While Kathleen poured him a second cup of coffee, he glanced around the room. 'How did you manage to find a nice little pad like this?' he asked. 'There's not much to rent close to London.'

'I was lucky. When Jane's brother, Jack, married Sheila, they moved into his prefab. I was looking for something and Sheila's flat was ideal.'

'Sheila? The attractive redhead?'

Kathleen nodded.

'Quite a challenge, taking on a widower with a handicapped boy like that,' Tim went on. 'Sandy tells me he's been looking for a specialist who might be able to help.'

'But not in this country, I'm afraid. Sheila has worked wonders with exercises, but unless we win the pools ... ' Kathleen pointed to a framed painting of Brixham harbour on the wall. 'Johnny did that.'

'Really?' Tim stood up to have a better look. 'He's a very talented lad. I like his use of colour.' He looked round at Kathleen. 'Right. Shall we go?'

'Will you wait just a moment?' she laughed. 'First I want to know where we are going?'

'Oh, didn't I tell you? Sorry. Just thought we'd have a run down to Hampshire. Could drop in on Ma and Pa for lunch.'

'Tim! You can't drop in and expect lunch, just like that.'

'Why not? They're used to me doing that,

24

and there's usually a Sunday roast big enough to feed an army.'

'But they don't know me.'

'Well, that won't take long to put right.'

Kathleen shook her head. 'I'm sorry, Tim, but I can't possibly just arrive on someone's doorstep, uninvited.'

'I'll phone them, if that will make you any happier.'

She hesitated. 'It's not only that. There's Bridie.'

The little dog responded to her name and nuzzled into Kathleen's hand, before turning her loving attentions to Tim, who tweaked her silky ears.

'I'd love to take you with us, Bridie,' he murmured, 'but those two enormous wolf-hounds would go berserk if I tried to introduce you.' He looked at Kathleen. 'What did you do with her yesterday?' he asked.

'My neighbour fed her and took her for a walk.'

'Well, that's all right then. I'm sure she wouldn't mind doing it again.'

'Tim! I can't . . . '

'Yes you can. Please?'

He looked so appealing that Kathleen began to relent.

'If Mrs Andrews *does* agree,' she said slowly, 'I can't be out too late. It's not fair on my very good neighbour, and I have a million things to do this evening.'

'Cross my heart.'

'OK. The phone's over there.'

While Tim was waiting for the operator to connect his toll call, Kathleen popped next door to speak to Mrs Andrews.

'Noticed the nice-looking young man sitting in that gorgeous little car,' she said. 'Who is he?'

'Tim Henshaw. He was Sandy's best man.'

'Another doctor?'

Kathleen nodded.

Mrs Andrews smiled knowingly. 'Well, that should make Desmond sit up and take notice.'

Kathleen couldn't help laughing as she said: 'It already has. But it's only a run out to the country.'

'If you say so, dear.' Mrs Andrews looked as though she didn't believe a word of it, but she changed the subject. 'Did the wedding go well?'

'And wasn't everything as perfect as could be?'

'You'll have to tell me all about it. And I'd love to see the photographs.'

'As soon as I get them I'll ask you in for a cup of tea.'

Mrs Andrews smiled happily. 'Off you go

then, dear, and enjoy yourself. Don't worry about Bridie. She's no trouble.'

Kathleen made a mental note to buy some flowers for her neighbour.

Back in her flat, Tim was replacing the telephone receiver.

'Mother said she's looking forward to meeting you,' he said.

'Another kind lady, like Mrs Andrews.'

'So your pooch is fixed up? Good. Have you phoned Mrs Harrison?'

'I'll do it now.' Kathleen had a thought. 'Am I all right like this?' She had chosen a turquoise-print dirndl skirt and white cotton blouse.

'You look as fresh as a daisy. Better take a headscarf, though, and perhaps a cardigan for coming home. It can be a bit breezy.'

At the cemetery, Kathleen laid Jane's bouquet on Rose's grave, thought a prayer, then moved on down the path to the two graves with the name O'CONNOR on the headstone and placed her own posy on the grave with the long list of engraved names, thinking how ironic it was that there had been so little left to bury of her nearest and dearest, just like Rose, whereas Theresa, in her little grave, had been unmarked, but just as dead. Theresa had been Jane's first friend at the grammar school. She should have been a bridesmaid yesterday. Deeply thoughtful, Kathleen moved the posy to Theresa's grave.

Tim stood quietly behind her, reading the inscriptions.

'So many names,' he murmured. 'Was it a direct hit on your house?'

'On the shelter. Flying bomb.'

'How come you were OK?'

'I was staying the night with Jane.'

'Thank God.' His gaze went to Theresa's grave. 'Why is this sister not with the others?' he asked.

'Theresa was killed by the blast from a stray jettisoned bomb when she was evacuated.'

'God, that's rough.'

Kathleen nodded. 'Theresa was the clever one, the first in our family to pass the scholarship.'

'Do you have any other relatives?'

'Only Great-aunt Bernadette in Ireland. She wanted me to take holy orders, but Mr and Mrs Harrison offered me a home, and Jane's Uncle Len became my guardian. The war was still on and he wanted to make sure I would be taken care of if anything happened to the Harrisons. He was a bachelor then, and still at sea, but when he married Laura, she agreed that he should put me through university. They are all saints.'

'And did Great-aunt Bernadette keep in touch with you?'

Kathleen shook her head. 'I don't even know if the poor soul is still alive.'

'Poor soul, indeed. Not much Christian charity from your only relative.' Tim glanced around at the neat rows of well-tended graves. 'Shall we go?'

The Morgan whizzed them through London and the suburbs until they climbed the Hog's Back and stopped to admire the stupendous view and stretch their legs.

Tim hadn't talked much so far, but now he told her about his sisters. Kathleen lost track of the number after he mentioned one who was married with two small children, one who was a GP, one who was mad on sport, or was that the one who was at university? Suddenly, he stopped talking, and looked out across the Surrey and Hampshire countryside.

'Sorry for rabbiting on so,' he eventually said. 'It was just — seeing all those names on the grave, some of them so young, I realized how lucky I am to have a family.'

She smiled. 'Are you the only son?'

'Yes, and it has its advantages. Lots of their gorgeous friends around the place, and never had to help with the dishes or things like that.'

'Yet you helped me?'

'Ah, well, I've had my own little bachelor pad for a while now, and the nurses soon put me in my place. Not that I minded the place they put me in.' His grin was mischievous.

Soon they were swerving around a network of narrow winding lanes until they slowed and stopped between a pair of imposing iron gates, opened to reveal a long drive with a circular turning-area in front of one of the loveliest houses Kathleen had ever seen. The Virginia creeper climbing up one side of the front door glowed in the early autumn sunshine, while a rambling-rose splashed pinkly against the wall on the other side. The windows had tiny diamond panes and were open, as though to welcome the sunshine, and visitors. Sweeping lawns flanked the drive, softened by a variety of shrubs and trees.

'It's beautiful,' she breathed.

'I have to admit I've always been rather fond of the old Henshaw residence,' Tim said. 'Funny thing is, none of us could wait to get on with our lives somewhere else, but it's the one place we all come back to as often as we can manage.' The gravel scrunched beneath the tyres as the car moved slowly along the drive. 'Let's see how many of us wanderers will be sharing Sunday lunch today.'

3

The succulent aroma of roasting meat followed Tim's mother as she came out of the kitchen, wiping her hands on a towel.

'Ah, there you are, my dear,' she said, quickly shaking hands and offering her cheek to Tim. 'Come and talk to me while I baste the joint. Tim will get you something to drink.' Before Kathleen could answer, she looked over her shoulder. 'You're not Jewish, are you?'

Bewildered, Kathleen shook her head.

'Only it's pork, and when I saw your lovely dark hair . . .'

Crouched in front of the oven, she glanced up at Kathleen. 'If I'd noticed your eyes first, I would have realized. My goodness, what a magnificent colour. And those lashes. You're Irish, aren't you?'

Kathleen laughed, realizing that Tim had inherited her talent for hopping swiftly from one sentence to another. 'Yes, I am — and it really is very good of you to allow Tim to bring me at such short notice.'

'Nonsense. We're used to it by now. They all do it. Lovely to have a house full. Do sit

31

down, dear. Shove those newspapers under the table. Now, where did I put that thingy?'

Kathleen found the glass baster under the potato-peelings and watched as the older woman went about her task. She was fair, like Tim, probably mid-fifties, and slim. Looked attractive in her floral dress and tiny frilly apron tied around her waist. Must have been very pretty as a young girl. Now she was telling Kathleen about the local butcher.

'All through the war I saved our scraps for his brother.'

Kathleen guessed that all would be explained in time.

'And in return,' Mrs Henshaw went on, 'we were provided with a very nice leg from time to time.' Kathleen concentrated, trying to work out the story behind the words. 'I wonder whether he'll still want our scraps when rationing ends? Next year, they think, don't they?'

'They hope so. So — your butcher's brother is a farmer?'

'Of course. Only pigs. Best in Hampshire.' Her face slightly flushed, Mrs Henshaw closed the oven. 'I wonder where my son has got to with those drinks?'

On cue, Tim arrived with a tray. 'Gin and lime for you, mother.'

'Thank you, darling.'

Tim handed a tall glass to Kathleen. 'Thought you might prefer a shandy, after that dusty ride.'

It was just what Kathleen needed.

'Father at the golf-course?' Tim asked his mother, who nodded.

'With Olivia. They should be home soon.'

'When does Olivia go back to Oxford?'

'Not until next month. Still, she helps to keep Charles out from under my feet when he's not in London.' She put her glass down. 'Now, I do want to talk to you — sorry — I've forgotten your name.'

'Kathleen. Kathleen O'Connor.'

'Beautiful name. Suits you. And you must tell me all about yourself.' Mrs Henshaw's attention wandered to the cooker. 'Cauliflower, carrots, runner-beans — that's the last of them, I'm afraid. Ah, yes. Mustn't forget the apple-sauce.' She selected two huge cooking-apples from a garden trug standing on the table.

'Can I help at all?' Kathleen asked.

'That is kind of you, my dear. Perhaps you could lay the table in the dining-room? Tim knows where everything is.'

'How many of us today, Mother?'

'Only five, dear, although Phyllis did say she might come over for supper when we get back from evensong.'

They had just folded the last napkin when Tim's father and sister arrived, heralded by the frantic barking of two enormous dogs, who pushed their way past his legs and into the dining-room, to jump up at Tim with enough force to make him stagger backwards.

'Whoa! Romulus. Remus. Down.' His orders were completely ignored as he stood in front of Kathleen and warned: 'Whatever you do, don't let them jump up at you. They won't bite, but they could flatten you with excitement.'

Kathleen didn't think that being flattened was much of an option, and was thankful when Tim's sister took control.

'Bad dogs!' she snapped. 'Go to your kennels.' She pointed to the door. 'Behave yourselves.'

Kathleen still cowered behind Tim as the two hounds slunk out of the dining-room.

'Gosh! How did you do that?' she asked.

'Easy — who said that?' Tim's sister looked astonished.

Mr Henshaw shook hands with his son. 'Have you taken up ventriloquism?' he asked. 'It's very good. I didn't see your lips move.'

Tim stepped to one side and revealed the tiny figure of Kathleen.

'No, but I wouldn't mind having Kathleen sit on my knee,' he joked.

'Tim!' She knew she was blushing scarlet.

'Oh, ignore him,' his sister said, holding out her hand. 'I'm Olivia, one of his siblings. Are you one of his nurses?'

'No. We only met yesterday.' Kathleen felt as though she was saying all the wrong things but couldn't find the right things to say. Tim rescued her.

'Kathleen is Jane's closest friend. She was her bridesmaid.'

'Ah, yes. Sandy's wedding.' Mr Henshaw's handshake was almost as powerful as his daughter's. 'Pleased to meet you, Miss . . . ' He raised an eyebrow.

'O'Connor,' Kathleen murmured, trying not to wince.

Mrs Henshaw swept into the room, carrying a bottle of wine which she handed to Tim.

'Don't be so stuffy, Charles. I'm sure the child would rather be called Kathleen.'

'Yes, please.'

'Thought so. Tim, there's a corkscrew somewhere.' She turned to her husband. 'You two had better clean up. Lunch is almost ready. You can bore us with the golf details during lunch.' At the door, she turned back. 'Not for long, mind. I want to know all about Kathleen.'

Just like the dogs, Mr Henshaw and Olivia

made a hasty exit. Stunned, Kathleen caught Tim's eye, and they both burst out laughing.

'You'll get used to them,' he said eventually.

'I think your family are wonderful,' she said.

'Do you?'

'Well, Auntie Nell is kindness itself, but she would go mad if anyone brought a stranger home for a meal.'

'Why?'

'Because she has to have two weeks' notice to clean the house from top to bottom, and everything has to be just so.'

He chortled. 'Oh, God, she sounds like Mrs P.'

'Mrs P?'

'Mrs Peak. The lady who does for mother. Lives in the village, cycles up here every morning, Monday to Saturday. Keeps everything in order. But on Sundays, mother has the kitchen all to herself. Total chaos, but we always have a splendid lunch.'

'The garden is huge. Is that your father's domain?'

'Good God, no. Mr P comes in twice a week to mow the lawns and look after the vegetable garden. Mother does the flowers and fiddly stuff.'

The roast pork was delicious. While Mr Henshaw and Olivia argued over various points of their game of golf, Kathleen was able to study them quietly. Mr Henshaw had an air of authority about him, like an officer in the army, and his eyes were watchful rather than distant. She wondered what he did in London. Olivia, too, had an air of no-nonsense. Not at all like her brother, or her delightful mother, who flitted through the conversation like a butterfly.

It wasn't until she was dishing up the apple-and-blackberry-crumble that Mrs Henshaw turned her attention again to Kathleen.

'What did you say you do, my dear?' she asked. 'Cream jug's over there.'

Tim laughed. 'She hasn't had a chance to get a word in yet, Mother, and I confess I haven't asked her. Very remiss of me.'

'That's all right.' Kathleen said. 'Actually, I start a new job tomorrow, with a legal firm.'

Olivia held out her hand for the cream jug.

'Secretarial?' she asked.

'No. As an articled clerk. It's my first job, actually.'

Mr Henshaw stopped eating.

'Are you planning to take it further?'

'A solicitor is probably about as far as I can go.'

'No aspirations to become a barrister?'

Kathleen smiled. 'Aspirations, yes. Finances, no, I'm afraid.'

He nodded. 'Costly business, going to the Bar, I agree.'

Mrs Henshaw interrupted. 'It took you a long time to reap your just rewards. More crumble, Tim?'

'Thanks.' He motioned to the sideboard behind Kathleen, cluttered with family photographs. 'Did you notice father's photograph?'

'No, I'm afraid I didn't.' Her head swivelled around. There it was, tucked behind the larger frames of a wedding picture. A younger Mr Henshaw wearing his barrister's wig.

'Father's a QC now.' Tim's voice had a hint of pride.

'Really?' Kathleen gasped. Why hadn't Tim told her? But then, she hadn't asked, either.

'Where did you take your law degree?' Mr Henshaw went on.

'Exeter. And I've just completed my year at the Chancery law school.'

He nodded. 'Good college, Exeter. About time they had university status.'

'With luck it will be within the next couple of years.'

'Isn't this nice?' Mrs Henshaw seemed to be thinking aloud. 'I'll get the coffee. Shall we sit in the garden?'

Half an hour later, Olivia decided she

needed some exercise.

'Do you play tennis?' she asked Kathleen.

'Afraid not.'

'Not to worry. I expect Tim will give me a game. Do you mind?'

A few minutes later, Kathleen watched as brother and sister wandered down to the tennis court that was only just visible through the trees.

'I'll do the dishes if you like,' she suggested to Mrs Henshaw, who shook her head.

'Olivia and Charles usually do them later on,' she said. 'We like to let our meal settle first.'

Mr Henshaw stood up. 'Think I'll have a turn around the garden. Would you like to accompany me, Kathleen?'

'Very much. Are you coming, Mrs Henshaw?'

'Oh, no, my dear. I'm quite comfortable here. Did you see where I put the Sunday newspapers?'

Kathleen retrieved them from under the kitchen table, feeling guilty about the saucepans and dishes strewn around, but it wasn't her place to insist.

'Now, off you go, and don't let Charles bore you with all that legal talk.'

'I shan't be bored, I assure you.'

'Good. Charles — remember you are in the

garden, not in court.'

He smiled. 'Yes, dear.' He whistled the dogs. They made no attempt to jump up at Kathleen, just frolicked behind.

As they watched the tennis players, Mr Henshaw said; 'Sometimes I think Olivia should have decided to be a jolly-hockey-sticks gym-teacher instead of a politician.'

'Is that really what she wants to be?'

'Oh, yes. Now she's got her degree in economics and politics, she's working for her PhD.'

Kathleen was impressed. 'You must be very proud of your family,' she commented. 'And they of you.'

He paused to light his pipe. 'Dora hates it in the house,' he explained. After a few moments of sucking and puffing, he went on: 'Proud of them? Yes, of course I am. And I suppose they are proud of me in their own way. At least they've been able to make their own career choices, and not worry about surviving on baked beans.'

'Was Mrs Henshaw an academic as well?'

'Dora?' He burst out laughing. 'Good heavens, no. Straight out of one of those rather exclusive girl's boarding-schools without a clue where she was going.' His expression softened. 'Everything was changing after the Great War. I didn't want to stay

40

in the army, but I knew Dora and I were right for each other as soon as I set eyes on her.'

Kathleen remembered her father making the same remark once.

'So.' He shook the flame from the match and they walked on. 'What made you decide to take up law, Kathleen O'Connor?'

She thought about it. 'Several things, actually. The Harrisons gave me a home during the war, and I desperately wanted to do something worthwhile to show my gratitude.'

'Are you an orphan?'

'Yes. Jane's uncle became my guardian and the dear man supported me through college. But I suppose it was Jane's aunt who really triggered my interest in the legal profession.'

'Was she a solicitor?'

'No. Head of the typing pool at Wainwright's. Aunt Grace encouraged me to think about becoming a solicitor, and introduced me to one of the partners. They said they would take me on if my exam results were satisfactory.'

He nodded. 'Good firm, Wainwright's. I've known Humphrey Grierson for many years. Play a round with him from time to time.'

They had almost reached the river before he spoke again.

'There is something I often ask my

students when I am lecturing, and the answers interest me a great deal. May I ask you the same question?'

She nodded.

'If you were asked to defend someone who you felt was guilty, what would you do?'

This was something that Kathleen had often wondered about, and she thought carefully before she answered.

'I realize that a solicitor or barrister must never become judge and jury,' she said. 'And everyone is entitled to a fair defence.'

'Even a murderer?'

'Yes. Until all the evidence is given, the jury cannot decide whether the accused planned the murder, or it happened in self-defence, or a fit of anger.'

'As in *crime passionnel*?' he suggested.

'That's one example,' she said. 'As you know only too well, there is a world of difference between the mentality and motives of one person who takes life without remorse or conscience, and another whose anger spirals out of control for one tragic moment.'

'What are your views on capital punishment?'

'The premeditated killers are certain they have planned the perfect murder and will get away with it, whereas the person who reacts to sudden anger doesn't have time to think about it. If it was a deterrent, there wouldn't be any murders,' she said simply. 'Also, there is always the risk of the wrong person being sent to the gallows.'

'So you would like to see the death penalty abolished?'

'Yes. It allows no room for error, and is so — final.'

As they stood on the riverbank, a heron swooped across the water, scooped a fish from beneath the surface, and victoriously flew off with its next meal.

'What category would you put that bird into?' Mr Henshaw asked, as they watched the creature disappear.

'They only kill for survival.' She smiled. 'I think a 'not guilty' verdict would be given without too much trouble.'

'I agree.'

They stood in amiable silence, watching the hoverflies skittering near the low branches of the huge willow tree that drooped into the water and gave the house its name. Further along, a rather dilapidated boathouse still housed a rowing-boat and a collection of old canoes and fishing equipment.

'I really should clear it out,' Mr Henshaw said. 'But sometimes parents are reluctant to accept that their children have grown up.' He picked up a landing-net. 'Still usable. Perhaps

I'll leave it until the grandchildren are old enough to help.'

It was a world apart from the council estate of Kathleen's childhood, and she thought how her brothers and sisters would have loved to grow up in this idyllic paradise. She also wondered if Tim realized how very lucky he was. The Willows wasn't just a beautiful house and garden. It was filled with love, just as her house had been.

After a few minutes, Mr Henshaw led the way across to the orchard, his thoughts obviously still on a legal plane.

'So there are no circumstances where you would refuse a defence brief,' he said.

'Two. If I felt certain that someone had harmed a child, I don't think I could take on their case.'

'And the second?'

'Rape. I would have to refuse if I thought for one minute that he was lying.'

'Could you be sure, with conflicting evidence? It is usually one person's word against another in such cases.'

She paused under a tree laden with russet apples.

'I might have to rely on my instinct.'

'The law doesn't allow for women's instinct, I'm afraid.'

'Instinct doesn't have a gender.' She smiled

'And I'm sure one or two male lawyers have been influenced by what is known as gut feeling.'

He reached for an apple and handed it to her. 'But we never admit to it.'

They had almost reached the tennis courts before he spoke again.

'Just a word of warning.' His voice was serious. 'Even in this year of our Lord nineteen fifty-three, there are still men who resent women as competitors. The legal profession is no exception.'

'Aunt Grace warned me about that. I can only hope that if I work hard they will realize that a female solicitor is an asset, not a threat.'

'Ah, but Kathleen — clever women are always seen as a threat.' He watched his children on the tennis court. 'So I'm afraid you will have to work twice as hard as your male colleagues. Not fair, I know, but when is life ever fair?'

He was right of course.

'And there's Dora waving the teapot at us. Excellent timing.' He paused to knock out his pipe on the heel of his shoe. 'I have enjoyed our little chat, Kathleen.'

'Thank you. So have I.'

'Given half a chance, you'll make a worthy solicitor. No chance of your going to the Bar, I suppose?'

She laughed. 'Not unless I win the football pools.'

'I'll ring Grierson tomorrow, ask him to keep an eye out for you.' He raised his voice to reach the tennis players. 'Come along you two. You know everything stops for tea.'

4

Tim was as good as his word, and drove Kathleen home after tea, despite his mother's pleas that they stay for supper. The sunset had bathed the roads in crimson and gold, promising a fine day tomorrow. By the time they reached London, the sun had dipped below the horizon and twilight darkened the picture.

'It was a lovely day, Tim. Really lovely. I will write to your mother,' said Kathleen.

'She'll like that.' He helped her out of the car, and waited, leaning casually on the bonnet. 'Well, I'd better get along.'

'Yes. I've got a million things to do after I've walked Bridie around the block. Guess you have as well.'

'I'm on call again tomorrow, so I should get an early night.'

'Yes. Well — thanks again for — everything.' She didn't know whether to hold out her hand, kiss him on the cheek, or just walk away.

'I'll phone you,' he said.

Taking her door key from her handbag, she nodded.

'Kathleen . . . ' His hand was on her shoulder.

'Yes?'

'I've been wondering all day . . . '

'Yes?' she repeated.

Suddenly, he pulled her into his arms and kissed her. It wasn't a particularly passionate kiss, but it was warm, and enjoyable — and she found herself responding.

He lifted his head and nodded.

'Yes,' he murmured. 'Just as sweet and lovely as I had imagined.' He looked up at the flats above the shops. 'I suppose there's no chance . . . ?'

She guessed he didn't mean a cup of coffee this time, and shook her head.

'Thought not. Well, it's always worth a try.' Grinning mischievously, he lowered himself into the car. 'Good luck with your new job. Who knows? You might end up as Miss Kathleen O'Connor, QC.' Without waiting for an answer, he had revved the engine, and was roaring away, scarf flying in the breeze, one arm in the air, waving.

About to turn away, she noticed a car parked in a lay-by at the far end of the shops. Desmond's car.

Before she could call out, the little Austin Seven suddenly shot off at an alarming speed, leaving her standing on the pavement, watching two sets of rear lights disappear in opposite directions. How much had he seen, or heard?

Mrs Andrews was waiting by her front door, Bridie in her arms.

'Heard the car,' she said. 'Did you see Desmond?'

'Yes, but he shot off down the road before I could speak to him. Would you know how long he'd been waiting?'

'About an hour, I think. I asked him in for a cup of tea, but he wouldn't. It was the second time he'd been over.'

'Oh?'

'He was here when I got back from the park with Bridie this morning. Asked me where you'd gone. I think he guessed you were with that other young man, so there was no point in my lying.'

'No, of course not. I'm sorry you were troubled.'

'Oh, it's no trouble, dear. Did you have a nice time?'

'Lovely, thanks.' Kathleen took Bridie from her arms. 'I'd better take her for another run around the block. Has she behaved herself?'

'Perfectly. I've just given her a bit of chopped beef and gravy with some mashed potato for her supper, so she'll only need a few biscuits.'

'Thanks. It really is good of you.'

'Not at all. Well, I'd better let you get on. You've a big day tomorrow, haven't you?'

★ ★ ★

Kathleen's telephone didn't stop ringing on Monday evening. Auntie Nell, Uncle Len, Aunt Grace from Devon. They all wanted to know how her first day at Wainwright's had been, and talked about the wedding — everything had gone off so well, hadn't it? At about ten o'clock it rang again. She grabbed the receiver, hoping it was Desmond, but it was her closest friend from college.

'Cecilia!' Kathleen gasped. 'What a lovely surprise.'

'Sorry it's a bit late, but I suddenly remembered you were starting your new job this month. How's it going?'

'Actually, I only started today, so I'm still a bit bewildered, trying to remember all the names, and who runs what department.'

'Tell me all about it.'

'Not much to tell, really. I have a mentor, Mr Jarvis, who will take care of me while I'm learning the ropes.'

'What's he like?'

'A pleasant young man. Quiet. Answered all my questions.'

50

'Good-looking?'

'Not handsome, but nice enough.' Kathleen chuckled. 'What are you getting at?'

'Just wondered if he might be available, that's all.'

'Aunt Grace told me he's married. Not that I'm attracted to him, anyway, and you really are a terrible person, Cecilia Pedlar.'

'Aren't I just?' Cecilia giggled. 'Are you and Desmond engaged yet?'

'No. And the way he's feeling about me right now, I don't think it's likely.' Kathleen explained about Tim.

'Now *he* sounds rather delicious. When are you seeing him again?'

'How should I know? I can hardly phone and ask him, now can I?'

'Suppose not. But I think I'd make some excuse. Apart from anything else, his old man could be very useful to your legal career.'

'If you keep on trying to lead me astray, I won't have a legal career. Now, will you tell me what you have been up to since graduation day? Your Christmas card didn't say much.'

'It said *Happy Christmas*. What else do you expect?'

'Oh, ha, ha. You know what I mean. Have you found a job?'

'Yes — and no.'

'That's very helpful.'

'Well, the job found me. And it isn't teaching, or anything to do with languages.'

After a pause, Kathleen asked: 'Are you likely to be telling me before midnight?'

'To be truthful, my feet haven't quite touched the ground since they contacted me, and I can't believe it myself.'

'Can't believe what?'

'I'm going to be a singer.'

Now it was Kathleen's turn to be silent. She knew what a glorious voice Cecilia had, but her training . . . her degree . . .

'I know,' Cecilia went on, 'it had the same effect on Mum and Dad. They gave me all the usual warnings, but I have to go with this, Kathleen. If I don't, I shall be thinking *what if?* for the rest of my life.'

'Are you training to be a concert singer, or for opera?'

'Neither. It's the other end of the scale.'

'Musical comedy?'

'No. I suppose the best way to describe it is popular music. Ballads, and that sort of thing. I've started writing my own songs, as well, and really do enjoy it.'

'How did it all come about?'

Now Cecilia's voice became really excited. 'It's a bit like a fairy tale, really. I'd gone to a party in Plymouth. We were singing around the piano when some guy said he worked for a record company in London. I thought he was kidding, but he gave me his card and asked me to contact him.'

'Wow! Are you going to make a record?'

'I've just cut a single — oh, how I love saying that. It will be out in a couple of months.'

'Cecilia! That's wonderful. I'll be the first one through the door at Keith Prowse to get a copy. What's it called?'

'*There's always tomorrow.*'

'Pardon?'

'That's the name of my song. Let me know what you think, won't you? And when Desmond phones you, or Tim, just play hard to get. They'll be all over you. Could lead to pistols at dawn.'

Kathleen giggled at the thought. 'And what about your own love-life? Anyone nice hovering around with a bunch of roses just now?'

'Too busy to notice.'

'Anyway, I do wish you well with your new career.'

'Thanks. And likewise with yours. We really must keep in touch. This is more fun than a serial in *Woman's Own.*'

★ ★ ★

Two weeks later, nothing had changed for Kathleen. No phone call from either Desmond or Tim. Twice she had begun to dial Desmond's number, but really didn't know what to say to him, so hung up. If he hadn't behaved so childishly at the wedding she might not have gone out with Tim the following day — but it had been such a lovely day. So why should she feel guilty?

She was still learning the ropes at Wainwright's, not having much responsibility, and not yet having had much chance to make new friends. The girls in the typing-pool were nice, but she felt slightly 'on the other side of the fence', whereas she was not yet senior enough to be included in the élite group of solicitors. This must be how governesses felt in the grand houses, Kathleen thought, not one of the servants, nor yet one of the family.

Jane had been so busy when she returned from her honeymoon, settling in at the flat in East Grinstead, visiting her parents, and catching up on an enormous backlog of work, that it was Tuesday before she phoned Kathleen. It was a fairly brief call, by their standards. The honeymoon had been wonderful, delightful, and would Kathleen like to come over for lunch on Sunday?

'We'll meet you at the station,' she said. 'And bring Bridie. Come early, so you can tell me all about your new job while I'm peeling potatoes.'

Not that there was much to tell, Kathleen thought, as she replaced the receiver. She had learned the location of the stamp- and petty cash-box, sat in with Mr Jarvis when he talked to clients who were having problems with their house purchases, thoroughly read their files, checked the surveyors' reports and local searches, struggled with the technicalities of the cylinder recording-device and then dictated one or two case-notes to go down to the typing-pool, making sure they were put in the right OUT tray.

What she desperately wanted to do was to be in court, where it was all happening. Mr Jarvis had said that she could take some documents along to the Court of Appeal on Friday morning so, for now, that was the best she could hope for. Next week, she should be working in the probate department so, on the Friday evening, she had just settled down to study a relevant file when the telephone rang.

'Hi.' It was Tim. 'Sorry I've not phoned earlier, but life has been a bit hectic.'

She took a deep breath. 'That's all right. I know how busy you are at the hospital.'

'Actually, it's a bit more than that. I've been having interviews, and finally been accepted as registrar in orthopaedics.'

'That's wonderful news, Tim. Where?'

'Southampton. So I'll be able to live at home when I'm not on call. Much more comfortable. Mum's tickled pink.'

'I'm sure. And how are your parents?'

'Fine, thanks. They send their best.'

'That's kind. When do you start?'

'Straight after Christmas. So I thought I'd celebrate the good news by taking my favourite bridesmaid out for a meal and a show.'

Kathleen couldn't believe her ears. 'That's very good of you, Tim. What do you have in mind?' She reached for her diary.

'Well, I've heard that the *The King and I* is pretty good. Do you like musicals?'

'Love them. But it's only just opened, so I would imagine it will be some time before you can get a ticket.'

'That's what I thought, but I went round to the box-office today and they'd just had a cancellation, so I grabbed the tickets.'

'That was lucky. What date?'

'Tomorrow. You are free, aren't you?'

'Yes. Where do you suggest we meet?'

'How about the Corner House in the Strand? I'll see you in the brasserie at six o'clock.'

They both had steak and chips, and chatted non-stop, mainly about Tim's new post. The show surpassed her expectations, and they were both laughing at the antics of the children in the cast when they made their way into the bar during the interval.

'Glass of white wine?' he suggested, after he'd found two vacant stools in a quietish corner.

'That would be lovely, thank you.' She smiled up at him, and then began to read the programme notes about Valerie Hobson. Suddenly, she became aware that she was being watched, and glanced up. Her instinct was right. As a group of people moved closer to the bar, she saw Desmond, standing alone. At first, she thought he was going to look away and pretend he hadn't seen her. But common sense came to his rescue and he looked back and nodded in her direction.

This has gone on long enough, she thought, so she smiled brightly and beckoned for him to join her. After all, they were grown-ups, weren't they?

'How are you, Kathleen?' he said, standing by her stool.

'I'm fine, thank you. And you?'

'Very well, thank you. Busy.'

'Yes, I guess you would be, with the new term. The more you learn, the harder it becomes, doesn't it?'

He nodded, then asked: 'How's the job going?'

'Grand, thank you. I actually went to court yesterday. Not that I did much. I'm still only a glorified dogsbody.'

His smile was still a little tense. 'What do you think of the show?'

'Isn't it the most breathtaking thing you've ever seen? No wonder it's a sell-out.'

'I was glad I ordered my tickets ages ago.'

Kathleen wondered how long ago, and whether he had intended the two of them to come together. Better mention Tim. No point in pretending she was here alone. He would be back with the drinks at any minute.

'Tim managed to get a last minute cancellation. He only phoned me last night.'

'Yes, I saw him just now.'

'It's a celebration, actually . . . ' Before Kathleen could tell him about Tim's new job, which would take him miles away, and might defuse the situation between Kathleen and Desmond, a pretty blonde girl joined them, taking Desmond's arm in a familiar way.

'Sorry I've been so long,' she said. 'The queues in the ladies-room are horrendous. You men don't realize how lucky you are.'

It was strange to see the blush rise from Desmond's shirt collar until his whole face was scarlet. Heart thumping, Kathleen waited to see whether Desmond would introduce her to the blonde, who didn't seem aware of Kathleen at all.

At that moment, Tim arrived.

'One glass of wine for you, Macoushla, and a beer for me.' Suddenly, he noticed Desmond, and grinned. 'Hello, there,' he said, holding out his hand. 'I don't think we met properly at the wedding. Can I get you a drink, and one for your friend, of course?' He beamed at Desmond's companion.

'No, thanks. I'd pre-ordered, so ours should be over there on that shelf.' Desmond looked decidedly uncomfortable as he shook hands with Tim. 'Sorry, I haven't introduced — this is Sylvia. Sylvia, this is Kathleen, and Tim.'

Sylvia! Kathleen was tempted to ask whether Sylvia's mother had been taken ill again, but bit back the sarcasm.

As they all shook hands, Sylvia said: 'It's nice to meet you at last, Kathleen. Desmond mentioned that you've known each other since you were children. Nice to keep those friendships going, I think. Perhaps we can all go out together some time, as a foursome?'

Not if I have anything to do with it, Kathleen thought, as she dabbed an imaginary splash of wine from her skirt.

'Are you feeling OK, Desmond?' Tim asked. 'You look a bit hot around the collar.'

'I'm all right, thanks,' Desmond said, rather abruptly. 'It's just a bit warm in here. If you'll excuse us, we'd better get our drinks before the bells start ringing.'

As they moved away, Kathleen heard Sylvia say:

'I was hoping you'd bring the drinks over so I could talk to . . . ' the rest of her words were lost in the hubbub.

Tim pulled a face as he took a swig of his drink.

'Ugh! Lukewarm,' he complained.

Kathleen pretended to immerse herself in the programme, but Tim wanted conversation.

'Sylvia is a pretty girl, isn't she? Not a patch on you, though.' He took another sip of his drink, and then went on: 'Actually, I don't mind a foursome night out, if you want to arrange something before Christmas?'

Surprised, Kathleen looked up. Was he being sarcastic? Or serious? She didn't think Tim was capable of malice, but he might be capable of practical jokes.

Eventually, she murmured: 'I'd rather not, if you don't mind.'

His expression was bland as he nodded.

All through the second act, Kathleen found her attention wandering as she glanced around, wondering where Desmond and

Sylvia were sitting, and whether they were watching her.

Oh, this was all too silly. Here she was, seeing one of the most raved-about shows in London, with a good-looking young man who was a great companion.

So why did she feel as though she had lost something and was afraid she wouldn't find it again?

5

Christmas Day at the Harrison's was the jolliest it had been for many a year. Thanks to Uncle Len, they had the biggest Christmas tree they could get through the door, and the downstairs rooms were bedecked with holly, mistletoe, and paper-chains. They were even able to buy some new ones from Woolworth's. All morning, Auntie Nell fussed around the kitchenette, wearing a paper hat and making sure the turkey was cooking properly, and that the saucepan holding the precious Christmas pudding didn't boil dry. Uncle Fred was dispatched into the garden to dig up the finest cauliflower he could find, not forgetting the Brussels sprouts; and potatoes and parsnips were crisply roasted. Despite all the flapping, Auntie Nell had the gift of bringing everything to completion at the same time, so that the gravy was being poured into the jug at the same moment as Uncle Fred carved the last slice of turkey.

With three excitable dogs trying to dislodge the tree-lights, and crackers exploding across the table, it was anything but a quiet household, and Kathleen was delighted to see the smile of satisfaction on Auntie Nell's face as the plates were cleared, to exclamations of praise.

'Couldn't have been better at Buckingham Palace,' Jane's grandfather commented, as he popped the last piece of Christmas pudding into his mouth.

After they had washed up and listened to the Queen's speech on the wireless, Jane and Kathleen decided to take the dogs for a walk before dark.

'Do you think Esther recognizes that our puppies came from her litter?' Kathleen mused.

'I've often wondered that myself. She certainly makes a fuss of them.' Jane called Esther to heel. 'By the way,' she went on, 'I love the record you bought me. Heard it on the wireless the other day. Didn't realize it was your friend.'

'It is rather good, isn't it. Bought one for myself. Mind you, I had a devil of a job finding it. She forgot to tell me she'd changed her name.'

'Well, Cecilia Saint does have a nice ring to it. I should imagine it would sell well for Christmas. Lovely melody.'

Kathleen nodded. 'And the lyrics are like poetry. Did I tell you she wrote it herself?'

'No! Clever girl. She should go far with

talent like that.' Midge decided to run in a circle around her sister, so the next few moments were spent untangling dog leads.

'This is more tricky than a maypole dance,' Kathleen giggled, as they swapped leads.

'Talking of tricky things, how are you getting on with the dictating machines in the office?'

'Not too bad, except that most of them are very old and decrepit, like the typewriters.'

'Aunt Grace used to moan about everything dating back to Charles Dickens.'

'The one machine I hate doing battle with is the Gestetner.'

'Oh, that reminds me of poor Miss Dawson. She used to get in such a mess, with ink everywhere. I did the copying for her whenever I could. She was never brought up to go out to work, not even as a book-keeper.'

'Dear Miss Dawson, a casualty of two wars.' Kathleen sighed. 'I loved her cottage, with the roses around the door, and that beautiful painting over the fireplace. Rather remote, though, on the edge of Dartmoor like that. Is she all right on her own?' Kathleen waited while Midge investigated a fluttering leaf. 'It's such a different world for her, after living in Knightsbridge.'

'It's strange; despite her genteel upbringing, Augustine Dawson has become quite a tough cookie, through necessity. She's an active member of the local church and Women's Institute, so she won't be bored. And she has her cats for company.'

'True, and she's over at Aunt Grace's hotel most days, helping out. Now there's another maiden lady I admire greatly.'

'Best decision she ever made was to give up working in that stuffy office and take over the hotel in Babbacombe.'

They chatted of this and that for a while, until Jane asked; 'Have you seen anything of Desmond since you bumped into him at the theatre?'

'No, although I had a nice card last week. I suppose he'll be at Laura's tomorrow?'

'Bound to be. Wonder if he'll take Sylvia?'

★ ★ ★

The restaurant was full when they arrived, and old Mr Davies soon settled by the fireside to chat with Laura's mother, Bea, who had stayed overnight. As usual, the decorations were magnificent, as was the meal. Desmond sat at the far end of the table, next to his grandmother. There was no sign of Sylvia. Afterwards, they retired to the flat upstairs and exchanged gifts. This time, Desmond sat next to Kathleen.

'Did you have a good Christmas Day?' he asked, his voice a little strained.

'Grand, thank you. And you?' Her voice was also a little uncertain.

'Once the pub had closed, we had the restaurant to ourselves, which was nice.'

'It's not often you have the chance to just be a family together, although a pity Lawrence couldn't get home. Where's his ship now?'

'Last we heard, just off Gibraltar.' There was a long silence, until he reached inside his jacket pocket. 'Here,' he said. 'Hope you find it useful.'

As soon as she saw the slim package, Kathleen realized it was the same shape as the one she handed to Desmond.

'Snap!' she cried, as they unwrapped almost identical fountain-pens.

'What's that saying, about great minds thinking alike?'

As they laughed, the ice was broken, and she found she could relax.

Desmond looked at Bridie, who was sitting hopefully by the door.

'Does she want to go out?' he asked.

'Oh, my goodness, yes.' Kathleen stood up. 'I'd better take her straight away. Laura . . .' she called to her hostess, 'Would you like me to take Patch out for a walk with his sister?'

'Yes, please. He's much more excitable than Bridie, so I had to shut him up in the bedroom.'

'I'll come with you,' Desmond offered. 'I was going to take Patch for a run, anyway.'

They walked on the common for a few minutes until Desmond broke the silence.

'I should have phoned you before now.'

'So should I. But we've both been busy.'

'Ye-es, but it wasn't that really.'

'Oh?'

'I've been wanting to talk to you since the wedding, but I couldn't get things clear in my head.'

'What things?'

'How I felt about you, about Tim, about Sylvia — and about my future.'

'And have you come to any conclusions?'

'Yes. Actually, Sylvia helped me to sort myself out.'

Kathleen waited, expecting him to tell her that he was going to marry Sylvia. But that was far from the truth.

'She's a nice girl, but when we were out, she kept looking in jewellers' windows, admiring engagement rings, and dropping hints left, right and centre. It was embarrassing.'

'Not what you had in mind?'

'No! I'm only twenty-two, and won't get a

permanent teaching-post until next year. The last thing I want to have on my mind is marriage. Not for quite a while, anyway.'

'Have you told her how you feel?'

'It all came to a head last week. She wanted me to spend Christmas with her family, and everything she said had an undertone of wedding-bells, so I had no choice, or I would have been dragged off to see the vicar before I knew what was happening.'

'It must have been difficult for you.'

'It was. Floods of tears. I felt so guilty, even though I'd never suggested for a minute . . . to tell the truth, I thought she wanted to establish her career, like you, but all she wants is a husband and children. I don't understand it.'

'Would she be good, as a special teacher?'

He thought for a while before he answered 'Not really. She's too soft, and gets involved.'

'Isn't that what those children need?'

'To a degree, yes. But they need a firm hand as well as a caring one.'

Kathleen nodded.

'But Sylvia isn't the only person I feel guilty about,' he went on.

'Oh?'

'I behaved very badly towards you at the wedding, then waiting outside your flat the next day and driving off without speaking to you. You must have thought I was spying on you.'

'To be honest, I didn't know what to think.'

'And then, when I bumped into the pair of you again at the theatre . . . '

'Ah, yes, that was a little — awkward.'

'But I realize now, I have no right to object to you going out with someone else.'

'And neither have I.'

'Just because we've known each other for years doesn't mean that we can pick and choose each other's friends. So there's no reason at all why you shouldn't go out with Tim, although I hope we can still be friends.'

'Me too. But I doubt whether I'll be seeing much of Tim in the future. He's got a new post, in Southampton.'

'Really?' Desmond sounded — relieved? Pleased?

'That's what we were celebrating.'

Laughing, Desmond shook his head 'I was exactly the same with Len when I realized he was in love with Mum,' he said. 'Stupid and possessive, expecting her to remain a lonely war widow for ever. Lawrence said it was none of our business, and he was right. I'm sorry, Kathleen.'

They walked on for a bit, deep in thought, until Desmond said:

'I've missed your company, you know.'

'So have I.'

'We do get on well together, don't we?'

'Usually.' Kathleen tried not to giggle.

'You know what I mean. It's a special kind of friendship.'

'I like to think so.' It was quite dark now and much colder. Kathleen tussled with her coat-collar.

'Here let me.' Before he pulled her scarf across her face, he briefly kissed her lips. 'To friendship,' he murmured, then scooped up Bridie and tucked her inside his overcoat. 'Come on, Patch,' he commanded his mother's dog. 'Let's get back and ask Granbea to make us one of her famous hot toddies.'

Feeling happier than she had since Jane's wedding, Kathleen quickened her step and slipped her hand into the crook of his elbow. As he hugged her arm close to his body, she thought back over the events of the year. So much had happened. The Coronation; Jane and Sandy's wedding; meeting Tim and his family; her job at Wainwright's . . .

'Penny for them,' Desmond said, glancing down at her face in the glow from a streetlamp.

'Oh, I was just wondering what nineteen fifty-four holds in store for us,' she said.

★ ★ ★

70

By the time Sandy and Jane celebrated their first wedding anniversary, Jane was pregnant, Desmond had a teaching-post at a local special school, and Cecilia had been one of the supporting acts in a gala night at the London Palladium.

As for Kathleen, she knew she had found her niche in law, especially criminal law, and was happy to study night after night to learn even more. And that was what she was doing when Uncle Fred phoned.

'A letter came for you today. It's typed and has an Irish stamp, so it might be important. Can I pop over with it? It's such a nice evening, I'll come on my bike.'

'If you're sure you don't mind. Thanks. I'll have the kettle going.'

For the rest of her life, Kathleen knew that whenever she heard the shrill whistle of a kettle, she would remember that heart-stopping moment, standing with the letter in her hand, Uncle Fred watching anxiously.

'Is it bad news, dear?' he asked. 'You've gone very pale.'

'Yes — and no. Great-aunt Bernadette has died — without leaving a will.' She handed him the letter, from the same solicitor who had written to Uncle Fred nine years ago, informing him that Miss Delaney wished to have nothing further to do with the ungrateful child. And now, this . . . Kathleen began to pour water into the teapot, until Uncle Fred stopped her.

'I'll do it,' he said, chuckling. 'It will taste better with some tea in the pot.'

While they waited for it to draw, he read the letter stating that as Miss Delaney's brother had died in the monastery two years earlier, Miss O'Connor was now the sole beneficiary.

It was the last paragraph, giving the estimated amount of the estate that made Uncle Fred turn as pale as Kathleen, and reach for a chair.

'Blimey!' he croaked. 'It's like winning the pools.'

6

'How much!' Jane's voice screeched over the telephone.

'I know. My feet haven't touched the ground since your dad brought the letter over last night.'

'Have you told anyone else?'

'Only Uncle Len. I wanted to tell him that now I can repay all the money he's spent on putting me through law school.'

'And what did he say to that?'

'He said he wouldn't dream of taking a penny, but I shall insist. It's the least I can do.'

'Did you know the old dear was as rich as that?'

'Not at all. Mam and Da' often said they thought she must be worth a bob or two as the farm was so big it was split into several lots when Great-aunt Bernadette sold it off. And I think some of it was sold as building land, so I suppose that's where most of the money came from.'

'Plus the fact that she probably never spent a penny that she didn't have to, and just hoarded all the interest. Kathleen . . . ' Jane hesitated. 'Are you sure there are no other relatives who can suddenly pop up from nowhere?'

'No. I telephoned the solicitors today and they've checked every possible avenue, and advertised for any claimants. There was one crank, but he couldn't prove any relationship, so they discarded him.'

'Well, that's a relief. Did you go into work today?'

'No. I hardly slept a wink last night, and my stomach was all over the place this morning, so I phoned Mr Jarvis.'

'You need a few days to take it all in. Thank goodness it's the weekend tomorrow. Do you have any plans?'

'Some. I want to make sure your mam and da' are taken care of. And Johnny can have that operation. Then, of course, there's yourselves and the little one. You'll be needing a deposit for a house now, and — '

'Whoa there! At this rate you'll have given all your inheritance away and not spent a penny on yourself. You must think about this very carefully, Kathleen.'

'That's what the Irish solicitor said.' Kathleen knew her friend was right. 'So I'll have a word with Mr Grierson on Monday. He's very good on personal investment and so on.'

'Good. But I wouldn't spread it around the office, if I were you.'

'But surely they'll be pleased for me?'

'Not necessarily. A large amount of money has a funny way of bringing out the green-eyed monster in some people. Just keep it between yourself and Mr Grierson. For the time being anyway.'

'If you think so.'

'I do. And Kathleen — I am so pleased for you. Believe me, it couldn't happen to a nicer person.'

'Thanks. But I would like to talk to Desmond about it.'

'OK. He's level-headed enough to not let it change his friendship with you.'

★ ★ ★

Level-headed or not, Desmond was so excited he was at Kathleen's flat within half an hour, clutching a bottle of champagne. After he had hugged and danced her around the kitchen, he popped the cork from the champagne and carried the two glasses into the living-room, still beaming from ear to ear.

'Fancy the old girl leaving everything to you,' he commented, 'after all those rotten things she said.'

'She didn't exactly leave it to me — she

just didn't make a will, so I inherited it as her only relative.'

'Really? I would have thought she'd have insisted on making a will, leaving everything to the cat's home or something, just to make sure you didn't get a penny.'

'That's what I thought, except that it would probably have been left to the church. The solicitor said he had tried to persuade her to make a will several times, but she always had some excuse.'

'Too mean to pay his fee, I expect.'

Kathleen shook her head. 'I think it was more a case of not wanting to think about death. I've come across similar cases at work. They just don't realize the problems they will cause when the inevitable happens.'

'You could be right. Anyway,' he raised his glass, 'here's to you — and congratulations.'

After the bubbles had tickled their noses, Desmond put his glass down on the table and became more serious.

'Will you need to go over to Ireland? Sort things out?'

'I'd like to go over, anyway. See her grave; meet some of the people who may have helped her over the years. Reward them.'

'I expect Len would be only too glad to go with you if you want him to.'

'Oh, yes. I'd like that.' Kathleen looked

appealingly at him. 'I suppose you couldn't . . . ?'

He shook his head. 'Sorry, but I've only just started at the school and it's difficult to have time off unless you're sick.'

'Of course. I understand. But if Laura can spare him, I'd be glad of his company and advice.'

'I'm sure that won't be a problem. But be careful, Kathleen.'

'How do you mean?'

'There might be some people who would think they have a better claim to her money than you. Don't allow anyone to talk you out of what is rightfully yours.'

'I won't, although I do want to be fair.'

'Well, just make sure you talk everything over very carefully with the solicitor, and with Len.'

Smiling, Kathleen agreed. It still didn't seem real.

'You know what else this means?' Desmond went on.

Kathleen thought for a moment. 'I can learn to drive,' she suggested. 'That would be useful.'

'Yes, it would. And you could buy a brand-new car.'

'So I could, and all.' Kathleen knew little about cars, but it was nice to dream.

'But that's not what I was thinking of,' Desmond said. 'This inheritance could make your biggest dream come true.'

It took some while for the penny to drop. Kathleen gasped. 'You mean . . . ?'

Slowly, he nodded. 'It means you can become a barrister.'

As the impact hit her, she murmured, 'But I'm half-way through my training as an articled clerk. I couldn't drop everything now. It wouldn't be fair to Wainwright's.' The thoughts rushed around her mind. 'Although — it will be months before probate is finalized. Irish law is even more complicated than English. It will give me a breathing period to think about my future.'

'Exactly. And I'm sure you won't be the first person to change horses once they have become a fully fledged solicitor.'

Kathleen wasn't sure what would be involved. She'd never come across anything like this before.

'I'll talk to Mr Grierson on Monday. Ask his advice.' A smile spread slowly across her face. 'Oh, Desmond. To think I might be able to train for the Bar!'

* * *

Mr Grierson listened intently to every word, made one or two notes, then sat back in his chair and studied Kathleen across his desk.

'You do realize that it will be several more years before you can actually be earning fees, don't you?'

'Yes, although I don't think the money will be a problem.'

He looked at the figure he had noted on his pad. 'If you invest the money wisely, you should be able to manage for quite a while,' he commented, with a wry smile.

'I'm hoping you can advise me about that, please,' she said.

'With pleasure. I can draw up a plan for you, if you wish.'

'Thank you.'

'Now,' he peered at her over his spectacles. 'There just remains the question of whether your future will be with Wainwright's, or the Bar.'

Biting her lip, Kathleen waited for him to continue.

'I'll be honest with you, Kathleen. I had high hopes of you becoming a partner here, eventually. We need new blood to replace those of us who are coming up to retirement age, and you have so much promise.' He thought for a while before he went on: 'I can understand that your circumstances have opened another door, but have you investigated exactly what is on the other side?' He raised his eyebrows and waited.

'Well, no,' she answered truthfully. 'I have a rough idea, but never thought it would be possible, so I didn't go into it thoroughly. And now all this has happened so suddenly.'

He nodded. 'What you need is some expert advice.' He tapped his pen absent-mindedly on the pad, and then looked up. 'And I think I know the right person to give it to you.'

Kathleen wondered who he had in mind, and was quite shocked when he said: 'Charles Henshaw.'

'Oh, no. I couldn't ask him. I've only met him once.'

'Well, I have known him since we were at law school together, and we still meet socially from time to time, even though he has moved much further up the legal ladder.' He smiled. 'He always asks how you are getting along, and I know he respects your abilities.'

'Does he?' she faltered. 'That's very kind — but I still don't feel I could . . . '

He raised a hand to silence her. 'My wife suggested only the other day that it was time we asked the Henshaws over for dinner again,' he said. 'I can mention your situation to him, if you wish, and ascertain whether he is willing to talk to you.'

7

A week later, Kathleen found herself having lunch with Charles Henshaw in his club, at his invitation. He seemed genuinely pleased to see her, and ordered a sherry for Kathleen and whisky for himself. They chatted of other things as they sipped their drinks. She asked after his wife, and how Tim was getting along in Southampton.

'Very well, thank you, although he makes sounds from time to time about going to Canada or the United States.'

'Any particular reason?'

'Money mainly, and opportunity. He's young, and needs to find his feet before he settles down.'

Kathleen thought about her conversation with Desmond. It was as though young men still found it difficult to settle down, even though the war had ended nine years ago. But it made sense to explore all possibilities.

The very formal waiter brought the menus. It did not take long for Charles Henshaw QC to make up his mind.

'I can recommend the cream of asparagus soup,' he said to Kathleen. 'And the chef has a beautifully light hand with pastry, so I will order the steak-and-mushroom pie, but you order your own choice.'

'They both sound perfect to me, thank you,' she said.

After the waiter had draped snowy napkins over their laps and poured water from the jug, Mr Henshaw smiled at her.

'Sandy brought Jane over recently, when Tim was home. Did they tell you?'

'No, but we've all been so busy we haven't had a chance for a social evening together for some time. Had you met Jane before?'

'No. Sandy, of course, several times, but not his wife. Very intelligent young lady. Pleasant personality. I understand that they will have a new addition to the family next spring.'

'Yes. They are both incredibly excited.' Kathleen looked around the room at the other diners, most of whom would be barristers, or possibly judges, and wondered what it must feel like to be a member of their élite society. Then she realized that Mr Henshaw was watching her, an amused expression on his face.

'This is so very kind of you,' she said. 'I know how busy you are, and to give your time like this . . .'

'Not at all, my dear. I'm very happy to have

82

such a young and attractive companion. And I do rather relish the thought that there might be a little speculation from one or two of the older members, maybe even a little gossip.'

Eyes wide, she noticed an elderly man staring curiously at her, and quickly turned back to Mr Henshaw, who was now smiling broadly.

'To tell the truth, I am certain that most of them would dearly love to change places with me, so let us enjoy the moment.' He raised his glass in greeting to the elderly man, and then became thoughtful for a while.

'Tim told me what happened to you in nineteen forty-four. That must have been a terrible blow, to lose your family at such a young age.'

'Yes, it was. But wasn't I blessed to have good people like Jane's family to take care of me?'

'Indeed. But now it appears that you are to become a woman of substance. Did you realize that your aunt intended to leave everything to you?'

'Goodness, no! Great-aunt Bernadette disowned my father when he married my mother. Mam was from Belfast.'

'Ah. Differences of faith.'

Kathleen nodded.

'Was she informed that you were orphaned?'

His voice was matter of fact, as though in court, but not unsympathetic.

'Yes. The garda traced her address, and . . . ' Kathleen hesitated for a moment, the memories still painful to acknowledge, even after ten years.

'And did she offer any assistance at all?' he probed.

'Yes.' Kathleen sipped some water. 'But it was on condition that I finish my education at the convent school in Ireland.'

'And you didn't want to leave your friends.'

'Not really. But I would have gone, if it hadn't been for the second condition.'

'Which was?'

'That I take holy orders.'

His eyebrows rose. 'Why should she insist on that?'

'She felt she had been cheated from her calling because her parents needed her on the farm.'

He nodded, and then said, 'But you did not have such a calling, I presume?'

'No. I have the greatest admiration for the nuns I know, but they all have a sense of vocation, of being called to work for God. I don't have that.' She frowned. 'Perhaps I am not such a devout Catholic as I imagine.'

'Or — perhaps — has it occurred to you that you might be destined to be called to the

Bar, rather than a religious order?'

Startled, she looked at him.

'There is more than one way of serving the Lord, Kathleen,' he said simply.

While she was thinking about this, the soup arrived. He was right. It was delicious. And he was probably also right about there being more than one way of serving the Lord.

After the waiter had removed their soup-plates, Mr Henshaw leaned towards Kathleen. 'I gather from Humphrey Wainwright that you would like to know what to expect should you decide to go to the Bar?'

'Yes, please. At the moment I am a little confused.'

'I'm not surprised my dear.' He thought for a moment, and then said; 'Let us assume that you successfully complete your articles next year, which would qualify you to act as a solicitor.'

Kathleen waited for him to go on.

'Before you could be accepted as a pupil by the Bar Council you would have to sign a declaration that you will not be a practising solicitor.'

She nodded.

'Then you can apply to one of the Inns of Court. Do you have any leanings towards a particular area of law?'

'I do feel a greater interest in criminal law.'

'Really?'

'Yes. In my exams, I always had higher marks regarding criminal and civil law, and I love delving into old cases and trying to find a similarity.'

'There will be plenty of opportunity for that,' he remarked drily. 'And I would suggest you apply to the Middle Temple. I may be able to put in a word and, if accepted, you would certainly receive an excellent grounding in criminal law.'

'Thank you.' Kathleen was finding it difficult to contain her bubble of excitement.

'It will be like going back to college, but with a far deeper intensity of learning. There will be times when your head will buzz and you will feel as though you cannot absorb one more iota. But you will think of the impending examinations, and study even harder, regardless. And, of course . . . ' He paused as the waiter quietly set the main course before them, and said, 'I should have asked earlier — would you like a glass of wine, Kathleen?'

'Thank you, no.' She smiled. 'I want to be able to take in every word you say. The water is sufficient, thank you.'

He smiled, looked approvingly at the meat-pie and vegetables, then went back to his original sentence: 'And, of course, you would have to complete a specified number of dining-terms.'

'Dining-terms?'

'Oh, yes. The dinners are a very important part of the process. There will be some role-playing, questions, and discussion of various points of law. They are not necessarily of cordon bleu standard, but they are compulsory.'

'Are there many — dinners?' Kathleen asked.

'Could be upwards of twenty. You would have to pay for each one, of course, in addition to the fees for the lectures and examinations.'

Now Kathleen began to understand why it was such an expensive process. 'And if I am fortunate enough to pass the necessary examinations, would I then be qualified as a barrister?'

'You would then be 'called to the Bar', Kathleen. A momentous time in your life. But you would still require pupillage. I expect you have heard of that?'

'Yes. Although I am not sure exactly what it entails.'

'To put it briefly, you will need a pupil master, who will take you under his wing for a year or so and attempt to teach you everything he knows.'

'Similar to Mr Jarvis, I suppose, but at a higher level.'

'Exactly. You will work from his chambers, accompany him to court, and have regular tests — to make sure that you have been listening.' He seemed to enjoy his little joke.

'And if I pass all these tests, what next?'

'You will need to apply for chambers. Not as straightforward as it sounds, and many bright young legal minds fall by the wayside if the waiting period is too lengthy. However, it often helps if you know someone.' He lightly touched his nose.

For a while they concentrated on their food, although Kathleen was digesting his words as avidly as the crisp pastry.

As Mr Henshaw neatly laid his knife and fork on the empty plate, he asked, 'Do you have a good memory for facts?'

'I think so.'

'Good. You will need it.' He leaned towards her. 'Kathleen, the path to the Bar is long and arduous, and sometimes you will wish that you had chosen anything but law.'

'Did you ever have that wish?'

'Oh, yes, my dear. Many times. When the children were little I became almost a prisoner in my study, surrounded by books and documents.' His eyes saddened a little at the memory, as he went on: 'In fact, I barely saw my first two girls as toddlers. They appeared one day as young ladies, and I realized how much I had missed.'

'Do you think that is why Mr Grierson did not choose that path? I have often felt he would have liked to become a barrister.'

'He had his dreams, as we all did when we were young. However, practicalities prevented him from following that dream. As you will see, the financial burden is significant, membership fees, fees to the pupil master, rental of chambers before you earn a penny. Grierson did not have a wealthy father, as I did.' His lips quirked in a small smile. 'Nor did he have a great-aunt who was foolish enough to die intestate.'

Kathleen smiled back. 'He is a very good solicitor, just the same. And a very kind man.'

'True. But he is also astute enough to realize your potential and not want to stand in your way for pointless reasons.' He paused, before he went on: 'There is another consideration, of course. I am sure there must be a young man in the background. Could that be a problem?'

'The only young man in the background is the stepson of my guardian, but Desmond has his own dreams and understands how much this means to me. In fact, it was his suggestion that I use my legacy to train for the Bar.'

Slowly, Mr Henshaw nodded. 'Good' He signalled the waiter. 'Now, my dear, have you decided upon your dessert? I do hope treacle-pudding is on the menu. It's one of my favourites.'

Kathleen chose the sherry trifle and watched with amusement as her host tackled his large helping of treacle-pudding and custard with great enthusiasm. The staff were obviously trained to match the portions to the appetites of the members, she thought, noting the smaller portions at another table. Yet he appeared to have no excess fat on his frame.

As though reading her mind, he said, 'Fortunately, I have good metabolism and am almost addicted to the golf-course at weekends, otherwise I fear that my appetite would be of grave concern to my doctor.'

Over coffee they discussed the highs and lows of the training-period. At last he sat back and studied her face for a moment, as though trying to assess her reactions.

'Obviously you will need to think deeply about all this, Kathleen,' he commented, as he swirled his brandy in its glass. 'It will steal several years from your youth, and you will work harder than you have ever done in your life. Not only that, despite the fact that our monarch is female, and making a fine job of her role, there are still many who believe that a woman's place is in the kitchen and the nursery, not competing with the male species in a world they regard as exclusively their own.'

She nodded. 'Already I have found one of the partners to be disapproving of my presence in the firm.'

'Does it bother you?'

Truthfully, she answered: 'No. I feel it is his problem, rather than mine.'

He smiled. 'Good girl.' Again he studied her face carefully before he said, 'My final question — why do you wish to become a barrister?'

She chose her words carefully. 'I could have died with my family, that night. But I didn't, and I would like to think that God has some purpose for me, and that is why I have been given this wonderful opportunity. So many people have helped me, that I want to go as far as I can, within my capabilities.' She smiled. 'My eldest sister told me of her dreams of going to university and becoming a teacher.'

'But you didn't wish to go into the teaching profession?'

'No. I chose law because I love it, and everything it stands for. If I don't go ahead, all my life I will wonder if I could have made a worthy barrister. The years of hard work must be worthwhile, surely?'

'They are, Kathleen. Believe me, they are.' He covered her hand briefly with his own. 'And Theresa must have been a remarkable sister, to inspire such dreams. She would have been proud of you.'

'Thank you.' Kathleen blinked back a tear and glanced at her watch. 'Oh, my goodness, is that the time?' she said. 'I should have been back in the office half an hour ago.'

He dismissed her fears with a wave of his hand. 'It's all been taken care of. Grierson said you were to stay as long as necessary. It's too important a decision to rush.'

Outside the club, he insisted on hailing a taxi for Kathleen. 'I shall walk back to chambers,' he said, 'Maybe I did overindulge a little with the lunch. It will also enable me to give some thought to your needs.' He handed her into the taxi. 'Leave it with me, my dear,' he said, 'Humphrey Grierson and I have arranged to play golf at the weekend. Between the two of us, I am sure we can come up with a few names that will be of assistance.'

He gave the driver instructions and payment and touched his hat.

Kathleen wound the window down. 'I don't know how to thank you,' she said.

'It was only lunch, my dear. I hope you enjoyed it.'

'Oh, I did, thank you. It was lovely. But everything else is beyond thanks.'

'The expression on your face is enough. I will talk with Grierson and see if we can get you started on your way to the Bar.'

'Do you have any idea when that might be?'

'Assuming good results from your final articles test, and satisfactory completion of the probate, I see no reason why you should not join the Michaelmas term next year.'

8

There were so many names added to her prayer list over the years that sometimes Kathleen fell asleep before she had finished mentioning each and every one. But she always gave thanks for Uncle Len. He had been a tower of strength when they visited Ireland, comforting her during the rough crossing, hiring a car and driving her to the beautiful county of Cork, accompanying her to appointments with the solicitor, and advising her about the bequests.

It appeared that Great-aunt Bernadette had promised many people that they would be remembered in her will — her house-keeper, gardener, nurse, doctor — even some of the shopkeepers, to whom she constantly owed money. Fortunately, most of them regarded her promises as 'just blarney', so they made no demands upon Kathleen. There was no sign of resentment that the young lady from England had inherited everything. Many of them remembered her father and mother with affection, and said that the money was hers by right — after all, she was family. When she insisted that she would clear all her aunt's debts as soon as probate was finalized, they were grateful. Privately, she arranged with the solicitor that generous amounts should be paid to those who had taken care of her aunt in her last years, also the church and the convent school.

Kathleen had but vague memories of her early years in Ireland, but soon recognized and loved the feeling of peace and genuine warmth. It was almost like being back with Mam and Da' again, she thought, as they were invited into the homes of welcoming strangers. It had been Uncle Len's first visit to Ireland but he, too, felt the magic, and admitted that he had been aware he was in the 'land of the little people'.

Auntie Nell and Uncle Fred were also high on her list of thanks to God, as was her 'nearly sister', together with Jane's children, Nicholas and his baby sister, Gillian.

Then there was Mr Henshaw. Not only had he helped her to join the Michaelmas term in November 1955, he had offered to become her pupil master once she was called to the Bar. He had certainly been right about the amount of antagonism she might have to face because of her sex. There were only two girls that term, and her heart ached for the student who did not return after Christmas because the barrage of sneers and jibes was more than she could bear. Somehow, Kathleen managed to build a wall of defence around her, shielding her from the unpleasant remarks so that she could focus on Roman law, constitutional law, the law of tort, and any other laws with strange names that might be on her schedule for the day. The fact that her marks remained among the top of the class seemed to be a constant source of irritation to most of the male students but, just as constantly, Kathleen reminded herself that it was their problem, not hers.

Even so, it would have been difficult to keep going without Desmond. Dear, dear, Desmond, who would sometimes appear late in the evening, carrying a newspaper bulging with fish and chips, because he knew that she wouldn't have stopped work to cook a proper meal. Desmond, who also had piles of books to study, but realized the importance of taking some time out to recharge the batteries, so would insist on driving her over to East Grinstead to play with the children, or to Upminster for a Sunday lunch so that she could chat to Laura and Len, something she usually only managed briefly on the telephone. Although she argued that she couldn't really spare the time, Kathleen had to admit that she felt refreshed after these little breaks. One of the nicest, and most thoughtful treats was when Desmond produced two tickets for the show at the London Palladium, where Cecilia Saint was a supporting act to the handsome Hollywood icon who had star billing. As she watched her friend sitting at a white grand piano, singing song after wonderful song, Kathleen knew why the world of show business had recognized the unique voice and talent. After the show, they walked round to the stage-door in the hope that they might be allowed in to congratulate Cecilia, but there was no way they could have pushed through the huge crowd waiting for autographs. So Kathleen penned a little note to Cecilia, who wrote back saying how disappointed she was that they hadn't been able to meet. Perhaps when she returned from her tour of America?

Desmond was the only person who really understood the loneliness of being shut away with only books for company. Bridie was all very well, but she was a wee bit one-sided when it came to conversation. There were times when Kathleen wondered why Desmond didn't have other girlfriends. After all, they weren't engaged, and they had a clear arrangement that they were free to socialize with other friends. The situation worried her a little and she brought up the subject one evening when they were musing about this and that. It was towards the end of her course and the weather had turned rather chill, so she had lit the fire and they sat on the floor, toasting thick slices of bread.

'Don't you ever want to go out with other girls?' she asked, giving the last piece of toast to Bridie.

'Not really. Why? Are you fed up with me coming round?'

'Of course not. But I don't want you to think I take you for granted.'

He shook his head. 'I wouldn't come if I didn't want to. To tell the truth, I find other girls a bit dull compared to you.'

'Really?' She looked at him in surprise.

'Yes, really. All they talk about is film stars and fashion, or the weddings of their best friends, which bothers me no end.' He laughed. 'Come here, you silly goose, and I'll show you why I prefer your company to that of anyone else I know.'

She shuffled across the rug on her knees, causing Bridie to whimper with annoyance as her favourite place in front of the fire was disturbed, and snuggled into the comfort of Desmond's arms. Although she responded to his kisses, she was careful not to allow herself to become too passionate. Who knows where that might lead?

As if following her line of thought,

Desmond lifted his head and shifted so that she was leaning back against him, his arms around her. It felt very comfortable.

'There,' he said softly, 'see what I mean? We can enjoy being together, without being carried away. I don't know another girl who wouldn't feel slighted if I stopped kissing her.'

'But . . . ' she didn't know how to put her thoughts into words. 'Surely you will want more one day, with someone.'

'Maybe,' he said, thoughtfully. 'But the last thing I want is to be forced into marriage because I have been daft enough to get a girl pregnant.' He stroked her hair. 'And I thought you were happy with things the way they are.'

'Oh, I am. It's just that . . . '

'What?'

'Well, you are so very good to me, and I don't feel I'm giving enough in return.'

His arms tightened around her. 'You give me your friendship and affection, and I'm very happy with that. I'm not ready to settle down with anyone yet, and I know you want to be established before you consider it.'

She nodded.

'Well, then, what are you worrying about?'

'Not so much worrying, as wondering how someone like Rose Heilbron manages to combine a demanding career with a private life.'

'Is that the judge?'

'Yes. The first female judge at that. She must be incredibly clever.'

'Nearly as clever as you, I reckon.' He eased her up into a sitting position. 'Time I was going home, or the neighbours will be talking.' He yawned. 'And you look as though you could do with a decent night's sleep.'

Kathleen stood up and switched on the lamp.

'I just want to read a couple of points on practical conveyancing. It's not my best subject.'

'Hmm. I suppose it's useless saying don't stay up too late.'

She smiled. 'I'll try to be a good girl, honest.'

'You are a very good girl, Kathleen O'Connor.' Desmond bent his head to kiss her goodnight. 'I'll pick you up on Sunday.'

'Sunday? Are we going somewhere?'

'To Jane and Sandy's.' His gaze was whimsical. 'Don't tell me you've forgotten it's our godson's birthday party?'

She clapped her hand over her mouth. 'Holy Mary! I haven't bought a card for Nicholas, let alone a present. Thanks for reminding me.'

At the door, he turned back. 'By the way, I should warn you that if some gorgeous blonde rides up on a white charger, I'll be off like a shot. You won't mind, will you, dear?'

Kathleen hurled a cushion at his head, but he fielded it expertly. She watched from the window as he walked to his car, waving cheerily up at her. Although it had been a joke, she hated the thought that Desmond could, and might, fall in love with someone else. She couldn't imagine him with another girl, any more than she could imagine herself with another boy, but no point in wasting time thinking about what might happen in the future. As he said, there was plenty of time before either of them needed to think about settling down. It was a very nice understanding between two friends.

★   ★   ★

Despite the hard work and the barbed remarks from fellow students, sometimes even from tutors who seemed surprised that a mere female could not only hold her own, but excel at her chosen subject — despite all that, she loved every minute of the lectures. She read books until every word was stored in a mental compartment. It was as though she couldn't grasp enough knowledge of law to satisfy her appetite. She even enjoyed the dinners, not noticing the food, but entranced by the feeling that almost four centuries of echoes whispered from the magnificent oak-panelled banqueting-hall. As much as that, she loved the opportunity to converse with those who had already been called to the Bar, delighting in mock debates and trials, and listening carefully. She almost giggled when she learned that if counsel said: 'Watch his Lordship's pen,' the significance was that there was a small spotlight trained on his pen as he took down spoken evidence to remind the jury of crucial points. If he put the pen noisily down and folded his arms, it could indicate that he regarded the evidence as irrelevant, or the witness might be speaking too quickly. It could even be that the jury were not paying sufficient attention. But certainly a point worth looking out for.

Notebook after notebook was filled with points to look out for, particularly regarding criminal law, the subject that interested her above all the others. Even so, no one was more surprised than Kathleen when she was awarded a fifty-pound prize for the best examination result in Part I, Section V.

'Looks as though you're destined to be a criminal lawyer to rival Clarence Darrow,'

Desmond teased, when she showed him the letter.

'Now wouldn't that be something?' Kathleen laughed. 'But I could quite happily settle for getting through Part II of the exam, and earning the right to wear a splendid new horsehair wig. In the meantime ... ' she beamed at him, 'I am going to treat you to the grandest meal you've eaten, and best seats at a show of your choice.'

Kathleen was delighted at the show of Desmond's choice, but he insisted that he had so enjoyed *South Pacific* first time around that it would be a pleasure to see it again. She also suspected a tinge of guilt.

The next celebration, the following year, was to see *The Boy Friend*, as a reward for passing Part II with flying colours. Not the highest marks, this time, but very satisfactory, nevertheless. Laura gave her a sumptuous dinner-party in the restaurant, and Kathleen found herself answering a barrage of questions.

Mr Davies wanted to know whether she would have to wear one of those curly wigs, or was that only the men.

'Actually, it's not long ago that some judges felt that only men should wear wigs, not the new lady barristers.'

'I suppose they were scared you might turn

up in court wearing trousers, as well?'

'Something like that. Fortunately, they were out-voted so, yes, I have a brand-new wig in a lovely box with my name painted in gold on the lid.'

Auntie Nell wanted to know all about the final dinner in the Middle Temple Hall.

'Do they touch you on the shoulder with a mace, and pronounce you madam barrister?' she asked.

Chuckling, Kathleen shook her head, and then was solemn for a moment.

'Much simpler than that,' she answered softly, 'but wasn't I the one holding my breath as the Treasurer of my Inn said, 'I do hereby call you to the Bar and do publish you barrister'? Even then I was scared stiff someone would stand up and announce that there had been a terrible mistake, and it was someone else, not me.'

'I know what you mean, dear,' Uncle Fred commented. 'That's how I felt when the vicar asked if anyone had any objections to my getting married.'

'Then what happened?' Auntie Nell went on. 'After the announcement. Did he kiss you on the cheek, like the Royals do?'

'No, he just shook my hand. But the poor man will never know how much I wanted to throw my arms around him.'

'You should have done it,' Desmond laughed. 'I don't suppose the old fogies are hugged by pretty young lady barristers very often.'

When the laughter died down a little, Auntie Nell had another question.

'What was that bit about drinking from a loving-cup? I was so excited I couldn't take it all in when you phoned.'

'Oh, yes. We had to drink a toast to the pious, glorious and immortal memory of Good Queen Bess. Granny O'Connor would not have approved at all, but I feel very proud to be able to take part in these old traditions, quaint as they are.'

Uncle Len held up his champagne glass. 'Not half as proud as we are of you, love.'

'But I couldn't have done it without your help, Uncle Len, and Great-aunt Bernadette's legacy, God rest her soul.'

'Help and money would have been a fat lot of good without your brains to do something with it. And don't you think it's about time you called me Len? It was different when you were a little girl.'

'But now you're a five-foot-nothing little woman,' Desmond teased. 'You'd better carry a couple of extra books into court to stand on, or the judges will keep asking you to stand up.'

'Little and good, that's what she is,' Mr Davies protested.

'I know,' Desmond agreed. 'And I'd rather have Kathleen in my corner than someone twice her size.'

Kathleen was feeling a little embarrassed by so much praise, and was relieved when Laura asked about the next step.

'You know that Charles Henshaw has agreed to be my pupil master?'

'Desmond told me. How long will that take?'

'About a year, if I'm lucky. I shall work in his chambers and accompany him to court whenever possible. It's another form of learning, but I will be a junior barrister and entitled to wear the wig and robe in court.'

'You must be so excited.'

'Oh, I am. Can't wait for the next term to commence.'

'Kathleen . . . ' Auntie Nell interrupted, 'I know you told me that you are now qualified as a junior barrister. How long will it take before you are a senior barrister?'

'It doesn't quite work like that, Auntie Nell. I will be a junior barrister for ever, unless I decide to take silk.'

'Does everyone have to take silk, whatever that means?'

'It means becoming a QC — Queen's

Counsel — and being able to wear a silk gown. No, it's not compulsory. Some judges are junior barristers before they are called.'

'Called what, dear?'

'To the Bench.'

'I see.' Auntie Nell looked as though she was far from seeing. 'Do you want to take silk, as you call it?'

'I'd like to, of course, but you have to apply to the Lord Chancellor, and it can take several years before he calls you to the inner Bar.' Kathleen noticed Desmond's frown as she continued: 'I think it highly unlikely, Auntie Nell but, in any case, I need to get a few more years' experience under my belt before I even think about applying.'

Auntie Nell looked even more confused before she asked something that Kathleen could answer more easily.

'Have you told Grace your good news?'

Kathleen nodded. 'She said Auntie Peg cried and Uncle Joe is going to plant a rose tree in my honour.' Kathleen smiled at the thought. 'I had a lovely bouquet from Cecilia — you remember, my friend from college. By the way, did I tell you that Exeter has received the charter as a full university?'

'That's very good news. And your friend is becoming quite famous. Always reading about her in the papers. Do you still visit the family?'

'No, and I feel sad about that. But we've both been so busy. She's always on tour somewhere and I've hardly had time to come up for air yet. We haven't met since we graduated, but we do write from time to time, even if it's only a message on a Christmas card.'

Uncle Fred pushed back his empty plate with a satisfied sigh.

'That was lovely, Laura. Very tasty piece of beef. Never had it wrapped up in pastry like that, before. Made a nice change from steak and kidney pie.'

'Was that the beef Wellington recipe you were telling me about, Laura?' asked Nell Harrison. 'Thought it might be. Very nice too. Pity Jane and Sandy couldn't come.'

'They were wise, though, not to bring the little girl out if she has a cold.'

Desmond topped up the wineglasses. 'But Kathleen and I are going over there at the weekend.' His sigh was exaggerated. 'Then we have to go to Devon for a few days. More celebrations, I suppose. Don't know how much more of this wild living I can take.'

'You don't need to accompany me, sir, if you prefer not to,' Kathleen said, in a mock haughty tone. 'Now I have passed my test I am quite capable of driving to Torquay without an escort.'

'True. But I think I should come, just to warn the other road-users there is a new lady driver on the loose.'

'Ha, ha! Very funny.'

The jocular banter continued throughout the dessert, and up to the flat where they had coffee. At one point, a framed snapshot caught Kathleen's attention; a family group of Laura with her first husband, her father, and the boys, on the deck of a small fishing-boat. It had always stood on the sideboard, but she had never examined it closely before. It must have been taken just before the war, because Kathleen knew that Laura's husband and father had been killed on that boat, helping to ferry soldiers from the beaches of Dunkirk.

As she leaned forward to study the photograph, Uncle Len — Len — picked it up and handed it to Kathleen.

'Just as well they didn't know what was ahead of them,' he commented.

'True. We've all got photographs like this, haven't we?'

'Sadly, yes. Rose, of course. And your family.' He replaced the photograph. 'Do you have your photographs on show?'

Slowly, she shook her head. 'No. I keep

them in the album that Mam used. It's rather tatty, and Da' only had a cheap little box-camera, so the snaps weren't up to much.' She fingered her locket. 'The two best ones are in here, so they are with me all the time.'

He kissed the top of her head.

'Come on, love. I think Desmond is ready to run you home.'

9

It wasn't until a few weeks later that Kathleen realized just how fortunate she was to have Charles Henshaw as her pupil master. Not only did he clearly explain his own opinion of a case, he gave her plenty of time to read all the necessary documentation before they went into court. Most important of all, he made sure that his schedule allowed time for him to finish each trial before his presence was needed in another court. There were other pupils who were left alone to handle a defence, completely unprepared, while their leader dashed from court to court. Some pupils did not seem to mind being thrown in at the deep end, as it were, but most were so petrified they relied on the judge to remind them what they should say and do next. Even the thought filled Kathleen with fear, but Charles Henshaw QC believed in allowing his pupils to gain as much experience as possible before putting them in a position where they had to stand up and address the court. Plenty of time for that later, he said.

Only one thing marred Kathleen's happiness with her new role. The other juniors told her that it was customary to refer to each other by surname only, including the silks. At first, she thought they might be winding her up, because she was new, and female at that. So she listened, and realized that they actually were calling each other Grieves, Robinson, Townsend — and only called her O'Connor, never Miss O'Connor or Kathleen. But she had not heard any of them address Mr Henshaw personally, although they referred to him as Henshaw when in discussion. Was it a hoax, to embarrass her?

Eventually, she decided to speak to her pupil master direct.

'Actually, they are correct,' he confirmed. 'And it is in order for you to address me as Henshaw.'

'Would it not be also in order for me to call you Mr Henshaw?' she pleaded. 'Don't you think it sounds as though I am lacking in respect to call you anything else?'

'It does rather smack of public-school jargon, I agree.' He regarded her thoughtfully for a moment, and then smiled. 'Why don't we have our own arrangement?'

'And what would that be, sir?'

'When you are with the other juniors, refer to me as Henshaw, but address me as Mr Henshaw, if that will help you to feel more comfortable.'

'Oh, it would, Mr Henshaw. Indeed it would.'

'And to tell the truth, O'Connor doesn't quite suit a young lady barrister. So I will refer to you as Miss O'Connor, but call you Kathleen in private. Will that suit?'

'Admirably, sir. Thank you.' Beaming, she turned towards the door, but he called her back.

'Almost forgot. My wife asked me to invite you to lunch on Sunday week. Tim is off to America shortly, and we thought it would be nice to combine a family meal with some of his friends. Sandy and Jane are bringing their little ones, also my married daughter, so it should be quite jolly. Will you come?'

'I should love to. Thank you — should I telephone Mrs Henshaw?'

'No need.' He scribbled on a message pad. 'If I put this with my keys, I should remember to tell her this evening.'

★ ★ ★

The Willows was as beautiful as she remembered, even on a damp, chilly day. A pretty child with sparkling eyes opened the door.

'Hello I'm Susan Grandma said to go through to the kitchen can't stop we're

113

looking for Tommy,' she said almost in one breath, before she raced off. Kathleen found Mrs Henshaw working happily amidst the chaos that represented her kitchen.

'How nice to see you again, my dear.' Mrs Henshaw kissed Kathleen on the cheek, and then turned back to the table. 'I hope I've enough vegetables,' she commented.

Kathleen surveyed the heaps of potatoes, carrots, swedes.

'Looks enough to feed an army.' She picked up the biggest cabbage she had ever seen. 'Did this one win the local flower and vegetable show?' she laughed.

'Goodness, no. You should have seen the one that did. Now, where did I put my sharp knife?'

Kathleen rummaged behind the cabbage. 'This one?' she asked.

'Thank you, dear. It's just that I always forget to count the children and they have such hearty appetites. Are Sandy's children fussy eaters?'

'I don't think so. Gillian is only a toddler of course, but Nicholas will eat anything that is put before him.'

'Good for him.'

A younger version of Dora Henshaw came out of the larder, carrying a large crock of salt, her right hand extended.

'You must be Kathleen. I'm Sally, the mother of those noisy brats racing around the house.'

'They certainly seem to be enjoying themselves.'

'I'm not sure if I warned them that father's study is out of bounds,' Sally said, reflectively. 'Last time one of them hid under his desk and thought it would be a better hiding-place if he surrounded himself with as many of Grandpa's files as he could drag in.'

'Oh, no! And your father is such an orderly person. Was he very cross?'

'Let's just say that he was not exactly pleased. But Pa can never be cross for long, especially with the children. Still, I'd better just round them up and remind them. Their memory span for rules is virtually non-existent.'

Kathleen asked: 'What can I do to help?' just as Mr Henshaw came in.

'I told you this young lady was bright, Dora.' He smiled as he shook hands with Kathleen. 'Anyone else would have said, 'Is there anything I can do to help', expecting you to say, 'No, thank you.' But Kathleen O'Connor actually wants to help, and there's the difference.'

'I'm not quite sure I understand your legal way of looking at things, Charles, but there is something Kathleen can do, if she doesn't mind.'

'Of course not.'

'I need some mint for the sauce. The herb garden is down near the vegetable plot. There are scissors around somewhere. It's still a bit damp out there, so you'd better find some galoshes.'

'Galoshes?'

'There's a pile of them in the back porch. Bound to be two that will fit you, even if they're not a pair.'

Kathleen found the scissors, and galoshes, but paused for a moment, scanning the garden, before she ventured outside. The last thing she needed was two bouncing dogs knocking her flying into the compost-heap.

Carrying a huge, empty basket, Mr Henshaw appeared at her side.

'Would you like me to get the mint?' he asked. 'It is rather muddy out there.'

'Oh, no, that's not a problem, thank you. It's just that — I wondered if Romulus and Remus were out in the garden.'

'No, but I don't blame you for being apprehensive. They are somewhat boisterous. Come on, I need more logs, and can show you where the herb garden is.'

'Thank you.'

'Actually, the dogs are with Olivia. She's

116

taken the horse for a ride, now it has stopped raining, so she thought it would be a good idea to let the dogs have a gallop at the same time. Expend some of their energy.'

While Kathleen cut the mint, he filled up the basket from an enormous pile of logs stored in an open, barnlike structure, which also gave some protection to a stack of straw bales, obviously for the horse. Their whole world was different from anything Kathleen had experienced and, as she looked down towards the river, she again felt that calming atmosphere that had affected her on her previous visit. Even without the sunshine, there was an air of tranquillity that warmed her soul.

Mr Henshaw glanced across at her, as if reading her mind.

'This is my haven, from all the battles of the courtroom. You feel it, too, don't you?'

'Indeed I do,' she said softly. 'No wonder your family come here so often on a Sunday. And your wife is at the heart of it, keeping everyone happy, just like my mam . . . '

He smiled. 'You'll be that type of wife and mother one day, Kathleen,' he said. 'Have you thought that far ahead?'

'Yes — and no. Of course I would like to marry one day, and have children, but for now I want to put everything I have learned, especially the things you are teaching me, into practice for a while. It would seem such a waste, otherwise.'

'I agree.' He tucked another log into the basket. 'And I do appreciate that it's not quite so straightforward for a woman. However . . . ' he brushed the sawdust from his hands. 'It is possible to go back to law after time out to get the family started on their way, you know.'

'Yes. I might consider that option.'

'No reason why it shouldn't work, as long as you keep revising and watching out for changes in law. It would be a sad loss to the legal profession if you gave it up altogether.'

'Thank you.' They both looked towards the house as the noise of a fast-moving car screeching to a halt on the gravel drive shattered the peace and quiet.

'That sounds like my son,' Mr Henshaw said, ruefully, and then paused to listen to voices raised in protest. 'And that sounds like my daughter.'

'The doctor?'

He nodded. 'We asked Tim to pick Phyllis up, or she would still be browsing through her medical journals at teatime. But she hates him driving so fast. Better go and act as referee, I suppose.'

'If I hold one of the handles, it will be

easier to carry the basket back to the house.'

'That would be most helpful, thank you. Dora is always chiding me for filling the basket so full that I can hardly carry it.'

In the kitchen, Mrs Henshaw and Sally were struggling to lift an enormous saddle of lamb out of the oven, just as Tim and his sister came in from the hall.

'Phyllis, dear,' Mrs Henshaw calmly interrupted their argument, 'would you clear a space on top of the Aga? And we could really do with some help here, Tim, if you don't mind. I'm not sure I can hold on to this heavy beast for much longer.'

The heavy beast was deposited on top of the Aga in no time, and Tim kissed his mother and gave Sally a bear hug.

'Haven't seen you for ages,' he said. 'Are you putting on a bit of weight, or in the pudding-club again?'

She cuffed him playfully. 'Actually, I am pregnant. Didn't think it showed much yet.' She patted her slightly rounded stomach.

'Well, I wouldn't be much of a doctor if I couldn't diagnose a pregnant woman. Is Jeremy here?'

'No, he went back to sea last week. God knows when I'll see him again.'

'Perhaps it's just as well. Every time he gets shore leave, you're left holding the baby

— literally. But I must say, it suits you. You're blooming.'

'Blooming awful when I'm offloading my breakfast,' Sally said, wryly. She smiled at Kathleen. 'Just dump it anywhere, I'll deal with it in a minute.'

'Would you like me to chop it for you?'

'Kathleen!' Tim grabbed her around the waist and lifted her to his face-level before he kissed her full on the lips. 'Nearly fell over you. I'd forgotten how tiny you are.' He set her back down on the floor. 'You look wonderful. Hello, Dad. I'm just going to pinch your protégée for a minute. Want to hear if you're browbeating her.'

He hadn't changed at all, Kathleen thought.

'In a minute,' she laughed. 'After I've chopped the mint.'

Phyllis had a better idea. 'You can really do us a favour by taking our Stirling Moss drive-alike far away from the kitchen, before I find myself with a heavy object in my hand and his head in the vicinity.' Her tone was quite good-humoured. 'I'll do the mint. Chat to you later. And Tim — a large whisky might help to settle my nerves after that hairy ride.'

'Right. We'll do drinks and lay the table.' Tim sounded equally good-humoured. 'Too many cooks in this kitchen, anyway.'

The large damask tablecloth slid backwards

and forwards on the highly polished dining-table before it was straight.

'Sherry for you, Kathleen?'

'Yes, please. How many place-mats do I need?'

'Oh, gosh. Let's see.' He counted mentally for a moment. 'Thirteen I think — no, fourteen. Although we may have to use the old family high-chair for Sandy's youngest.' As Kathleen smoothed the tablecloth, he glanced at her hand. 'No ring I see.'

'No.'

'Do you still see that fellow who got pie-eyed at Sandy's wedding?'

'Desmond? Yes, we're good friends.'

'In the sense that film stars say, 'We're just good friends'? When everyone knows they are lovers.'

'Is it really impossible for you to believe that a man and a woman can be just good friends?'

'Let's just say that I would find it impossible to remain just good friends with someone as beautiful as you. In fact, if I wasn't booked to sail on the Queen Elizabeth tomorrow, I might be tempted to give your good friend a run for his money.'

He really was incorrigible, Kathleen thought, as she took a handful of knives from the drawer.

'Oh, well. That's life.' Tim handed Kathleen a glass of sherry. 'I suppose this is the point where I should change the subject?'

'Yes, please.'

'What shall we talk about? Not the weather. Too boring. Not religion or politics. Too dodgy. Not the job. We hear enough about it as it is. I know! Travel. How did you get here? Train?'

'No. I drove.'

'Really?'

'Yes, really. What's so strange about that.'

'I don't know. I suppose I still think of you as being too young, and too little.' He glanced out of the window. 'That wouldn't be your car, would it? The white Anglia?'

'As a matter of fact, it is.'

He moved over to the window for a better look. 'Crikey, it's a brand-new 100E,' he observed. 'Nice drive?'

'Very nice. Haven't had it long — ah, here's Jane and Sandy.'

★ ★ ★

After all the hugs and kisses, Sally's trio dragged Jane's children into their game of hide and seek. Susan practised her budding maternal-instinct skills by taking charge of Gillian, who squealed with delight as she trotted after her new friends.

Smiling, Jane watched them disappear into the house.

'They are so trusting and uninhibited at this age. Why can't we all make new friends that easily?'

'Wish I knew.' Sandy lifted a bag of children's clutter from the boot of his car. 'There just seems to be a point in our lives when we decide that we're too old to smile and speak to someone without a proper introduction. Daft, isn't it?'

'I don't have a problem,' Tim said, cheerfully.

'That's because you haven't grown up yet.'

'I hate to admit it, Sandy, but you're probably right.' Tim reflected for a moment before he went on: 'And if it means I've got to be stuffy and suspicious, I'll put a hold on growing up for as long as possible.'

They were still laughing when Olivia appeared from the house.

'We're dying from withdrawal symptoms, Tim,' she said. 'What happened to our drinks?'

'We're very well, Olivia,' Tim said, 'and thank you for asking.'

'Hello, everyone. Sorry. It's just that Winston slipped on some wet leaves, and I finished up in the ditch. A very muddy ditch. And don't you dare laugh, Timothy Henshaw.'

'Wouldn't dream of it.' Tim fought back his

grin, and then said, 'You don't look as though you've rolled in the mud. Are you OK? No broken bones or anything? There are enough doctors here today to give you a second or third opinion if you want confirmation that you're alive.'

'No, I'm fine, you idiot. A quick shower restored me to something resembling a human being. A drink might just finish the job. Come on, I'll give you a hand.'

'Is Winston OK?' Jane asked.

'He ought to be, all the fuss and attention he gets. There are times when I think the edict that animals have to be fed and watered first amounts to cruelty to humans. I'll have to ask Pa.' She turned towards the front door.

'Don't need to,' Tim said 'You've a very capable barrister right behind you.'

Olivia swung round and looked down at Kathleen.

'I've done it again,' she said. 'Sorry, Kathleen. And congratulations. How's it going, working with Pa?'

'Wonderful. Your father is the grandest pupil master anyone could have.'

In the dining-room, Tim and Olivia poured drinks, still chatting to Kathleen, while Jane and Sandy went through to the kitchen.

'Do you get much sexist discrimination in chambers?' Olivia asked.

124

'A bit, but nothing I can't handle.' Kathleen grinned. 'And I have a feeling that they have too much respect for your father to make it too blatant.'

'Could be.' Tim found a tray for the glasses. 'Phyll found it tough, the way some men behaved, just because she was a woman. Even now, she gets the odd male chauvinist who refuses to allow her anywhere near his body.'

'How does she deal with it?' Kathleen asked.

'She just tells them that they'll have to wait at least a week to see a male doctor, and their condition could deteriorate to a dangerous level. Most of them fall into line.' Laughing, Olivia picked up the tray. 'Let's take these through before they all droop with thirst.'

After the magnificent lunch, it was decided that a walk was absolutely necessary. The air smelled damp, but fresh, and at one point they actually caught sight of the spire of Winchester Cathedral in the distance.

Despite their numbers, it was a remarkably quiet little crowd. The children thought up a private game of their own, something to do with the number of farm gates. Even the dogs seemed to have worn themselves out and trotted sedately behind Olivia. Sandy and Tim were discussing the pros and cons of

125

working in New York, and Kathleen walked with Jane, Gillian fast asleep in her pushchair.

'You're looking remarkably well,' Kathleen observed, 'considering your hectic lifestyle keeping these two in order. Not to mention Sandy.'

'Actually, I am, and I'm hoping it's for the same reason as Sally, but I won't have the results of the tests for another week.'

'Oh, Jane. That's wonderful. I'll pray for a positive result.'

'Isn't it ironic, that I should be the one who had all the ambition, and now I'm completely fulfilled with a husband and children.'

'Truly?'

'Yes, truly.' Jane stopped to tuck the blanket more securely around Gillian's legs. 'I do understand your need to go as far as you can in the legal profession. But don't leave it too long before you start obeying your instincts, or he might have flown.'

'I presume you're talking about Desmond?'

'Of course. Who else?'

'Neither of us is ready to settle down yet, and we have agreed that we are both free to go out with others if we wish.'

'But sooner or later one of you is going to want to settle down. Then what will you do?'

'Whatever happens, it will be God's will. And Desmond has another year of exams before he is eligible to apply for a deputy headship, so it is all rather academic.'

As Jane hurried ahead to rescue Nicholas, who was stuck on top of a farm gate, Kathleen mulled over the comments that had been made by Tim, his father, and now Jane. Sooner or later, Kathleen knew she would have to face up to a decision that would affect the rest of her life. But it would be later, rather than sooner.

Meantime, her thoughts for the future must focus on finishing her pupillage training, deciding which of the many chambers she would wish to join, and hoping and praying that one of them would accept her. That could take quite a time.

10

'There.' Aunt Grace set the tray down on a small table in front of the corner window-seat, where Kathleen dreamily enjoyed the afternoon sunshine and the view along the road towards Babbacombe Downs; Bridie curled up asleep at her side.

'That's just what I need. Thank you.' Kathleen welcomed the pretty flower-sprigged teacup.

'Now, I want to hear all about your new chambers. How did you manage to get fixed up so quickly? I've known of some juniors applying for years before they are accepted.'

'I know, and I truly thought that would be so in my case, although Mr Henshaw did say I could stay on at his chambers in the meantime. But the dear man knew I really wanted to handle more criminal and civil law, so he phoned several of his legal friends and, thanks be to God, one of them was losing a junior and offered me the place.'

'Was the other barrister giving up law?'

'No. His wife hated London and persuaded him to return to Northern Ireland.'

'What luck for you.' Aunt Grace replaced

her teacup on the tray. 'Where are your new chambers?'

'King's Bench Walk.'

'That is a lovely spot. Whenever I had to take a brief to Middle Temple, I would always pause and admire the view towards the Thames.'

'I do that, every day. Aren't I the lucky one?'

'No more than you deserve, dear. Who is head of chambers?'

'Merrick Soames. Do you know of him?'

'Oh, yes. I remember him before he took silk. Such a nice gentleman.'

'He is certainly very kind to me.'

'Who are you sharing with?'

'Neville Shorter. I doubt whether you would know him.' Kathleen pulled a face. 'Come to that, you wouldn't want to.'

'Oh, dear. Does he give you a hard time because you are a woman?'

'No. He leaves that to the others.' Kathleen raised her eyes to the ceiling. 'But he does tend to think he is God's gift to the ladies, and delights in telling me every detail of his latest conquest, along with some rather tasteless and very unfunny jokes.'

'Really? He doesn't — well, you know — with you?' Aunt Grace sounded slightly flustered.

'Not at all.' Kathleen chuckled. 'When he starts talking dirty, I pretend I am totally deaf. He gives up eventually, but I think it is all in his dreams, really.'

'Whatever has happened to the little Irish girl who blushed every time the word sex was mentioned?' Aunt Grace commented, spluttering slightly into her teacup.

'She worked on some very explicit and extremely sad divorce cases, not to mention breach of promise and prostitution trials.' Thoughtfully, Kathleen returned her gaze to the view from the window. 'I didn't enjoy them, of course, but after a while I stopped blushing.'

'Yes — remembering some of the statements I typed, I can understand that. In a way, I suppose it's like nurses, who learn to accept the death of a patient.' Changing the subject, she pushed a plate of scones towards Kathleen. 'These are still warm from the oven, and quite delicious,' she said. 'Peg might be getting on a bit, but she's still the best cook I know.'

Kathleen nodded her agreement. 'I thought she looked wonderful. But Uncle Joe seems a little tired.'

'He is, and I worry about him.' Aunt Grace spooned jam on to her scone. 'Dad was like that in his last months. Nothing you could put your finger on, but a feeling of ageing.'

'I know what you mean.' They were silent with their thoughts for a moment, until Kathleen continued: 'Mr Davies was the grandfather I never had — but such a peaceful way to go, in his sleep like that. Who could wish for more?'

'I know.' Aunt Grace's smile was sad. 'And he adored being a great-grandfather. Pity he didn't live to see Jane's latest little boy.'

Kathleen nodded 'Philip is a darling. They all are.'

Aunt Grace refilled Kathleen's cup. 'Tell me about your chambers,' she said. 'How do you get on with the clerk?'

'Very well. George is lovely. I would find it difficult to not get on with him.'

'I bet there are some that don't, though.'

'Oh, yes. Julian Mountford for one. He thinks that because George has never read a law book in his life, he knows nothing. But he knows more than the rest of us put together.'

'Well, I'm sure he will appreciate your opinion of him. And you will need someone like him in your corner. Another scone, dear?'

'Yes, please. Oh, how I love coming here. It's so refreshing after . . . '

'London?'

'I suppose so. It's a more peaceful world.'

'True.' They munched in silence until Aunt

Grace asked; 'Will you visit your friend while you are here? The singer.'

'Sadly, no. I had hoped to, but Cecilia is in Australia. I haven't seen her for years.'

'Well, I know one person who would love a visit from you. Augustine Dawson. She fell off her bicycle and can't get out at the moment.'

'Oh, the poor soul. Is she badly hurt?'

'Mainly bruises and grazes, but her knee is quite swollen. Nobby took me over there a couple of days ago and she was hobbling around with a stick.'

'How does she manage, on her own?'

'Her friends in the village have rallied round, so she's all right for shopping and so on, but she misses getting out and about.'

'I'll run over there tomorrow. Show her the latest pictures of Jane's little brood.'

'She'll like that. And do remind her to lock her front door before she goes to bed. She's been leaving it unlocked so that her friends can come straight in, and I worry about her.'

'If a burglar was tempted by the Turner painting, the insurance company would pounce on an unlocked door, whatever the circumstances. I'll warn her.' Kathleen finished the last morsel of scone. 'While I'm here, I want to visit Jack and Sheila. Would you like to come?'

'That would be nice, dear. We're not too

busy just now, and I'd like to see their little ones. They grow up so fast.'

'How is Johnny?'

'You won't recognize him. He walks much better since that operation you paid for, and is such a handsome young man, just like his father. Making quite a name for himself with his paintings, too.'

'Good.' Kathleen turned her face back towards the sun. 'Do you know, I could sit here for ever.' She sighed with pleasure and closed her eyes. 'Do tell me about your visitors. They must find this place really heavenly.'

'Most of them do.'

'No regrets? You had so many problems to start with.'

'Goodness, yes. Mum gave us a hard time; she was so upset that I was moving away. And, of course, she felt I would be labelled as a loose woman by sharing a house with Nobby Clark. Poor Mum couldn't understand that it was only a business partnership.'

'I can imagine. But Jane told me he was secretly in love with Laura. Was it true?'

'Probably. But his best friend pipped him to the post.' Aunt Grace sipped her tea. 'Nobby did offer to marry me, but we're both too set in our ways.' She smiled. 'It's worked out very well, actually, and I've never regretted it. Despite all the hard work, it's satisfying to know that we've helped some people to have as normal a holiday as possible, despite their handicaps.'

'Maybe one day other hotels will follow your example and put in ramps and special bathroom fittings. You've even got books in Braille.'

'And I can communicate in sign language when necessary.' Aunt Grace poured them both another cup of tea, still talking. 'When I read some of the lovely comments in the visitors' book, I know I made the right choice. You must know what I mean, after all your hard work to get on to the legal ladder.'

'Yes, and like you, I know I made the right choice.' Thoughtfully, Kathleen sipped her tea, and then went on, 'But we both know there is even more hard work to come before I achieve my dream of leading a really important trial at the Old Bailey.'

★ ★ ★

Kathleen was reminded of those words many times as she wrote opinions, prepared pleadings, worked on breaches of contract and bankruptcy applications, occasionally a brief relating to the nuisance of noisy dogs or a pathetic burglar who elected to be tried by jury. She attended conferences with solicitors and managing clerks in the draughty corridors of the Old Bailey, but seemed no nearer to addressing the jury, until the day when George beckoned her from his own private little cubby-hole.

'Got a good one for you here, miss,' he said, waving the brief under her nose. 'From Moorhead and Foster. Know them?'

'No. I've not worked with them at all. What's it about, George? Judgment on trust funds or something equally exciting?'

'Better than that. They're representing a celebrity on a minor assault and damages charge. Normally, it would be dealt with in the magistrate's court, but the lady in question wants to put her case before a jury. There will be reporters and cameras all over the place on this one.'

'I don't understand why you're giving the brief to me. Shouldn't one of the more senior members be defending?'

'Not this one, miss. They've particularly asked for you.'

'Are you sure?'

'Apparently the client was impressed with the way you worked out the truth in that trial about the radiators. Reckons she was deliberately provoked, and needs a bit of your detective work.' George tapped the letter on top of the brief 'This could be the chance you've been waiting for, Miss O'Connor.' He grinned. 'It's that lovely girl who plays the piano. Cracking voice, too.'

As the penny dropped, Kathleen stared at him open-mouthed.

'They've got her down here as Cecilia Pedlar,' George went on, 'But you'll know her better as Cecilia Saint.' He crossed the hall to open the door to her office. 'By the way, our Mr Julian is representing the newspaper.'

'Newspaper! What newspaper?'

'The one that the Duke of Edinburgh can't stand. Never read it myself. It's all in there.' He glanced at her face. 'Don't worry, miss. Nothing you can't handle.'

Cecilia Saint! Opposing Julian Mountford! A national newspaper! As she flopped into her chair, Kathleen hoped and prayed that George was right. It could be the chance she was waiting for. On the other hand, it could be a disaster.

11

As she slowly walked towards the robing-room, Kathleen wondered what the reaction would be from her learned friends. Now, there indeed was a misnomer. OK, maybe one or two were friendly — too friendly in one particular case — but the words of Julian Mountford, as they left the court, still rang in her ears.

'A word of advice, O'Connor. You may have won this case, but you cannot always rely on further evidence dropping into your lap at the eleventh hour, so it would be a mistake to become too euphoric.'

'Actually, Mountford, I thought it was my closing speech that had influenced the jury to give a not guilty verdict,' she had retorted, muttering 'and I'd rather be euphoric than a sore loser' at his retreating back as he swaggered along the corridor.

But the words stung. In part they were true. Without that witness, who certainly hadn't dropped into her lap, it was unlikely that the jury would have been unanimous in their verdict, however impassioned the closing speech. And no doubt other barristers would air opinions similar to those of the Hon Julian Mountford, son of a viscount, heir to a fortune, and possessor of a formidable ego.

Even though she could match his verbal thrusts and parries, he still managed to get under her skin and leave her feeling more like a callow undergraduate than a young woman approaching her thirtieth birthday, who had passed all her examinations with flying colours.

In the ladies' room, Kathleen splashed cold water on her cheeks and turned to the mirror. The deep-blue, almost violet eyes, with their fringe of dark lashes, studied her reflection, but mainly concentrated on the curled wig, which confirmed to her that she was indeed a barrister. Although still regarded in a junior capacity, nevertheless, she *was* a barrister. It had taken years of hard work to earn that right, and she was proud that at last she could stand up in courts like the Old Bailey, whatever her colleagues might say. The fact that they came from privileged backgrounds did not give them the right to cast doubt upon her ability to do her job as well as any of them. But it did succeed in making her feel inferior.

Suddenly, she remembered something her mother had said, the morning Kathleen was to start at the county high school.

'Listen to me, my darling girl,' she had said softly, the rich brogue like music to Kathleen's ears. 'So far you've only been to Catholic schools, so you have been accepted as one of them. Now you will mix with girls and boys from all sorts of families. They won't all live in council houses like us, and they might not all be friendly at first. Some are quite — posh.'

Kathleen had looked around the cluttered living room.

'I'm not in the least ashamed of living here,' she said.

'Indeed I should hope you're not.' Mrs O'Connor had sounded quite indignant. 'Isn't that what I've been trying to tell you? Never be afraid of your home, or your faith.' She had tucked a stray curl under the unflattering hat. 'And never ever be ashamed of being the clever girl that you are.'

Now, almost eighteen years later, Kathleen smiled at the memory as she went back into the corridor. 'I'm not ashamed, Mam,' she murmured. 'But I do so wish you were here to see me wearing this. And to tell me how to face those high and mighty snobs in the robing-room.'

For a moment she hesitated, her hand on the doorhandle. Then the O'Connor courage took over and she entered the lion's den.

Brian Copeland was the first to break the silence.

'Just heard the news, Kathleen. Congratulations.' His handshake was warm.

Kathleen had known she could rely on Brian. He was one of the few who had welcomed her into chambers.

'Thanks, Brian.' She looked expectantly at the others. One murmured something completely incomprehensible, one gave a curt nod and left the room, and the third decided he had to say something dismissive.

'Of course, you were extremely lucky to be given such a high-profile brief so soon.' Frederick Willoughby continued to place the wig carefully upon his balding head.

Kathleen kept her gaze upon his reflection in the mirror. 'Luck had nothing to do with it. My name was particularly requested by my client's solicitors.'

'Ah, yes, your client ... the common expression is a pop star, I believe.' A significant pause while the wig was slightly straightened, then the wounding shot. 'I understand you were at school together. Would that have been the secondary modern?'

Gritting her teeth, Kathleen matched his terse tone.

'No. That would have been the University College of the South-West. My client was a language scholar before her phenomenal singing voice was discovered.'

'Really? Oh, well, I suppose it takes all sorts.' He looked bored. 'Now you will have to excuse me. I'm due in court fourteen. Interesting case defending a Member of Parliament. Poor chap has been accused of a dodgy share deal. Absolute rubbish, of course. Shouldn't take long.' With a last gaze at his reflection and a twitch of his gown, Frederick Willoughby swept from the room, closely followed by Julian Mountford. The prosecuting counsel did not even glance at Kathleen, but his expression spoke volumes.

Alone, Kathleen felt far from euphoric. How long would this hostility continue, she wondered? Even the judge had that air of slight disapproval when he realized that the defending counsel was a woman, questioning every point of law she voiced. And there was still the reaction from other colleagues in chambers to come. Would they be pleased at her first significant success? Or envious, disparaging?

Was this what it would always be like? Constantly struggling to be accepted, trying to pick herself up again after they had burst her precious balloon? Just because she was female. There couldn't be any other reason, and the sixties were supposed to be the start of a second era of emancipation, according to one newspaper.

Perhaps it would have been better if she had settled for becoming a solicitor. If it hadn't been for Great-aunt Bernadette's money, that would have been her destiny. But it wouldn't have been that much easier, she mused, thinking of colleagues from law school who had come up against similar prejudices, where some clients did not think they should be trusted to handle their conveyancing or probate, let alone criminal charges. Anyway, it was too late now for regrets.

Kathleen removed the treasured wig and carefully placed it in its box. Then she unpinned her hair and allowed it to flow down to her shoulders, combing it into some semblance of order. Time to return to chambers.

Outside, the press were packed into a huddle surrounding her client, until they noticed Kathleen. Then a small bevy of clicking cameras broke away and dashed towards the defence counsel, like shoppers on the first day of a Harrods sale. They jostled with each other, calling her name, pushing microphones up her nostrils. It was almost impossible to hear, let alone answer, the questions they hurled at her. Clutching her brief-case in one hand and robe-bag in the other, she was unable to move for fear of losing her footing. Blinking at the flashbulbs, Kathleen tried appealing.

'Would you please let me through? I have to get back to chambers.'

Her words fell on deaf ears.

'Tell me how you feel . . . '

'Is it true that you were at school . . . ?'

'Did you expect to win?'

They shouted each other down, not waiting for an answer. Even if she had given one, Kathleen was sure it would be misreported in the early-evening editions. She had never experienced anything like it and looked around for someone, anyone, to rescue her. Behind her, a familiar face smirked slightly as its owner tried to edge his way around the crowd. Leaning towards the ear of the nearest newshound, Kathleen shouted:

'If you want a good interview, try my learned friend.' She glanced towards Julian Mountford and smiled sweetly, then turned back to the reporter. 'I think he rather enjoys it,' she yelled, her voice not carrying far in the hubbub.

The brief lull as the reporters turned towards the prosecuting counsel was enough for her to side step in the opposite direction, but the path to freedom was still blocked, until her arm was grabbed by a giant of a man, who hustled her across the pavement.

'What on earth?' she gasped, before she recognized her rescuer. His other arm was clutching her client with equal tenacity. The crowd of cheering onlookers parted before them as surely as if he had been driving a tank, until they were thrust into the back of the most ostentatious Rolls Royce Kathleen had ever seen. Falling on to the fur-covered seat, piled high with leopardskin cushions, she stared open-mouthed as the bodyguard nimbly jumped into the front of the vehicle and the chauffeur nudged through the screaming fans, who were acknowledged by the singer with a dazzling smile and a regal wave.

'Does this happen to you all the time?' Kathleen asked incredulously.

'Sure. It goes with the job.'

'Don't you find it frightening?'

'Only when they try to cut off bits of hair or my clothes. That's why I need a good minder. And Les here is the best.' She was rewarded with a beaming smile from the man in the front seat. 'He could see you were in trouble and knew exactly what to do.'

'Thank you very much, Les,' Kathleen said, recovering her breath. 'I don't know how I would have managed without you.'

'My pleasure, Miss O'Connor.' The smile was now for Kathleen, and a little concerned. 'Hope I didn't hurt your arm too much.'

'Not at all.' Kathleen knew she would have a rare old bruise tomorrow, but what was that compared to being trampled on? 'But I really don't know why the press should be interested in me. I'm only a lawyer, for goodness sake, not an entertainment icon.'

Cecilia, busy at the built-in cocktail cabinet, turned around.

'Ah, but you are young, beautiful, and a female barrister. A good one at that. Of course the press are going to be interested. Drink . . . ?'

Kathleen shook her head. She was longing for a cup of tea.

As Cecilia pressed a button, the drinks-cabinet slid silently back into its recess. 'How did you manage to persuade that woman to give evidence?' she asked. 'My solicitor said she really dug her heels in at first.'

'True. She was such a keen fan, I thought she would jump at the chance. But that was the problem. Her husband didn't know she was going to your performances. I think she felt embarrassed more than anything, being a — groupie, I think they call it — at her age.'

Les spoke over his shoulder. 'That's why I remembered her. Most of Miss Saint's fans

145

are teenagers or blokes. No wonder she didn't want her old man to find out. A bit weird, if you ask me.'

'I don't know,' Cecilia mused. 'Perhaps it was just a kind of surrogate yearning.'

'Surro — what?' Les asked.

'Surrogate. When someone else does something you can't do yourself.'

Kathleen nodded. 'You might well have the answer there, Cecilia. She told me she once trained to be a singer, but her husband made her give it up.'

'Oh, dear. The proverbial domineering husband.'

'Of the first order. He didn't want children, or holidays abroad. I think sheer boredom drove her to follow you around. You were doing all the exciting things she's dreamed about and couldn't do.'

'So what made her change her mind about the photographs?'

'I told her that if she didn't produce them, it was quite likely that you would be heavily fined, or even go to prison. Whatever, your career was in jeopardy, and the fear of harming you was greater than the fear of her husband, thank God.'

'I'll send her some flowers, and a little note of thanks,' Cecilia said, after a moment's silence. 'That won't be considered improper, will it?'

146

'Oh, no. I shouldn't think so. And won't she be just thrilled to bits?'

Thoughtfully, Cecilia sipped her Martini, then changed the subject.

'You are coming to my celebration party at the hotel, aren't you? I phoned from court to order the champagne and canapés. We can take you back to your flat now, if you like, so you can have a rest and change.'

'Thanks just the same, but I have to get back to chambers. My desk is buried under a pile of paperwork.'

'Then can we lunch tomorrow? In my suite at the hotel. More private than the restaurant.' Cecilia giggled. 'We can gossip like schoolgirls again.'

'That would be lovely.' Kathleen glanced out of the window. 'Could you drop me off here, please? It's not so far to walk.'

'No you won't. James . . . ?'

Kathleen burst into laughter. 'I'm sorry, but is your chauffeur really called James?'

'No. He's really called Sid. But 'Home, Sid, and don't spare the horses' doesn't have quite the same ring.' Cecilia met the chauffeur's gaze in the rear-view mirror. 'James, will you go to King's Bench Walk first, please?'

He nodded and smoothly steered the Rolls into the inner lane. The bus-driver who had been gathering speed didn't even toot.

As Kathleen walked into the entrance hall, she was certain that George would offer to make her a cup of tea, less certain whether he had found her another decent brief yet, and completely uncertain what to do about the latest letter relating to her aunt's legacy.

12

'Well done, Miss O'Connor. I knew if anyone could do it, you could. His nibs came back in a foul mood, though. Wish I could have seen his face when you turned the tables on him. Sit yourself down while I brew up. I want to hear it straight from the horse's mouth. Beg your pardon, miss, not that you're a horse.' George appraised Kathleen with a twinkle in his eye. 'Though you could be compared quite favourably to a thoroughbred filly, in my book. Hope you're not offended?'

Chuckling, Kathleen shook her head. Apart from making an excellent cup of tea, George had a great talent for cheering her day with his earthy humour. Maybe it was his cockney background that helped him to put things into perspective, although his observations were not always appreciated by some of the barristers, a fact which did not bother George in the slightest. He knew he was virtually untouchable, provided he continued to run the ship smoothly and efficiently, and the twenty-three barristers who depended upon his skills at juggling briefs and acquiring fees acknowledged without argument that he was the best of many excellent clerks to chambers.

Polio had left a legacy of a slight limp, keeping George out of the services during the war, but enabling him over the years to become a character of repute in Middle Temple, sometimes feared, but always respected. Junior barristers were quietly advised to 'keep on the right side of George' and certainly those who tried to outsmart him soon learned the folly of their ways, but Kathleen had never attempted to tell him how he should do his job. In fact, she frequently sought his advice, resulting in a harmonious working relationship.

Amused, Kathleen watched as George set out a tray with a dainty china cup and saucer and milk jug, opened a tin of biscuits, reserved for his favourite members, carefully arranged a selection on the matching plate, then lifted down the huge cream-and-brown cup and saucer that had sat proudly on the shelf since she brought it back from the Babbacombe pottery last year. He couldn't have been more pleased if it had been made of gold. As always, he read the inscription, 'The cup that cheers — never a truer word.' Then he continued the ritual of swirling hot water around the brown glazed teapot, measuring three generous spoonfuls into the pot and filling it with boiling water. 'There!'

He snuggled the teapot into its knitted cosy. 'Let that draw for a bit while you tell me what was so special about that woman's snaps. All I managed to get out of the solicitor's clerk was that the poor lady was shaking like a leaf.'

Kathleen opened her briefcase, took out Cecilia's file and spread the snapshots out on his desk. There hadn't been time to have them enlarged, but the evidence was clear enough. George examined them minutely, then whistled.

'The rotten sod is trying to rip her dress off. No wonder she clouted him.'

'And would you look at this one, George? The angle of the photographer's camera, the one behind the reporter.'

'Blimey! He's trying to get a shot of one of her tits — begging your pardon, miss. So why didn't they use that one on the front page?'

'Because they could get a better story by taking my client to court for assault and wilful damage. All the other papers had pictures of her smashing his camera, and they closed ranks. They knew they would get more mileage out of a court case as well.' Kathleen studied the photographs, taken outside the Talk of the Town after a cabaret performance, and the startled, then angry expression on Cecilia's face as the reporter's hand grabbed at the slender strap of her evening gown.

Then she pulled out an enlargement of a press photograph from the file, showing the back of Cecilia, her fist making contact with the reporter's face.

'This was the one that started the ball rolling. You can see Mrs Willis behind the two plaintiffs. She was the only other person with a camera facing that way. I just knew it was worth trying to trace her.'

'Brilliant idea of yours, to get that detective on her track.' George lifted the teapot. 'Shall I be mother, miss?' he asked. 'The pot's a bit heavy.'

'Yes, please.' Kathleen shuffled the photographs tidily. 'The real break, of course, was when my client's bodyguard recognized her. All I had to do then was to suggest that he assist the detective.'

'And once the jury saw that it was self-defence, not to mention deliberate provocation, Bob's your uncle, as they say.'

'Absolutely. And the newspaper has to pay costs.'

'Serve them bloody right. I'll keep on at the solicitors to get your fee through as soon as poss, miss.'

'Thanks, George.' Kathleen nibbled at a biscuit. 'Expect you'll be glad to get your share, too.'

'Not so bad for me. I've got a handy little

percentage coming my way from Mr Copeland's last case, plus the shillings from the guineas.' George reached into one of the many pigeonholes above his desk. 'Now, I was going to give you that one where the nurse persuaded the old boy to change his will and his poor old lady was left with nothing. It needs someone like you to find out if there is anything unsavoury in the nurse's background.'

'So what made you change your mind? It sounds interesting.'

'A nice juicy rape case has just come in.'

Kathleen almost choked on her biscuit.

'But isn't Neville Shorter the one who usually handles rapes?'

'Oh, yes, he likes a bit of titillation, does our Mr Shorter.' George frowned. 'Hope I'm not speaking out of turn, miss, but I have thought he gets a bit too familiar with you sometimes. If he becomes a problem . . . '

Kathleen held up her hand. 'It's not a problem. Although . . . ' she hesitated, 'it is something I am aware of. Thank you for your concern, George. It is appreciated, but I can handle the matter.'

'Well, if any time you can't, just let me know.'

Kathleen nodded, and then went back to her original question.

'So why wouldn't Mr Shorter be offered this brief?'

'Because it's another one where the solicitor has asked specifically for you. There's the covering letter, explaining everything.' George pointed at a paragraph. 'And there's your name, requested by the client.'

'Oh!' Kathleen gasped as she read the letter. 'The request is from Laura Davies. She's married to my guardian.'

'Is she now? I didn't know that. But I did know the name of the defendant. Well, everyone has heard of Paul West, haven't they? Do you know him well?'

'Not at all, actually. He mainly works abroad.'

'He's reckoned to be one of the top five fashion photographers in the world,' George mused, 'but I can't make out why Mrs Davies is the one instructing Wainwright's. I would have thought someone like him would have his own solicitor. Contracts and so on.'

'Possibly his agent handles everything like that, but he wanted the family solicitor for this case. It is extremely serious.' Sipping her tea, Kathleen read the covering letter again. 'The model alleges he assaulted her quite viciously before he raped her.' Thoughtfully, she shook her head. 'I've only met him once, briefly, but I cannot for the life of me imagine

Mr West behaving like that. He seemed quite charming.'

'Mmm.' George pulled a doubtful face. 'I've known a few men hanged in my time who have been described as charming.'

Ruefully, Kathleen nodded, then murmured: 'I'm still wondering why they asked for me. Wouldn't it make more sense for him to want a male barrister? It will be a difficult enough case as it is, without the risk of hostility emanating from the prosecuting counsel and judge — and probably most of the jury — because I'm a woman.'

'I reckon it's a clever move.' George picked up the teapot and raised his eyes questioningly at Kathleen, who shook her head. As he refilled his cup, George went on: 'Look at it this way. The prosecution will pick a jury of mainly middle-aged, middle-class, very respectable men. Men who think a good-looking bloke like Paul West, driving snazzy sports cars and swanning around with some gorgeous blonde on his arm, is just the sort of cad who could turn nasty if a girl didn't want to play the game by his rules.'

'We can object if we feel they are prejudiced. But why would it be clever to have a female defence barrister?'

'Let me ask you a question, Miss O'Connor. Would you take the case if you thought he was guilty?'

Kathleen didn't need to think for too long before she answered.

'I know we are supposed to be impartial, but no — I couldn't. Not for rape.'

'Exactly. A man might agree to accept the brief without wondering if the guy was guilty, but a woman couldn't. And any women on the jury will know that she is certain he is innocent. That's why it's a clever move.'

For a moment, Kathleen stared at him. Then she smiled.

'And aren't you the shrewd one, George?' she said. 'We're lucky to have you. And thanks for the tea.'

Back in her room, Kathleen was glad that Neville Shorter was out for the rest of the day. Despite her assurances to George, she did not particularly like sharing a room with a man who attempted to embarrass women if they did not respond to his advances. Even the girls in the typing pool were fed up with it.

She read the brief thoroughly. It would be a nasty case. A very nasty case. But Paul was adamant that the whole thing was a fabrication by a model who wanted to make the headlines. And he was Laura's brother.

An hour later, she read through her notes, questions that needed answers. Then she arranged an appointment for the solicitor to bring Paul and Laura to chambers the following week. Until she had met him, asked the questions, she would not decide whether to take the brief. If she felt he was innocent, she knew she would have a hard task ahead. Skeletons would be dragged out of cupboards. She would have to convince a jury that a beautiful girl had not been raped, or punched. There would be medical evidence to counter. Possibly emotional scenes. There were no witnesses, just the accused and the accuser. The press would have a field day.

But — and it was an enormous but — if she felt that he was guilty, the consequences would be equally unpleasant. She would have to explain the reasons to Laura, and to Laura's son. How on earth would she be able to tell this kindest, gentlest of men that she believed his uncle to be capable of beating and raping a young girl?

13

The hotel had that air of opulence befitting one favoured by visiting film stars, European royals, those who never looked at a price-tag, and celebrities who needed to be constantly in the public eye. On her way to the lift Kathleen passed a top model gliding ankle-deep in carpet, and an opera diva surrounded by an entourage of fussing managers, secretaries, maids with hat-boxes, and anyone who could get in on the act. The leather-padded lift purred its way upward, piloted by an immaculately uniformed attendant, and the heady perfume of massive floral displays greeted her as she walked along the corridor to Cecilia's suite.

Cecilia wore a white satin robe trimmed with swansdown.

'Wow!' Kathleen exclaimed. 'Just look at you.'

'Anyone would think you'd never seen a négligé before.'

'Only on the films. How do you manage to look so gorgeous and all, considering you've only just rolled out of bed?'

'You don't look so bad yourself and all,

considering you've spent hours poring over dreary old legal documents,' Cecilia teased. 'Come on in.' She kissed Kathleen's cheek. 'I've got some champagne on ice to start the ball rolling while we're looking at the menu.'

Laughing, Kathleen protested: 'You're forgetting I have to work this afternoon.'

'Perhaps just a small glass with your lunch?' Deftly, Cecilia released the cork with a slight plop. She acknowledged Kathleen's knowing glance. 'Yes, I have done this a few times before. It goes with the territory, like the screaming fans. I'm not knocking it. Without the fans, I wouldn't be earning more money per performance than my father earns in a year. And without the money, I couldn't afford the champagne.'

'And all this . . . ' Kathleen's glance embraced the tastefully furnished room.

'And all this,' Cecilia repeated, a tiny smile playing around her lips. Even without a scrap of make-up, she looked stunning, blond hair loose around her shoulders, green eyes concentrating on the champagne. Her *retroussé* nose wrinkled slightly as it encountered the bubbles, then she relaxed on to a velvet-covered sofa. 'I needed that,' she sighed. 'Hair of the dog and all that.'

'Sounds like it was quite a party.'

'My agent invited half of Fleet Street.

Officially, she said, to show there were no ill-feelings but, in reality, she was rubbing their noses in it.' Cecilia yawned. 'Didn't fall into bed till the dawn chorus of taxis. Fortunately, champagne doesn't give me too much of a hangover.' She picked up a glossy menu card from the coffee table. 'What do you fancy?' she asked Kathleen.

'Just something light, please. I have some more of those dreary documents to check before a con and I'll not be wanting to fall asleep in front of my colleague.'

'A con? What's that when it's at home?'

'A conference. With a solicitor.'

'Ah.' Cecilia scanned the list. 'How about lemon sole with baby new potatoes and a green salad?'

'Sounds delicious.' Kathleen waited while her friend phoned the order to room service, and then asked: 'Do you have a performance tonight?'

'Thank goodness, no. My contract with Talk of the Town finished last week. But I have a gig tomorrow at that new nightclub in Park Lane, so I might as well stay here for a couple more nights. Then it's back home for a break. Mum and Dad have been a bit worried about me.'

Kathleen noticed the shadows under Cecilia's eyes.

'And not without justification,' she commented. 'When would you last have had a decent night's sleep?'

'You sound just like my mother. Every time she phones she asks if I am sleeping properly, eating properly, getting enough fresh air.'

'And I'm sure you've been telling her whopping great fibs in reply.'

'Of course.' They laughed, and then Cecilia went on, in a more serious tone: 'I had to, Kathleen. Mum would have been on the next train if she had known the truth.'

'Would that have been such a bad idea?'

Cecilia shrugged. 'I admit I was tempted at times, but the sight of all those reporters and cameras outside the court each day would have really distressed her. Not to mention the phone calls.'

'More so than reading the newspapers?'

'Yes. At least I could tell her it was mainly lies. Anyway, it would have been very complicated for her, getting time off from the school, making sure Dad and Andrew had enough food, and sorting out the animals.'

Smiling, Kathleen nodded. 'Ah, yes. I'd forgotten your menagerie. How many would there be now?'

'At the last count, two dogs, umpteen chickens, a family of ducks, Andrew's pony and goodness knows how many cats. Mum was so upset about the trial, she forgot to take the last litter to be done. Now four of them have plump little bellies . . . ' for a moment she paused, grinning at Kathleen. 'I suppose you wouldn't want a kitten, would you? It would be company for your dog.'

Kathleen shook her head.

'I don't think she'd take too kindly to a flat mate, after seven years of ruling the roost. Anyway, I have to consider the neighbours. They're goodness itself, the way they keep an eye on Bridie and take her for a walk every day. It wouldn't be fair to expect them to kitten-mind as well.'

'No, you're right, but if you know anyone . . . '

'I could ask Jane. The children might like a kitten.'

'OK. Does she still live in East Grinstead?'

'Yes. They've moved to a gorgeous new house now that Sandy's a fully paid-up surgeon. Huge garden for the children to play in, although . . . ' Kathleen hesitated. 'On second thoughts, she might not be too keen on the idea, with another baby on the way.'

'How many will that make?'

'Four, but she's so big it's possible it might be twins.'

'Crikey! She's going to have her hands full. Imagine, five children under the age of

162

— what — seven?'

'The eldest is just six, and little Philip coming up to his second birthday.'

'How on earth does she manage?'

'She'll manage fine.' A wry little smile crossed Kathleen's face. 'Didn't my mam have eight, and another on the way, when . . . ?' Her voice trailed.

'Oh, Kathleen, I'm so sorry. I'd forgotten.' Concern clouded Cecilia's eyes.

The painful moment was interrupted by a discreet knock on the door, which announced the arrival of their luncheon. Swiftly and efficiently the waiter transferred the food from the trolley to a small table, accepted Cecilia's generous tip with a bow, and left.

'This is something I'm really looking forward to when I go home,' Cecilia commented, spooning potatoes on to her plate.

'What? Having your mother bring gourmet meals to your room, silver service and all?' Kathleen joked.

'Idiot! Although Mum does make such a fuss of me, and for a teacher she's a nifty cook.' Thoughtfully, Cecilia mixed her salad dressing. 'No,' she went on. 'It's the opportunity to have a good old chat without being interrupted.'

'Autograph hunters and such like?'

163

Cecilia nodded. 'They mean well, and I know it goes with the job, but sometimes they want to talk, or take a snapshot of me with them. By the time they've finished, my food is cold and I've lost the thread of the conversation I was having in the first place.'

'You'd think they would understand you need some privacy.'

'Once you're in the public eye, they feel they own you.'

'Well, I promise I won't ask you for an autograph, Miss Saint.'

'You've got enough already,' Cecilia retorted. 'Didn't you keep any of the letters I wrote after we graduated and went our separate ways?'

'Actually, I kept all of them. Aren't I the world's greatest hoarder?' Kathleen helped herself to a tiny triangle of brown bread and butter. 'But they were all from Cecilia Pedlar, not Cecilia Saint.' Kathleen ate for a moment, and then asked, 'What made you change your name? There's nothing wrong with Pedlar.'

'According to my agent, there's nothing right with it. Doesn't fit the image, she said. Anyway, when I mentioned that I was named after my grandmother, who was named after the patron saint of music, Dee pounced on it straight away.' Cecilia's knife cut easily through the fillet steak. 'And I have to admit it has worked very well,' she went on.

'True.' Kathleen nodded. 'Did your grandmother live up to her name, as well?'

'No. But *her* mother had a glorious voice. Trained to be an opera singer. Mostly chorus, but sang Violetta in *La Traviata* at Covent Garden once, when the lead singer was taken ill.'

'Really?'

'Sadly, it was her one moment of triumph.'

Kathleen was almost afraid to ask, 'What happened?'

'She was seduced by the tenor playing Alfredo and became pregnant.'

'Oh!' For a moment, Kathleen was speechless. 'And did the young man do the honourable thing?'

'He had no choice. When Great-grandmama's father turned up at the stage-door with his shotgun, the young man decided that discretion was the better part of valour, and went to see the vicar pronto.'

'Thanks be to God.'

'I'm not so sure about that. They were happy enough for a while, until he ran off to Italy with a soprano ten years his senior, a Merry Widow in more ways than one, but so rich, he was able to overlook her vibrato.'

'So what did your poor great-grandmother do?'

'There wasn't much she could do in those days, except go back to the farm and throw herself on the mercy of her father. Fortunately, he was a good man at heart, so he took care of her and the child.' Cecilia smiled as she mused. 'I was very close to my grandmother. In fact, she was the one who encouraged me to sing. Reckoned I had inherited her mother's talent. But I didn't agree at first.'

'Isn't that amazing? You have such a beautiful voice, I would have thought it would be obvious.'

'Thank you.' A slight frown furrowed Cecilia's brow. 'I suppose I was aware of how unpredictable any career in the arts can be. Afraid, perhaps. So I decided to go for something more secure. And I've always been interested in languages.'

'But you sang so well in the school concerts. You even won the Dufton music prize.'

Her fork half-way to her mouth, Cecilia looked astonished.

'Fancy you remembering that!'

'And wasn't I there, cheering like mad, at the presentation? After all, you were my best friend at Exeter.'

Cecilia nodded reflectively. 'Why on earth did we lose touch for all these years?' she wondered. 'Oh, I know we wrote and remembered birthdays and all that, but we didn't meet up.'

'It's the way of life, I suppose. I was in London, still studying law, and you were all over the place, being famous. So famous, in fact, that I kept a scrap-book about you.'

'You didn't?'

'And why shouldn't I? It's not everyone can say they've had their stockings darned by a celebrity.'

'Oh, gosh, yes. Are you still useless at sewing?'

'Completely. Take after my mam, I'm afraid. Good job Jane's mam was handy with a needle, or I don't know how I'd have managed, with clothes being rationed and all.'

'How are they?'

'The Harrisons? Older. Frailer. But truly good souls at heart. Wasn't I the lucky one to be given a home by such lovely people? And it was all thanks to Jane's uncle that I was able to go to Exeter at all.'

'That and the fact that you passed all the exams in the first place.' Cecilia sipped her champagne. 'They must be very proud of you. After all, you're becoming a bit of a celebrity yourself.'

'Go along with you.'

'It's true. You're one of the youngest barristers in your chambers, and a female to boot. When I read about you in the paper, I knew you were the right one to represent me.' Cecilia refilled her glass. 'So what's next? You should get a good case after my result.'

'Actually,' Kathleen paused, 'I've been asked to represent Laura's brother.'

'Which one?'

'Paul. The photographer.'

Cecilia looked impressed. 'That'll make some of them sit up and take notice. Who's he prosecuting?'

'It's the other way round, I'm afraid.'

'Crikey! You'll hit the front page. What's he supposed to have done?'

'I can't go into details, of course, but a girl claims he assaulted her. It will be a very difficult case, especially with my connection with his sister, so I haven't yet decided whether to take it.'

'How well do you know him?'

'I don't. Well, I met him once when I was out shopping with Laura, but it was no more than an introduction. He was rushing to catch a plane.'

Cecilia nodded. 'I would have liked him to take some decent pictures of me, but heard he'd been working abroad for years. How long has he been back in the UK?'

'I'm not sure. But I've arranged to meet him next week, with Laura.'

'It'll be a tricky one but, if you can pull it off, it will be good for your career. I'm assuming he's claiming innocence.'

'Yes. And I won't take the case if I suspect he might be guilty.'

'Good for you. But I hope you do take it.' Cecilia grinned. 'It'll be one in the eye for some of those stuffed shirts in your chambers.' She held a finger to the tip of her nose. 'Especially Mr Julian Mountford. Did you see his expression when the verdict was announced? If looks could kill . . . ' Her expression became serious again. 'Will they give you a hard time if you take Paul West's case?'

'Probably. Won't they all be expecting that I stick with corporate cases for quite a while longer, until I've proved myself worthy? So, to defend a photographer of his calibre straight after your trial would be rather like . . . '

'Rubbing salt into their wounds?'

'Well, yes. And I don't really want to upset them. I do have to work with them. But Laura thinks I can handle it and, even more important, so does George.'

'That funny little guy who watches everyone like a hawk?'

169

Kathleen nodded.

'He's no fool,' Cecilia went on, 'and I have a feeling he wants you to succeed. So if you think it's right, go ahead.' She waved her glass merrily in the air. 'And sod the stuffed shirts.'

For a while, they chatted in pleasant companionship, the conversation flitting from the legal world to music, nostalgic reminiscences from their days at Exeter, and speculation as to their futures.

'How are things with you and Desmond?' asked Cecilia, as she poured coffee into the minute cups. 'You've been going out with him for some time now, but you're still not wearing a ring.'

Kathleen didn't answer immediately. It was a question that cropped up from time to time when she visited Jane, or Mrs Harrison. Laura had never actually voiced the question, but sometimes it was there, in her eyes, and Kathleen knew Laura would welcome her as her son's wife. Eventually, she said, 'We have a sort of — understanding, I suppose. At first we were both so committed to our studies there was little time or money for anything else.'

'And now . . . ?'

'I don't know if I told you, but Desmond is working at a new special school in Kent. He's deputy head, but would like to be a headmaster one day, to give him more authority to put things into action that will help the children. So he is still studying, taking courses, and so on.'

'What about you? Are you aiming higher?'

Kathleen shrugged 'I'd really love to take silk, but that would delay any thoughts of a family for quite a few years.' She sighed. 'To be honest, we haven't actually discussed marriage in any detail. We just seem comfortable with things the way they are.'

'You sound like a pair of old slippers.'

Kathleen laughed. 'Perhaps we do take each other for granted a bit.'

'Do you love him?'

'He's my dearest friend, and I can't imagine being without him, so I suppose I must do.'

'Then why wait? You already have a flat and I'm sure you could afford to get married now, if you really wanted to?'

'It's not just the money.'

'So what's the problem?'

Again Kathleen hesitated before she answered: 'As things are, I can delay a marriage, but not a pregnancy.'

Cecilia stared at her. 'You really go along with all that birth-control thing?'

'Of course. It would be wrong for me to go against the teachings of my church.'

Silently, Cecilia poured them both another cup of coffee and gracefully raised her legs on to the elegant sofa. Then she slowly said, 'Does that mean that you and Desmond haven't . . . ?' As Kathleen shook her head, she went on, 'How can anything so delicious be considered a sin?'

'It is only considered to be a sin if it is outside marriage.'

'And Desmond has accepted this? The man must be a saint!'

'He is, for sure. You should see him with some of his disturbed pupils. They worship him.'

Cecilia placed her coffee cup back on to the coffee table.

'Could you combine being a barrister with having children?'

'I believe that a mother should be with her children while they are small. But there is no reason at all why I should not return to the Bar when they are at school.' Kathleen decided to change the subject. 'It's all in God's hands, anyway. And there is something else I want to ask you about. Perhaps you can give me some advice.'

'Fire away.'

Kathleen handed her friend the letter with the Irish postmark. The letter that had been on her mind ever since it arrived.

Eventually, Cecilia raised her head and pursed her lips.

'What's the legal position?' she asked.

'There isn't one, really, because there isn't a will. The issue is a moral one and I really don't know what to do, except to pray.'

'Poor Kathleen. Your life is full of moral dilemmas, isn't it?'

For a few minutes, they discussed the pros and cons of the problem, neither of them finding a satisfactory answer. Then Kathleen glanced at her watch.

'Can that really be the time?' she gasped.

Cecilia reached for the telephone. 'There'll be a taxi waiting for you by the time you get downstairs,' she said. 'We both work too hard,' she added, as they hugged goodbye. 'What we need is a break. There's a lovely thatched cottage with a tatty old hammock in the garden that I can recommend.'

'The one on the edge of Dartmoor?'

'That's the one. Why don't we go down there one weekend, and do nothing more arduous than watch Dad inspecting his roses for the first signs of greenfly?'

'Sounds grand.'

'It is. And we mustn't lose touch again.'

'No. I promise. And thanks for the lunch.'

'My pleasure.'

In the taxi, Kathleen thought about their

conversation. It was true, her life was full of moral dilemmas at the moment. But the most pressing one was the letter from Ireland. Perhaps she should discuss it with Len before attempting to make a decision. He would give sensible advice.

14

Kathleen had deliberately arranged the appointment at a time when Neville Shorter would be in court. It was difficult enough interviewing clients at the best of times, knowing that his ears were pinned back to catch every word. This particular case was much more personal, and she needed absolute privacy for the initial meeting. If she decided to take the case, there was nothing he could do about it, and if she decided not to, Kathleen knew he would be only too pleased to accept the brief.

As always, Laura Davies was simply but stylishly dressed, the soft green woollen suit with its pencil-slim skirt complemented her trim figure, while the neat matching hat sat forward from her sleek French pleat. It was easy to accept that she had once been a fashion model in Paris, but much more difficult to accept that she was now in her fifties.

She greeted Kathleen warmly.

'Thank you so much for agreeing to see us, my dear. I wasn't sure that you would, because we are so close, but I'm grateful.'

Before Kathleen could answer, Paul West stepped forward, his right hand extended.

'I'm so sorry I was in such a rush when my sister tried to introduce us once before. You must have thought me very rude.'

'Not at all. You had a plane to catch. And it was many years ago.' As they clasped hands, Kathleen felt a rush of blood to her head. Like Laura, Paul had inherited the dark good-looks from his Italian mother, but his eyes . . . deep brown and soulful, yet with a smile lurking near the surface. It took a moment for Kathleen to tear her own eyes away so that she could shake hands with Mr Jarvis, who had been so helpful to her during her time with Wainwright's.

Usually one of the junior typists would bring in a tray of tea. This time it was George. Kathleen was sure it was so that he could have a chance to assess her visitors. After tea and biscuits had been dispensed, Kathleen picked up the sheaf of papers lying on her desk.

'You don't need me to tell you that these are very serious charges indeed, Mr West,' she began.

'It would mean the end of my career if they were believed,' he said quietly, 'and that is a terrifying thought.' He replaced his cup and saucer on the tray before he went on:

'Actually, I would feel more comfortable if you called me Paul, Miss O'Connor, and may I call you Kathleen? Of course I would be more formal in front of other people.'

She nodded, and then referred back to the papers.

'This young lady, Miss Gloria Benson, alleges that you assaulted her while you were working together on a fashion-shoot in Scotland. She claims that you deliberately chose a remote area in the Highlands, sent your assistant away under some pretext, and then forced yourself upon her. When she resisted, she states that you became quite violent and threatening.'

'That is not true, or at least, not all of it.'

Kathleen raised her eyebrows, and waited.

'The only part that is true is the fact that I deliberately chose a remote area. That was exactly what the fashion editor of the magazine requested. Wild, rugged scenery, lochs and rivers. Look, I can show you some of the pictures.' He took a portfolio from his briefcase and passed it across to Kathleen. The photographs were good. Very good. And they were certainly wild and rugged, with the model posed on a rock, or near a waterfall. The girl was young, with flowing blonde hair tossed in the wind, and seductive eyes. She was wearing a variety of twin sets, cardigan suits and tartan skirts, and there was something about her that reminded Kathleen of Rose.

'They were for the autumn collection, as you can see,' Paul explained, 'but we always have to do it several months in advance.'

'May I keep these for the file?'

'Of course.'

'Now, Paul, tell me exactly what happened on the day in question.'

'There's not much to tell actually. Eric, Gloria and I had stayed the night at a small inn — Eric Coleman is my assistant — and we set off for the shoot immediately after breakfast. As the morning wore on, Gloria complained more and more about the cold.'

Kathleen picked up one of the photographs. It was taken on open heathland and there were patches of snow on the distant mountains. The model was smiling, but holding on to her tam-o-shanter.

'I'm not surprised,' Kathleen commented. 'This looks rather bleak and windswept.'

'I agree. It was a bitterly cold day.'

'So, what did you all do after you had finished taking the photographs?'

'Eric and I wanted to go on to Mallaig. I had another commission for a travel feature and thought I could kill two birds with one stone.'

And claim two sets of expenses, Kathleen thought, but said nothing. He wasn't the only one, and it had nothing to do with the case.

'Did Miss Benson accompany you?'

'No. She was so cold, we took her back to the inn and organized some hot food and drinks, which we took up to her room. She said she would rest while we were out, and we left her tucked up with a hotwater bottle.'

'How long were you in Mallaig?'

'Just long enough to photograph the fishing-boats as they came into the harbour. About an hour, I suppose. Gloria was fast asleep when we returned to the inn. It was a shame to wake her, but we had a long drive back to London, and it was getting dark.'

'Why didn't you stay another night in the inn?'

'We thought about it, but the weather forecast was ominous and it was already beginning to snow. The last thing I wanted was to be stranded up there for goodness knows how long.'

'Did Miss Benson object?'

'Not really. We bought her a small bottle of cognac to keep her warm, wrapped her in the car rug, and she was asleep again before we had gone half a mile.'

'Did you drive through the night?'

'Yes. Eric and I took turns.'

'And did Miss Benson sleep for the whole journey?'

'Yes. Apart from one stop when we topped up the petrol and she used the toilet. I think the combination of the cold and the brandy knocked her out.'

'Did you take her straight home?'

'Of course. She lives in Streatham, as you can see.' Paul pointed to her statement.

Kathleen nodded. 'Was her flatmate home when you arrived?'

'Yes. We told Veronica that Gloria wasn't feeling too good, and she helped us get her upstairs and into bed. Did I tell you about the tumble?'

'I've read about it in your statement, but I'd like you to tell me, if you don't mind.'

'Not at all. It was right at the end of the shoot, when we were in some sort of copse on a steep slope. A stag suddenly appeared, and I don't know who was the most startled, Gloria or the beast. She wasn't in any danger, but she tried to run towards me, lost her footing, and slithered down the slope. That's how she got the bruise on her face.'

'Did she need medical attention?'

'I offered to take her to the nearest doctor, but she said it wasn't much and she'd rather go straight back to the inn.'

Kathleen shuffled through the photographs again.

'Did you manage to get a photograph of the stag?' she asked.

'Unfortunately, I'd just used the last of the film, and by the time I'd reloaded, he'd vanished. It would have made a good shot, too. He was a handsome brute.'

'Pity. It would have helped. But I assume your colleague saw it, and the tumble?'

'Oh, yes. It should be in his statement.'

'He does say that he never left you alone with Miss Benson, but I don't recall anything about a stag.'

'Perhaps he didn't think it was important.'

'Perhaps. But it is a question that will be asked by the prosecuting counsel.' Kathleen read the model's statement again, then said, 'I have to ask you this, Paul. Did you assault her? Sexually, or physically?'

He looked straight into her eyes.

'No. I will stand in court, put my hand on the Bible, and plead not guilty. And that's the truth.'

'Do you have any idea why she should make such a dreadful accusation?'

'Not really. Except . . . '

'Except . . . ?'

'Gloria is very ambitious. Her agent told me that she once deliberately ran in and out of the ladies' room at a huge jazz concert at Earl's Court, in the hope that the press would notice and take some photographs.'

'And did they?'

'Oh, yes. She even managed to get an interview with a gossip columnist on a national newspaper, and claimed she would give anything to become an actress.'

Again Kathleen thought of Rose. 'Was she talented enough?'

'Sadly, no. She'd failed auditions for RADA and suchlike. She is a pretty girl and the camera likes her, but she's not got the charisma of Marilyn Monroe.'

'Well, she will have to call upon all of her acting abilities if your story is true.'

'It is true, I promise you. And Eric can verify it.' Paul sighed. 'I'm so very surprised and disappointed that she has done this to me. I thought we were friends.'

Kathleen turned to Mr Jarvis. 'We will have to verify these facts with the landlord of the inn and anyone who might have seen Miss Benson before they left Scotland.'

'I agree,' he said. 'If the girl had been attacked one would have expected her to be very distressed.'

'Exactly.'

'In my opinion, the whole thing is very flimsy, with nothing to substantiate it.'

As Kathleen began to gather the papers back into the file, Laura spoke for the first time.

'Have you decided to take Paul's case?' she quietly asked.

'Once I have had my notes typed up and I've studied them, I will inform Mr Jarvis of my decision. My diary is pretty full just at the moment.'

'And if you can't?'

Kathleen smiled. 'There are other options, but I would prefer to wait and see at this stage.'

'Of course. I understand. It's just that we are both so much hoping you can.' Laura looked at her brother.

Paul nodded agreement. 'We were very impressed with the way you handled the defence of Cecilia Saint.'

'Thank you.'

'There is one more thing.' He looked embarrassed.

'Yes?'

'It's a little delicate . . . ' he hesitated before he went on, 'but if you could stress the bleakness of the location, I am sure that the jury would understand that no man in his right mind would plan to seduce a girl half-way up a freezing Scottish mountain.' He laughed a little self-consciously. 'I'm no angel, Kathleen, but I do prefer a warm bed in a comfortable hotel for any amorous interludes.'

Kathleen was surprised to feel her cheeks flooding with colour. Why on earth should she blush at Paul's words, she wondered?

'I'm sorry,' he apologized. 'I have no wish to offend you, but I'm sure you will agree it is a factor to be taken into account.'

'I'll bear it in mind,' she murmured.

★ ★ ★

After they had left, Kathleen dictated her notes for the typist, which helped clarify various points in her mind. Gloria Benson hadn't even complained about Paul's behaviour for eight days. It must be that it had given her time to think about it, and wonder if she could gain some benefit from the situation. Why hadn't she said anything to the landlord in Scotland? And if she was afraid of Paul, as she claimed in her statement, why did she agree to travel back to London with him? It would have been simple enough to get a taxi from the inn to the nearest station.

Then there was the corroboration from Eric. There was no reason why he should risk perjuring himself in court. He was not accused of being implicated in the attack.

Added to that was the fact that Kathleen had known Laura for many years, and also her other brother, Robert, now living in Devon. Yes, it was possible that a rogue family member could exist but, remembering his expression, open and honest, nothing furtive at all, she knew without doubt that there was no way Paul West could punch and rape a girl.

15

'To tell the truth, Kathleen, I can't make head or tail of this.' Shaking his head, Len read the letter again. 'Do they want you to give the money back?'

'I shouldn't think so, although I don't understand it, either, and I'm a lawyer.' Kathleen smiled wryly. 'An Irish one at that.'

'You say the solicitor is off sick. Wasn't there anyone else who could help you?'

'His clerk is on holiday, his secretary has left to have a baby, and the new one hasn't started yet.'

'So who answered the phone? The cleaning-lady?'

'It could have been the cleaning-lady, for all the sense she made.' Kathleen slipped the letter back into the envelope. 'That's not fair, really. The poor child has just started her first job and suddenly she's the only one there to do everything.'

'That's the trouble with small firms, I suppose. Did she know anything at all?'

'Only that the mother superior had come into the office, and when she left, Mr Malone dictated this letter, or something like it, to the girl. But he wasn't feeling well, and she'd only begun evening classes for shorthand and typing last term, so she had to write some longhand and thought she might have missed some bits out.'

'No wonder it's such a mess. Didn't he read it before he signed it?'

Kathleen shook her head. 'Apparently he went off home to his bed and asked the girl to sign it for him.'

'What's wrong with him? Flu or something?'

'She didn't know. But she said he had a nasty rash so she wouldn't go round to his house in case it was something catching.'

'Well, there's nothing more you can do till he's back at work, I suppose.'

'Not really, except to write a letter of acknowledgement, wish him well, and ask him to phone me when he feels better.'

Before Len could say more, Laura came into the room. She looked anxious.

'I've just had a call from Nell,' she said. 'Jane has been taken into hospital so Nell and Fred are going straight over to look after the little ones.'

'But she's not due for some time yet,' Kathleen said. 'Is there a risk that she might lose the baby?'

'It's more a question of Jane being at risk,

I'm afraid. Her blood pressure has hit the roof and they are concerned about the possibility of toxaemia.'

'Holy Mother, that's terrible,' Kathleen cried. 'What can they do about it?'

'Complete bed-rest until the child is born. They'll probably keep her in hospital to make sure.'

'Best place for her,' Len agreed. 'I suppose Nell and Fred will stay over there for the duration?'

'Probably, although I'm sure Sandy's parents will take a turn.'

'Will we be able to visit Jane?' Kathleen asked.

Laura shook her head. 'No visitors except Sandy. Any excitement could be dangerous. Which reminds me . . . ' Laura hesitated before she asked Kathleen, 'Have you told Jane that you are defending Paul?'

'No. I haven't had a chance to phone, what with the letter from Ireland and all. Why do you ask?'

'Well — I don't know if you remember, but Jane went out with him a few times.'

Kathleen searched her memory. 'I remember her telling me about some grand function he took her to. She was so excited because she'd met Stewart Granger. That was years ago.'

'It didn't last very long, but I thought Paul's trial might worry her, so I decided not to mention it, not even to Nell.'

Kathleen nodded. 'As you know, I can't discuss it, anyway, although no doubt it will be in the newspapers when it goes to court.'

'Yes, but I'll explain to Sandy and Nell once it becomes public, and they'll keep the papers away from Jane.' Laura reached for a packet of cigarettes, lit one, and inhaled deeply. 'Oh, Kathleen, I shall be so glad when it is all over. I haven't slept properly since Paul told me, and now this worry about Jane . . . '

'She's in good hands,' Kathleen comforted. 'I'll phone later and see if there is any more news, or anything I can do.'

Len glanced at the clock. 'Better go down and get the bar open, I suppose.'

Laura stubbed out her cigarette. 'Wonder how Desmond is getting on,' she murmured. 'It's quite a challenge taking a group of normal youngsters camping, let alone those with the problems his pupils have.'

'He loves it,' Kathleen said. 'And don't they love him? I was very impressed when I went to the Christmas party. All the teachers are so dedicated.'

'They have to be, I suppose.' Laura stood up. 'Do you have plans for tonight?'

'Only to walk this pooch.' She nudged Bridie with her toe. 'And wash my hair. But if you need help in the kitchen, I don't mind.'

'No, thanks just the same. For once I'm fully staffed. But I've had a cancellation for a table for two, so you're welcome to eat here. I'll come and sit with you when I can get away.'

'That would be nice. I'll just take Bridie for her constitutional first. And Patch, too, if you like.'

★ ★ ★

Kathleen ordered one of Laura's special pasta dishes and a glass of red wine. Many of the diners were regulars whom she had noticed before, and a family party, with two tables pushed together, seemed to be celebrating a birthday. It was quite pleasant, listening to the gentle hubbub of sound and anticipating something much more appetizing than the cheese salad she had planned.

The waitress brought the pasta carbonara, Laura brought the wine, and lingered after the waitress had gone back to the kitchen.

'This smells delicious,' Kathleen said, wondering why Laura wasn't moving on to serve wine at other tables, as usual.

'It's becoming quite popular.' Laura smiled

190

as she fidgeted with the tiny vase of flowers. 'Kathleen . . . ' She sounded diffident. 'Would you mind sharing your table?'

'Not at all. You've certainly got a full house tonight.'

'Well, more people are eating out at weekends now. The thing is . . . ' Laura moved the vase an inch. 'It's Paul.'

'Oh, dear.' Kathleen chose her words very carefully. 'I'm only supposed to talk to clients when their solicitor is present.'

'I know. And so does Paul. Surely it wouldn't matter so long as you don't mention his case.' Laura looked around at her customers, all immersed in their own business. 'And I shouldn't think you'd need to worry about anyone here telling tales.'

Laura was probably right, but still Kathleen hesitated.

'I'm sorry, Kathleen.' Laura placed her hand on Kathleen's shoulder. 'I shouldn't have put you on the spot like this. It was just that he turned up out of the blue, said he was feeling a bit fed up and fancied some company.' She smiled. 'Don't worry. I'll give him some food upstairs and pop up later on if it gets a bit quieter.'

It didn't seem right that Paul couldn't get a table in his sister's restaurant, Kathleen thought. It would be lonely for him in the flat. And she might end up with a strange man as a table companion, anyway.

'No, don't do that,' she said. 'It's quite secluded here, so it should be OK. Just tell him . . .'

'He mustn't mention the trial.' Laura completed the sentence. 'Of course. And thanks, Kathleen I'll bring him over.'

'I'm so sorry to disturb your meal,' Paul said as he slid into the chair. 'I had no idea that it would be so busy, or that you would be here. All my chums seem to be away for the weekend, and the London eateries aren't much fun for a lone guy.' He smiled up at his sister. 'I'll have the carbonara as well, please, Laura.'

'It's very good,' Kathleen said, trying her first mouthful.

'I know. Laura used to cook it when we were little.' Paul poured himself a glass of water. 'Did you know that she brought us up after our mother died?'

'No. How old were you?'

'About three months. She succumbed to that awful flu epidemic. Poor Dad was so grief-stricken he sold the house and we just drifted around the world on the boat. It must have been tough on Laura. She was only just a teenager herself.'

Fascinated, Kathleen listened as he talked

about his wandering childhood and the many countries they had visited, only to move on when something more exotic beckoned. It wasn't until Laura had insisted that her brothers needed more than languages, geography, marine skills and rudimentary maths that they eventually put down some roots in England. Laura became a fashion model, Robert joined the merchant navy, and Paul turned to photography. Their father sailed with the tidal waters of the Thames and built a thriving business, selling his catch to the fishmongers around Southend and Canvey Island. When arthritis began to get the better of him, he took on a younger man as his partner — the man who became Laura's first husband and father of Lawrence and Desmond.

All Kathleen's anxieties about dining with a client had long disappeared by the time the syllabub was placed on the table. With Desmond away, the worry about the letter, and now Jane, Kathleen had expected a rather miserable evening. Instead, she was relaxed and happy. Paul had been grand company. Not a word out of place, just pleasant conversation.

Laura interrupted Paul's hilarious tale of a fading Hollywood star who had begged him to lose ten years from her age and ten pounds from her weight.

'Would you mind very much having your coffee up in the flat?' she asked. 'I've just had a call from someone wanting a table for two at eight-thirty and all the others are booked.'

Kathleen was still giggling. 'As long as I get to hear what that poor actress said about the photos when you'd finished.'

'It's a sad, sad story,' Paul said, standing up.

Laura turned to Kathleen. 'You can phone Nell while you're up there if you like. Sandy should be home by now.'

Sandy sounded tired, which was understandable. Everything had happened so quickly, and he'd been dashing backwards and forwards, taking the children to a friend until Jane's parents arrived, stocking up the fridge, picking up the Harrisons from the station, and then back to the hospital to sit with Jane for a short while.

'She's putting a brave face on it,' he said, 'but obviously she's worried, not only about the baby, but the other three as well. Once the novelty of having Gran and Granddad to stay has worn off, they might begin to fret, especially little Philip, who is going through a 'clingy' phase.'

'Can they talk to Jane on the telephone?' Kathleen asked.

'No. The doctor is afraid it might make matters worse. There's always a risk, with this condition, of having fits. That could be really serious, for Jane as well as the baby — or babies. There's a strong possibility it might be twins, but they can't be sure just yet.'

'Oh, Sandy. I'm so sorry all this has happened. Do give her my fondest love and tell her I'll be praying for her all the time. You take care of yourself as well.'

'I'll be fine, once I've had a whisky and a hot bath, in that order.'

'Away you go, then. Can I have a word with Auntie Nell?'

As expected, Auntie Nell was worried sick and Kathleen spent several minutes trying to reassure her, even though she felt far from reassured herself.

'I don't know what I'd do if anything happened to Jane,' Kathleen said, as she replaced the telephone in its cradle. 'She's like a sister to me.'

Paul didn't answer at first, just continued to pour the coffee.

'I'm sure she'll be fine,' he said eventually, handing the cup to Kathleen. 'Jane has hidden strengths.'

Thoughtfully, Kathleen sipped her coffee. 'You were quite close to her once, weren't you?'

Again he hesitated before answering. 'I wouldn't say close. We just went out together a few times. It was a long time ago.'

'Yes, I was away at college.'

'Did she talk to you about our — friendship?' Paul crossed to the window, staring out into the dusk.

'Not really. I remember her being thrilled when you took her to a gala film night. And she was so grateful that you helped her to get that lovely job on the magazine.'

Looking slightly uncomfortable, he shrugged his shoulders. Kathleen had the impression that he didn't want to talk about it.

'Auntie Nell needs some bits and pieces,' she said. 'So I'll take them over after Mass. Good job I still have a key.'

He nodded, but his thoughts seemed elsewhere as he took an expensive-looking silver cigarette-case and lighter from his pocket. Suddenly he looked back at Kathleen.

'I'm sorry,' he said. 'Do you mind?'

'Not at all.' She shook her head as he offered the case and watched as he flicked the lighter. He had good hands, she thought. Long, tapering fingers that would suit a musician. Then she realized that he was watching her, as she was watching him, and they both laughed, a little self-consciously.

'I'm sorry.' Paul sat down opposite

Kathleen. 'Didn't mean to stare. It's just that I was wondering . . . '

'And what were you wondering?' Kathleen prompted.

'It is rather personal. I don't want to offend you.'

Curious, Kathleen said, 'We'll never know if you don't say anything, now will we?'

Paul's smile was nervous, but very sweet.

'I was wondering about your friendship with Desmond.'

'Desmond?' Kathleen was surprised rather than offended.

'Laura said you are close.'

'Well, we have known each other since we were children.'

'I know. But is it serious?'

'It depends what you mean by serious.'

'Engagement rings. Wedding-bells. Children. That sort of serious.'

'Oh.' Kathleen thought for a long time before she went on: 'It's true that we are the closest of friends — and Desmond is the kindest man imaginable. Always there for me.'

'But has he asked you to marry him?'

'Not in so many words. We both wanted to establish our careers before we thought of marriage to anyone.'

'But you haven't made plans. Set a date?

Anything like that?'

'No. But we enjoy each other's company and support each other.'

'It sounds more like brotherly love than loverly love to me.'

Kathleen didn't answer. There were times when she wondered whether her relationship with Desmond was too platonic. Perhaps it was too much under control ever to become passionate?

Paul put another of her thoughts into words.

'Do you know what I think?' He didn't wait for her to reply. 'I think it has gone on for so long that everyone will assume you are going to marry. It's a habit, more than a romance.' He looked into her face. 'And if you're not careful, you could find yourself drifting into a marriage that doesn't have the necessary spark to keep it alive.'

'I haven't given it that much thought,' she murmured, feeling a little breathless at Paul's closeness.

'You're not a very good fibber, Kathleen O'Connor.' He laughed as he stepped back. 'So — now that I know I am not stepping on anyone's toes, I can take it upon myself to put some spark into your life.'

'No, Paul,' she protested. 'You know we cannot meet like this again.'

'Of course. But after the trial — and I have complete faith in your ability to convince a jury that I am innocent — once we are free of the restrictions . . . ' His eyes twinkled. 'I give you due notice that you will find me constantly on your doorstep, or on the end of your telephone line, until you agree to let me have another enchanting evening in your company.' He took her empty cup for a refill. 'And, who knows, it might even light a squib under the backside of that nephew of mine.'

Paul crossed to the sideboard and poured a small apricot brandy.

'Nearly forgot. Laura said this was your favourite tipple.'

'Thank you.' Kathleen relaxed now they were on safer ground. 'Are you not joining me?'

'No. Haven't touched a drop since . . . ' A frown crossed his face as he began to pace up and down the room. 'It's no good. I must tell you. It's driving me crazy that you might find out from anyone else.'

'Paul.' She held up her hand. 'You know I can't . . . '

'It's not about the trial,' he went on quickly. 'At least, not directly. It's something that happened a long time ago. When I was diagnosed with a medical condition. It has a long name that I can't spell, but basically it is to do with allergic reactions.'

'What kind of allergic reactions?'

'Champagne and cognac.'

'What happens?'

Paul took a deep breath before he answered.

'If anyone with this condition mixes those two drinks, it changes their personality.'

'In what way?'

'It's a bit like schizophrenia, I suppose. Apparently, one can become quite violent, completely unlike their normal character.'

'And did you?'

'That's the trouble. I don't know. Usually, my friends would take me home and put me to bed. I'd wake up feeling like death, but with no memory of anything that might have happened.'

'And that's why you stopped drinking.'

'Completely. I was so afraid I might hurt someone without realizing it.'

'So why are you telling me now?'

Paul flopped into an armchair. 'There was an incident.'

'An incident?'

'Ten years ago, I was doing the stills for an Italian film, and one of the starlets made it obvious that she wanted to go out with me. Both of us drank a lot that evening and, as usual, I had total blackout.'

Heart thumping, Kathleen waited for him to continue. There was no point in trying to stop him.

'The next morning, the studio boss told me she had complained that I went further than she wanted. I didn't know if she was telling the truth or not.'

'Did she take you to court?'

'No. Once the doctors diagnosed the problem, I was able to apologize and compensate the girl. I felt awful about it, but she seemed quite happy with the settlement.'

'And you haven't drunk since?'

'Not a drop. Laura sent me to a clinic in America that specializes in that type of problem. Now I won't even have a beer in case it triggers something off.'

'Does anyone else know, apart from those involved at the time?'

'No. Laura didn't want me to tell you. Said it was so long ago that there was no chance of anyone finding out. But I wanted to be completely honest with you.'

'Well, I'm glad you did, although you should have told your solicitor first.'

'Does he have to know?'

'Afraid so. Just in case the prosecutor has a talent for digging up anything that might weaken the defence. But don't tell Mr Jarvis you've already spoken to me. It's not ethical.'

'I understand. Anyway, thanks for hearing me out. Is there anything else I should do?'

'Tell Mr Jarvis all the details you can remember, such as the girl's name, the studio, doctor's report, dates, etc. Just in case.'

'Forewarned is forearmed, as they say.'

'Exactly. Now I really must go home.' Kathleen stood up. 'Goodnight, Paul.' She held out her hand. 'I expect I'll see you in my chambers some time next week.'

'Goodnight, Kathleen.' He raised her hand to his lips. 'I'll come down with you.' He waited while she clipped the lead to Bridie's collar, and then went on, 'Thanks for sharing your table with me. I enjoyed your company.'

She smiled. 'Me, too. Much nicer than eating on my own.'

'And I shall look forward to more of the same.' Paul's grin was infectious. 'Never thought I would be competing with my nephew for the hand of a lady.'

As she drove home, Kathleen went over his words again in her mind. When Paul said, 'for the hand of a lady,' was it a throwaway remark, or was he the one being serious?

She glanced at her hand on the steering wheel. Certainly this lady's hand was tingling from the memory of his lips.

16

'Shingles? Are you sure?' Kathleen found the girl's soft brogue difficult to understand.

'That's what his wife said. And wasn't she cross with me for phoning again! Said she had enough on her plate with a sick husband who was very irritable.'

'Well, it is a very painful complaint, so I can understand that he will not be in the best of tempers.' Kathleen thought for a moment, then asked, 'Did you mention my letter at all?'

'Mrs Malone didn't give me a chance, that she didn't, she was so busy telling me the office would have to manage until he is better, and goodness knows when that will be.'

'Has the new secretary started work yet?'

'On Monday, she did and all. Her shorthand is grand, but she couldn't read mine, and the clerk doesn't know what I'm talking about. I really don't know what else I can do to help you, miss, that I don't.'

'There is just one thing. Would you ask the new secretary if she would be kind enough to let me know as soon as Mr Malone returns to the office? It is important that I speak to him as soon as possible. Will you do that for me, please?'

'I'll put a note on her desk right now, I will, and she'll find it as soon as she's back from eating her dinner.'

After she had hung up, Kathleen sat for a while, deep in thought, and then dialled Mr Grierson's number. His advice was that she should call at his office with the letter, and he would telephone the convent to speak with the mother superior.

Relieved that it was out of her hands for a while, Kathleen was able to focus her thoughts on the cases she had in hand: a forged cheque, an injured electrician, a row of new houses suffering from subsidence, and scheduling the hearing for Paul.

He had kept to his word and not attempted to see her alone, although they had once accidentally found themselves in the same coffee bar, and that had been rather strange. Kathleen had heard about the new espresso bar, not far from chambers, and decided to try a frothy coffee for herself. Immersed in a *Daily Telegraph* report on the trial to decide whether the book, *Lady Chatterley's Lover*, was, or was not obscene, she was unaware of anyone creeping up behind her, until hands covered her eyes and a voice whispered in her ear.

'Would you be knowing that you've a delicious white foam around your mouth, begorra, macoushla and all?'

'Paul! That is the worst attempt at an Irish accent that I've ever heard.' She tried to lick the offending froth, but he shook his head.

'Here, let me.' He produced a handkerchief and dabbed around her lips. 'There.' He glanced at the newspaper. 'Ah, I see that even the most delicate of our ladies are interested in salacious literature. Have you read it?'

'No. But it is a major topic of conversation in chambers, as you can imagine.'

'I bet. You should read it, though, make up your own mind. I can lend you a copy if you like.'

'Far too busy, thank you. And you know very well that we mustn't be seen talking together.' She began to fold the newspaper. 'The coffee is very good, by the way.'

'I know. I'm working on a feature about these new coffee bars springing up all over the place. Just popped in to arrange a photo-shoot.'

'I'll leave you to it, then.' Kathleen had walked for some minutes before she realized that one of her gloves was missing. She turned back. She could see it through the window, on the floor by her chair. But it was something else she saw that disturbed her. Through an archway that led to the back of the shop, Paul was engaged in a heated argument with a swarthy man. He didn't look English, but he did appear to be threatening Paul. For a moment she hesitated, then decided to slip inside and retrieve her glove, hoping she would be out of sight. But Paul stormed out of the shop at the same time, colliding with her in the doorway.

'What on earth . . . ?' He sounded angry. 'Are you spying on me, Kathleen?'

'Of course not. Why should I?' Now she was angry. 'I left one of my gloves here, that's all. Look, it's still there. Satisfied?'

He picked up the glove and handed it to her.

'I'm sorry,' he said quietly. 'It's just that — I was so angry, but I shouldn't have taken it out on you. Let's go outside, shall we. This place is giving me the creeps.'

She glanced back towards the archway and realized the man was watching them, so she agreed.

Outside, Paul was thoughtful for a moment, before he spoke.

'It's a lot of fuss about nothing. He denied that I had phoned and made an appointment to see him, and I was livid that he'd wasted my time.'

'I would have thought it was beneficial for him, free advertising and so on. So why should he be so angry?'

'Oh, you know what these foreigners are like. Threatened to smash my camera if I went in there again. So that's one name crossed off the magazine's list.' He breathed deeply. 'Sorry you became involved, and of course I don't suspect for a moment that you were spying on me.'

So why had he said it, Kathleen wondered, but remained silent.

'Hope I'm forgiven?'

She nodded.

'Good. Must go and reschedule my day. See you on Wednesday. We've got a conference at two-thirty, haven't we? Or should I say con? Get in the spirit of the thing.'

'It doesn't matter.' She smiled. 'The time is more important as my colleague will be in court. I have to grab the room whenever I can, to give my clients privacy.'

The last thing she wanted was Neville Shorter overhearing anything about Paul's 'incident' with the actress. Her colleague was unhappy enough that she had another high profile defence, and had complained bitterly to George, who gave him short shrift.

George still made a point of personally bringing in the tea or coffee whenever Paul and Mr Jarvis were in conference with her. When she briefly discussed the case with George, and told him she was certain of Paul's innocence, his response was a non-committal 'Hmm.' He seemed to be reserving his judgment.

Then there was Desmond. To her surprise, he didn't seem too happy that she was representing his uncle. Nothing specific, just hints. The last thing she wanted right now was to have to confront her feelings about him, so she made partially true excuses: that she was bringing too much work home even to consider going to the pictures, or having a cosy evening in her flat. Truth was, she found herself dreaming of a cosy evening with Paul.

What was it about this tall, good-looking young man who kept intruding into her thoughts? It was more than the practicalities of his impending trial. It was much more to do with the chemistry between a man and a woman, and it troubled her. When he sat on the other side of her desk, she was conscious of his dark brown eyes fixed upon her face, as though reminding her of his promise. However hard she tried to dismiss the image, it remained with her long after he had left the building. She had never felt like this before, not with Tim, and certainly not with Desmond. Did that mean she didn't love Desmond, Kathleen asked herself?

Her thoughts were so confused, she had no choice but to push them into the background, at least until after the hearing.

The forgery case went her way, as did the houses with ever-widening cracks in the walls. Not so with the electrician. She'd had a feeling he wasn't being totally honest with her when she asked if he had followed all the safety procedures. As a result, the plaintiffs were able to play a trump card: a witness who claimed that Kathleen's client hadn't followed the cardinal rule of disconnecting the electric supply before starting on the repairs, so no negligence could be proved on the part of his employers. Still, as George frequently said, 'You win some, you lose some. Move on to the next one.'

The next one was Paul West, and at last she had a date for his trial at the Old Bailey. Even though Frederick Willoughby was leading for the prosecution, Kathleen refused to be intimidated. She had observed him for some time and felt that he was more successful with corporate law — the larger the corporation, the better. He could delve into contracts and agreements at length, but she wondered if he had the same 'nose' for exploring a person's past. She hoped not. Even if he did, she was convinced of Paul's innocence, and it was up to her to convey that conviction to the jury.

Nell Harrison phoned Kathleen the day before the jury were sworn in.

'I knew she was carrying twins,' she explained, tearfully. This time the tears were joyful. 'They're a bit on the small side, being premature, but the doctors say they are fighters, especially the little girl.'

'Take after their mother, then. How is Jane?'

'She's very weak of course. Had to have a caesarean in the end. So it's still no visitors, I'm afraid, only Sandy.'

'I bet you can't wait to see your new grand-twins. Do they have names?'

'David and Julie. I had hoped they might call the girl Rose . . . but never mind. Julie is a nice name.'

'So you and Uncle Fred will be holding the fort for a bit longer, I suppose?'

'I don't mind. The children are very good.'

'Are Sandy's parents helping out?'

'They can't just now. Mr Randall is ill. Nasty bout of flu that went straight to his chest. Always been a bit dodgy since he was gassed in the trenches.'

'Oh, I am sorry. It must be a real worry for Sandy.'

'If he's not careful, he'll end up in a hospital bed himself with all this rushing around, not to mention his own work.'

'Isn't it a blessing, then, that you're around to see he has some decent food inside him?'

'I try, Kathleen, but he barely sits down long enough to eat it. He really ought to rest for a few minutes, instead of dashing straight out. I told him only last night to sit and read the paper for a bit, let his dinner settle. You'd think a doctor would know better, wouldn't you?'

'Auntie Nell . . . ' The mention of the newspapers reminded Kathleen that, very soon, Paul's picture would be in most of the nationals. 'I don't want to add to your problems,' she went on, 'you've certainly enough at the moment. But there is something I must tell you.'

She explained as simply as possible, stressing that it was important that Jane didn't hear about it, at least until she was feeling very much better.

'You're absolutely right, dear. The shock of it might dry up her milk. She used to go out with him, you know.'

'Yes. Laura told me. Will you tell Sandy, please, so he can watch out for any newspapers in the ward?'

'Of course. I'll have to tell Fred as well. He reads every page.'

'I remember. Do you know when Jane might come home?'

'Not for a while, I shouldn't think. Let's hope the trial will be done with by then. Do you reckon you'll win?'

'I hope so. And — Auntie Nell . . . '

'What, dear?'

'Don't believe everything you read in the newspapers. You know what they are like.'

★   ★   ★

A light drizzle dampened the pavement as Kathleen stepped out of the taxi. The media presence wasn't quite so high as it had been for Cecilia's trial. Right now it was relatively easy for Kathleen and her small entourage to push their way through the eager reporters, into the security of one of the most famous courts of justice in the world.

'Be prepared for more cameras tomorrow,' Kathleen warned Paul. 'We might have to shove a bit harder.'

Seeming subdued, he nodded agreement.

Mr Jarvis stayed with their client while Kathleen and Michael Latham moved on to the robing-room. He was a newly qualified barrister whom she had selected to assist her, and felt sure he wouldn't let her down.

An old friend was already fastening his white bands in the robing-room.

'Miss O'Connor. How nice to see you.' Charles Henshaw shook her hand. 'I understand that you are defending Paul West on the alleged rape charge. And this is . . . ?'

She introduced him to the young man who was so highly thought of by Merrick Soames, and Michael behaved impeccably. Just the right amount of deference towards a QC, without gushing or fawning.

'Are you counsel for the shotgun murders?' she asked Mr Henshaw.

'Afraid so. He's guilty, of course, but I'll do the best I can for him.' The older man smiled wryly. 'Reminds me of our little chat in the garden the first time Tim brought you over.'

'In what way?'

'Well, the poor devil had had enough of his wife's infidelities and finally cracked when he found her in the barn with the man from the ministry. They definitely were not discussing milk quotas.'

'Will you plea for insanity?'

'Not sure, just yet. Depends on the medical reports.' He settled the wig firmly upon his head. 'And I assume that you are certain of your client's innocence, otherwise you would

213

not be representing him.'

She smiled. 'You remember.'

'Of course. And you have a very fair-minded judge, so you shouldn't have any antagonism just because you are a lady barrister.'

'Do you know Mr Justice Barker?'

'Played golf with him last weekend.' He made a slight adjustment to his gown. 'By the way, don't get within sneezing distance of Willoughby.'

'Why, has he the plague or something?'

'Streaming cold. And if I remember rightly, his junior only just scraped through his finals. So the gods may well be with you today.' He smiled at Michael. 'Pay attention to Miss O'Connor, young man. You'll learn a great deal.' With a satisfied nod at his reflection, he turned towards the door, murmuring: 'And let battle commence.'

17

The jury took less than four hours to reach their verdict. They had listened carefully as Kathleen cross-examined the landlord of the inn, who couldn't honestly say that the lassie seemed particularly distressed, although she couldn't stop the shivering. But what else did she expect in Scotland at that time of year? Not a hardy lass at all. No, she hadn't said a word about being attacked. In fact, she had barely spoken at all, just hurried up the stairs to her room. The two young men had asked if she could have a hot water bottle and some brandy — then left her snug in her bed while they went off to Mallaig. It would be about an hour they'd be away, then back to pay the bill and pack their bags. I did tell them it might be better if they stayed a wee while until my Annie was home, so they could have something warm in their bellies before their travels. But they said they wanted to be well on their way before the snow turned into a blizzard, just in case they were stuck up here. Aye, it happens often enough. Nice young gentlemen they were, made sure the lass was well wrapped in her blanket before they set off. I told them they could keep the hot-water bottle.

Then there was the flat-mate, Veronica, who agreed that Miss Benson had not mentioned the alleged attack for at least a week, although she did have a nasty bout of flu and took to her bed. Somewhat reluctantly, she also agreed that Gloria had boasted that she would do anything to further her career as a model and actress and yes, she had been known to invent scenarios to attract the attention of newspapers.

When Gloria Benson entered the witness-box, it soon became apparent that she was not the brightest spark in the court, and she became more and more confused, even at the simplest questions, including those from her own counsel.

Frederick Willoughby had looked as though he wished he were home in bed, anywhere but in a courtroom, as he wheezed his way through his cross-examination. His junior seemed painfully nervous when he questioned Paul's assistant, merely asking if Eric had seen the stag, supposedly the cause of the plaintiff's fall. When Eric replied that there had been herds of deer all over the place, the hapless young barrister shuffled through his papers.

'What a missed opportunity,' Michael

Latham whispered to Kathleen, as his opposite number sat down. 'Still, it adds strength to our case. Look at the jurors writing furious notes.'

Kathleen had been more than pleased with her own junior when he questioned the petrol-station attendant, who said, yes, there had been plenty of opportunity for the young lady to ask for help, but she had just gone into the ladies' toilet, then straight back to the car, not looking at him while he refuelled the car. And yes, he had thought that the two men seemed to be taking great care of her, wrapping her in a blanket and asking for the hot-water bottle to be refilled.

Charles Henshaw had been right, Mr Justice Barker was a fair-minded judge, stressing to the jury that they must examine the facts, not emotions, and that they must be certain, beyond reasonable doubt, before a guilty verdict could be justified.

After the summing-up, Kathleen had appealed, at the judge's discretion, that Paul be given into the custody of the dock officers, provided he remained within the precincts of the building, so that he could wait in the corridors with his legal team. She had already arranged for a room where she might deal with her paperwork uninterrupted, so she slipped away after a few minutes, leaving Paul with Mr Jarvis, Michael Latham, and the two officers, and a promise to provide some refreshments if the jury was still out at lunch-time.

As she munched her way through a ham sandwich while she updated her notes, the ring of the telephone startled her. It was George.

'Sorry to disturb you, miss, but I've a message for you. Will you please telephone Mr Grierson as soon as you get a chance? I take it the jury's out. How's it been going?'

'OK, I think. I'll tell you all about it when I get back.'

Mr Grierson was also interested in the trial.

'Are you optimistic?' he asked, when she had told him most of the relevant facts.

'Fairly,' she said, 'The plaintiff should have been advised to dress with some decorum, but poor Mr Willoughby was so unwell, he'd obviously said nothing.'

'So what did she wear?'

'Short skirt, tight jumper with a plunging neckline. More in keeping with a modelling assignment than a court.'

'I don't suppose that impressed the jury. Mostly middle-aged, I expect.'

'Yes, apart from one or two men who looked as though they were close to drawing their pension. One of them actually tut-tutted as Miss Benson stepped into the box.'

'And how did they react to our client?'

'As you know, Paul is very charming, and I think he impressed the two women jurors, who smiled at him throughout his evidence. Perhaps they thought he was too nice to ever strike a woman.'

'Probably. And is that what you think?'

Kathleen didn't hesitate. 'Of course. I wouldn't have taken the brief otherwise. Now, George tells me you wish to speak to me. Is it about the letter from Ireland?'

'Yes. I've had a long conversation with the new mother superior, and it appears that your great-aunt informed her predecessor, many years ago, that she was leaving her entire fortune to the convent.'

'But she left nothing in writing. Or did she?'

'Certainly nothing legally binding. However, when the old mother superior died, earlier this year, the nuns found a journal among her possessions, where she recorded Miss Delaney's promise.'

'I see. Are they trying to hold me to that promise, even though it was merely verbal?'

'Not quite. They appreciate that a large portion of your inheritance has already been spent, and that you donated a generous amount to the church. At first they had been quite prepared to leave well alone, respecting the fact that you are a blood-relative. However . . . ' he paused.

'However?' Kathleen prompted.

'They now have serious structural problems with the convent and church buildings, and wonder if you would be prepared to help them out? I told them that you would need time to consider this, particularly as most of the money is tied up in trust funds, etc., and cannot be easily accessed.'

'What did they say to that?'

'Just that they would leave it to you and your conscience, and asked that you would pray for guidance. Must admit it sounds a bit like emotional blackmail to me.'

Already the guilt was niggling at Kathleen, but quietly she said:

'Thank you. I certainly will think about it, and I will pray. Would you do something for me, please?'

'If I can.'

'I know that my annual statement of accounts is not due until April, but it would help my decision if I could have a breakdown of my financial assets at the moment, and some guidance as to access.'

'Of course. I'll get on to the accountants straight away. Shouldn't take too long.'

Kathleen tried to immerse herself in her paperwork, but the problem in Ireland intruded into her concentration — and her conscience. She tried doing a few rough sums, but it was guesswork, and she couldn't do anything until she had the correct figures.

Eventually, a court usher put his head around the door.

'Jury's ready to return to court, Miss O'Connor,' he said. 'I've already informed your colleagues and the defendant.'

In the dock, Paul looked pale as he waited, staring straight in front of him, tension in every muscle. The two counts were read out again and the jury foreman was asked if the verdict was unanimous. It was. Not guilty on both counts.

The expression on Paul's face was one of great joy. He took an enormous breath of relief, looked at Kathleen and mouthed the words 'thank you'. When the formalities were completed, he came across to the barristers' row, took her hand, as if to shake it, then raised it to his lips.

'I'd really like to hug you,' he murmured, 'but I don't think that would go down too well. Perhaps later?' Quickly he turned to his solicitor, and Michael Latham, shaking their hands warmly and thanking them.

Frederick Willoughby and his junior were

on the point of leaving the robing-room as Kathleen arrived. The junior looked very subdued and barely nodded to acknowledge her presence, but Willoughby only opened his mouth to sneeze. She was glad he wasn't looking in her direction.

Outside the court, a circle of reporters and photographers had swallowed up Paul, and Kathleen was relieved that Michael Latham swiftly hailed a taxi before any of them diverted in her direction. Being small, she was often overlooked by taxi-drivers, but Michael was tall enough to attract anyone's attention.

George was waiting with congratulations and the ever-ready teapot. As usual, only Brian and Mr Merrick Soames said: 'Well done' as they passed George's cubby-hole.

Back in her room, Neville Shorter looked up.

'I've heard,' he said, and put his nose back into his files again. Kathleen knew she shouldn't have expected more, but she did notice his nose and ears turning in her direction when Paul telephoned.

'You didn't think I'd forgotten my promise, did you?' he asked.

'I'm sorry — I'm not with you.'

'Well you will be, tonight.' He laughed. 'Our celebration evening. Remember?'

Now she remembered. That time when

they had shared a table in Laura's restaurant, and he had promised he would be waiting for her as soon as the trial was over. She had thought he was joking, and now found herself blushing furiously at the thought of spending an evening alone with Paul.

'I've booked a table at the Talk of the Town,' he went on. 'Laura tells me you were at college with the star performer, Cecilia Saint.'

Kathleen was almost speechless with delight.

'It sounds wonderful,' she gasped. 'Shall I meet you there?'

'Come to my flat first for a drink, and then we can take a taxi. You've got the address on your file. Now go home and put on your glad rags.'

As she hung up, Kathleen noticed a very curious expression on Neville Shorter's face. Very curious indeed.

Her next thought was to wonder whether Paul had it in mind to hug her and, if he did, how should she react?

18

Mrs Andrews peered through the largest bouquet Kathleen had ever seen. 'You'll need to borrow some vases,' she laughed. The card read: *How can I ever thank you? You'll have to help me think of something. P.*

They were working on the third vase when more flowers arrived. A bunch of bronze chrysanthemums, clutched by Desmond.

'Oh, my goodness. Mine look pretty puny by comparison,' he said, eyeing the mass of blooms still on the table. 'Who are they from?'

'A grateful client,' Kathleen answered, trying to slide the card out of sight under the wrapping-paper.

'Very grateful, by the look of it. Who is it? Rockefeller?'

Mrs Andrews rescued the card as she scooped up the rubbish.

'I'll just put this lot in the dustbin,' she said, leaving the card exposed. 'Mind you don't lose the card, dear.'

Desmond glanced at the card and raised his eyebrows.

'My uncle?' he asked.

'Yes. We won the case, and this is his way of saying thanks.'

'Mum phoned me at school, told me the good news.' His voice was subdued. 'I tried your chambers and they said you'd already left, so I thought I would come straight round here.' With a wry smile, he handed her his flowers. 'They didn't have much of a selection at the shop downstairs, I'm afraid.'

'They're lovely. Thank you very much.' Kathleen leaned forward and kissed his cheek. 'Would you like a cup of tea?' she asked.

'Sounds good.' He draped his overcoat across a chair. 'I was wondering if we could go to the pictures tonight, to celebrate your success. We haven't been out together for ages. Do you fancy seeing *Ben Hur*?'

Warming the pot in the kitchen, Kathleen hoped he would understand. 'I would have enjoyed that, but I'm afraid I'm already booked up for tonight.'

There was a moment's silence, until he asked: 'Celebration?'

'Yes.'

'Paul?'

'Yes.'

'I expect you are going somewhere more exciting than the pictures.'

'Actually, he's taking me to the Talk of the Town.'

'Isn't that where Cecilia's starring?'

'Yes.'

Again a small silence, and then he said:

'Knowing my uncle, you'll probably get a chance to speak to her this time.'

Kathleen didn't answer, but when she carried the tea-tray into the living-room, Desmond was shrugging back into his overcoat.

'I'll skip the tea if you don't mind. You'll want time to get ready.'

'Desmond — please ... ' But he was through the door, almost colliding with Mrs Andrews, who was carrying two more vases.

'He seems in a hurry.' Mrs Andrews gazed after Desmond as he hurried down the stairs.

'Would you like the other cup of tea?' Kathleen fought back the tears.

'Shame to waste it. Thanks.'

The two women quietly finished arranging the flowers. Then Mrs Andrews put her cup back on to the tray and gazed thoughtfully at Kathleen.

'It's none of my business, I know, but if Desmond hasn't bought you a ring after all this time, he can hardly blame you for going out with someone else.'

'It was as much my decision as his, Mrs

Andrews, but I don't want to lose his friendship. I suppose that's called wanting your cake and eating it.'

'Something like that. But Desmond will really have to make up his mind. There must be many a man out there who would love to settle down and have a family with a beautiful girl like you. It's not fair of him to expect you to sit at home with your books for ever.'

Kathleen smiled. It was true that she had been thinking more of marriage and less of career, but now that Paul had come upon the scene, she was more confused than ever. She didn't for a minute expect him to propose to her, but he was very attractive and she was looking forward to the evening. She stood up.

'I'd better take Bridie for her walk, and then get ready,' she said.

'I'll walk the dog, and clear up here. You have a nice soak in the bath, and go out and enjoy yourself. You've earned it.'

★　★　★

Paul's flat was above his studio, in a quiet street near the Strand. The furnishings were very modern, almost stark, but a handsome marble figure of a horse, rearing on its hind legs, caught her attention.

'That is exquisite,' she exclaimed.

'Lovely, isn't it?' he agreed. 'Found it in a New York gallery. Frightfully expensive, but I had to have it.' He nodded towards the framed black-and-white photographs displayed on the walls. 'What do you think of my work?' he asked.

He poured them both a glass of wine and watched intently as Kathleen wandered around, examining each one.

'I know nothing of photography, but these are beautiful,' she said. 'Such lovely use of light and shade.'

The black leather settee squished as she sank into it.

'How long have you lived here?' she asked.

'Not long. The rent is horrendous, but I need to be central to get the work, and it's very handy, living above the shop. I'll show you all the bits and pieces in the studio some time. But tonight, I just want to enjoy your company.' He sat beside her, took her glass and carefully placed it upon a chrome and smoked-glass table, then took her face in his hands. 'You are very beautiful, Kathleen, but I could light you to look even more beautiful. Those eyes . . . one day . . .'

It was the most passionate kiss Kathleen had ever experienced. Long, lingering and sensuous. She felt powerless to move, but content to stay in his arms.

Eventually, he raised his head and gazed at her.

'You know, I've wanted to do that since the day I first saw you.' Releasing her, he glanced at his watch. 'Time to go, my sweet. Drink up.'

The evening was wonderful. Paul held her hands across the table, and ordered champagne. Sitting at a white grand piano, Cecilia wore a clinging black gown that flashed rays of light around the room every time she moved. Her exquisite voice filled the room with lyrical melody. When the standing ovation had ended, she came straight to their table and hugged Kathleen.

'The manager told me that you were here and that there had been a request for me to join you for awhile,' she said, glancing at Paul. 'And I believe you had something to do with that, Paul West. By the way, congratulations on your successful verdict today.'

As he took her hand, Paul's charm was tangible.

'It was all due to Kathleen,' he said. 'She had faith in me and convinced the jury that I was innocent.' He pulled out a chair for Cecilia to sit down. 'And I must congratulate you in return. That was quite a performance. The audience were spellbound.'

They chatted about the songs, the night-club, the trial, until Paul excused himself.

'I've just seen someone I know and need to have a quick word. It's business, I'm afraid.'

'Wow!' Cecilia gasped. 'I'd heard he was a charmer, but didn't realize how incredibly sexy he is. If you don't want him, please send him in my direction.'

Kathleen laughed. 'It's not like that, really. This is just a thank you for winning the trial.'

'And pigs are flying all around the room. I'll bet he also sent you masses of flowers.'

'Actually, I think he sent the flower-shop.'

'Thought so.' Cecilia's smile was wicked. 'And I reckon his kisses are sizzling.'

Kathleen knew her face was turning scarlet, but could do nothing about it.

'They are, aren't they?' Cecilia laughed. 'He didn't waste any time, did he? I know you weren't allowed to consort with him while the case was going on.'

Kathleen spluttered into her champagne.

'Consort! Now isn't that a word to behold? And you are quite right, I made sure we obeyed all the rules.'

'So it must have been tonight. Good for you. Does Desmond know?'

After Kathleen told her friend about Desmond's brief visit, Cecilia sighed.

'Well, it's his own fault, the old slowcoach.

So make the most of it. Paul West is absolutely gorgeous. I'm green with envy. Here he is now.' She stood up. 'Time for me to change. I've another spot later on.'

The night was almost turning into the next day as they left the old Hippodrome Theatre.

Paul had been very quiet after he had talked to his business acquaintance, and now seemed uncertain.

'I had intended to ask you back for a nightcap and then take you home,' he said. 'But I've just discovered I have to fly out to South America tomorrow morning, and need to get my photographic equipment sorted first. Sorry, and all that. I'll get you a taxi.'

His goodnight kiss was brief, but full of promise. Then he gave the driver her address and some notes, and walked briskly away, having promised to phone her when he returned.

The next few days were so busy she barely had time to draw breath. She had several run of the mill briefs that demanded all her time and any free time was spent buying Christmas presents and phoning Jane, who had just come home with the babies. Auntie Nell said she was staying on to help out, and doubted that they would be home for Christmas as Jane was still too weak to take care of the children, so it would be a quiet

Christmas. Kathleen promised to go over to East Grinstead with the presents, but felt it would be better if she, too, had a quiet Christmas this year. Auntie Nell and Uncle Fred weren't getting any younger. They must be feeling the strain a bit, and the older children would want to have their mother to themselves for a while. Laura had said she was welcome to join them for Christmas, but Desmond hadn't phoned, and that could be awkward. She tried not to think too deeply about the future, short term or long term.

Katherine was about to leave to attend a county court when Paul telephoned. He sounded bright and breezy.

'Not free tonight, I'm afraid,' he said. 'But I've booked a table for tomorrow at the Coq d'Or. Meet you there at seven. OK?' It was more a statement than a question.

Bemused, she hung up. Had it not occurred to him to ask if she was free? Perhaps that was what it was like in his world. But she had to admit it was rather nice to be part of his glamorous life, even if only for a short while. She wrote the place and time in her diary and left chambers, knowing full well that Neville Shorter could hardly contain his curiosity about her phone call. Then her thoughts wandered. Would she have time tomorrow to dash up to Oxford Street? Her 'little black dress' had covered most of her social occasions, including her first date with Paul. Perhaps it was time she updated her wardrobe?

Pleased with her purchases, she called a cheery 'hello' to George as she passed his little office.

'I've a message for you, Miss O'Connor.' He tore a page from his notepad. 'Phoned five minutes ago. I said you wouldn't be long.'

The message was from Paul. Would she go round to his flat? It was very urgent.

'Are you sure Mr West means now?' she questioned. 'Only we've already arranged to meet this evening.'

'Yes, miss. He was most insistent that I pass the message on the minute you came back. Said for you to take a taxi and go round there straight away.'

'Did he give you any idea what it was about?'

'No, miss. But he did sound rather anxious.'

'Well, I'll just leave these bags in my room and be on my way. Could you call a taxi for me please, George?'

As she dumped the fashion bags behind her desk, Neville Shorter looked up.

'Rumour has it that your lover-boy might not be able to afford to take you wining and dining tonight, O'Connor,' he smirked, nonchalantly pushing back his chair and regarding her with a supercilious smile.

'First of all, he's not my lover-boy, and — what on earth are you talking about?' she retorted, 'Not that it's any business of yours, Shorter.'

He took his time before answering, seeming to relish every moment.

'I expect you remember a very interesting case I handled not long ago, when I defended a member of the nobility against a charge of sexually harassing his secretary?'

How could she forget it, Kathleen thought, when he had been bragging about it ever since.

'Well,' he drawled on. 'His lordship was so pleased with my work that he invited me to join him at the gaming-tables last night. Interesting place. Full of celebrities. And who should be engaged in an intense conversation with the croupier, but Mr Paul West.

'There's nothing surprising in that. He was probably working on an assignment.'

'Oh, no, no, no.' He shook his head. 'He didn't have much luck at the roulette wheel, nor at the blackjack table. Last I saw of him, he was being escorted to the manager's office.'

'That still doesn't mean it was anything

more sinister than his whiling away the time before he discussed a photo-shoot with the manager.'

'Maybe so, but his lordship told me in confidence that West has been losing heavily there for some time.'

As she sat back in the taxi, Kathleen realized that the news had disturbed her more than she had thought. It wasn't far to Paul's flat, but there was time enough for her to ponder as to whether he had really been working, or trying to recoup his losses. Could that have anything to do with his urgent message to her? He'd never mentioned, or shown any signs of being interested in gambling. But then, what did she really know about the rather dashing photographer?

Her fears increased as the taxi drew to a halt outside Paul's studio. As she was paying the driver, a man pushed past her and jumped into the taxi, rudely interrupting and telling the driver to hurry up. His voice was deep and had a strong accent. He seemed very angry.

The man glanced out of the window, stared at her for a moment, and then looked away. Now she remembered where she had seen him before. It was the man who had been arguing with Paul in the coffee bar.

19

'Oh, darling, am I glad to see you.' Paul dragged Kathleen into the living-room, and held her so close she could feel him trembling. It was the first time he had called her 'darling'.

'You're the only one who can help me. I don't know who else to turn to.' In between showering her face with kisses, his breathless voice raced on, 'I've been such a fool, but I know you won't let me down, my darling Kathleen. You saved my life in court and I know you'll save me again.' He dropped to his knees, his hands clutched around her legs.

This was a Paul West she had never seen before. It was disturbing. The thought crossed her mind that he must be drunk, even though there was no hint of alcohol on his breath. But something had happened to torment him to this extent.

Gently, she stroked his head, soothing him as though he was a child.

'Shush,' she murmured. 'Just calm down and tell me about it.'

He became even more agitated. 'These are evil men,' he gabbled. 'They won't listen to reason. I've lost everything.'

'Is it anything to do with the gaming-tables?' she asked.

Jumping to his feet, he pulled her down beside him on the settee.

'How did you find out?' he asked.

'One of my colleagues saw you last night. Do you owe much?'

His head nodded up and down but his words were incoherent.

'I don't . . . more than . . . but I can't . . . they'll kill me.'

'I'm sure they won't.'

'You don't understand . . . burgled.' He grabbed her hands in a vice-like grip.

'Burgled? What do you mean, Paul? Who's been burgled?'

'They've taken all . . . I'm finished . . . '

'Are you telling me you've been burgled?' She looked around the room. It looked immaculate. 'The flat?'

'No . . . downstairs . . . all my equipment . . . I don't know what to . . . ' He seemed incapable of finishing a sentence.

'You must telephone the police.'

He became even more distraught.

'I can't . . . don't ask me . . . anything . . . not the police . . . you've got to help me.'

'I'll do what I can to help. Of course I will.' But she was worried. Why wouldn't Paul call the police?

'Marry me . . . you love me . . . you know you do . . . Kathleen . . . darling . . . marry me.'

She tried to ease her hands from his grasp, but his grip became even tighter. 'Paul, you really don't know what you are saying.'

'I do, I do, I do. Special licence . . . that's what I . . . only a few days . . . get it before Christmas . . . say you'll marry me . . . then I'll be safe.'

'We'll talk about it later, when you're calmer. Paul, please let go of my hands. You're hurting me.'

It was as though he hadn't heard. Still holding her hands, he slid off the settee and dropped to his knees, burying his face in her lap, gabbling on and on.

'You must marry me . . . I'll be dead . . . they need the money . . . said they will kill me if I don't . . . ' He began to cry, heartbreaking sobs.

'Paul, you need help. Let go of my hands, and I'll phone your doctor. Is his number in that book by the telephone?'

'I don't want a doctor!' he raised his head and almost screamed at her. 'I want money . . . lots of money.'

Although his behaviour was distressing her, she kept her voice calm.

'The bank is still open. I can cash a cheque for a few hundred if that will help.'

'Not enough . . . I need more . . . '

'How much do you owe, Paul?'

'Fifteen . . . twenty thousand . . . don't know.'

'But that's a small fortune,' she gasped. 'Surely you didn't lose that much at the tables?'

'This place . . . too expensive . . . new car . . . cameras . . . didn't realize . . . '

'Oh, Paul. What have you done?'

'Made me bring the stuff in . . . told them I had it . . . but when I got back it was all gone . . . he didn't believe me.'

'What stuff. Who didn't believe you?'

'Ahmed . . . gone to get his brothers.'

Kathleen remembered the man who took her taxi. 'Was it the man I saw you with in the coffee bar?' she asked.

Miserably, he nodded. 'Didn't want you to know . . . thought if I did what they asked . . . it would have been OK . . . thieves got the lot.' He was becoming more distraught by the minute.

Her voice was quiet, but firm. 'Paul. Look at me.'

Slowly, he raised his head.

'If I'm to help you, you must tell me everything, from the beginning. Just take a deep breath.'

For a while she thought he was too immersed in his demons to respond, but eventually he gulped and sat back on his heels.

'The casino gave me a deadline . . . wouldn't wait. What I was earning wasn't enough. They threatened to take all my cameras . . . everything I owned. I wouldn't be able to work.'

'How does it link in with the man in the coffee bar?'

'They're all brothers . . . Ahmed has a string of coffee bars . . . Hasan a couple of massage salons . . . Mahmoud the casino. They said I could clear my debt if I did as I was told.'

'And what did they tell you to do?'

'Bring back things from South America . . . hidden in my cameras . . . give them to Ahmed.'

'What sort of things? Jewellery? Gold?'

His voice was muffled as he sank his head on his knees.

'Drugs.'

'Drugs!' Kathleen couldn't believe what she was hearing. 'Why didn't you go straight to the police? Better the bankruptcy court than a criminal one.'

'Wasn't thinking straight. Didn't want to do it. They said one trip would be enough. They lied.'

'How many trips have you made as a courier, Paul?'

'This was the third. I told them it was the last one. It was a big one, so I went round to the coffee bar.' He tried to moisten his lips with his tongue. 'Took some for Ahmed to test. Good stuff. Told him to come back with me and collect the rest. Didn't want to be caught with that much dope on me.'

'And while you were round there, the studio was burgled.'

'Yes. The charlady had left the door unlocked, but he didn't believe me. Oh, God, Kathleen. What am I going to do?' He was becoming agitated again.

'Do you think the burglars were after the drugs?'

'Cameras. It's all expensive equipment. They took the best . . . except for the one in the bedroom . . . even the tripods . . . '

'Well, they've got a surprise coming when they try to sell on their haul.'

'But they won't be able to go to the police, will they?'

'Unlikely. Unless they panic and try to get a deal.'

'Then I'm finished.' He buried his head in his hands.

'More likely they'll dump the drugs and keep the cameras. You've got to go to the police, Paul. They'll protect you.'

'No! I can't go to jail, Kathleen. I can't. These brothers have contacts. Nobody could protect me inside.' His breath came in such short gasps, she was afraid he would have a heart attack.

'Listen, Paul.' Kathleen tried to think straight,

and fought her conscience. 'Phone Ahmed. Tell him you can let him have a thousand pounds straight away and you'll get the rest by the weekend. It might be enough to buy you some time. And then I suggest you disappear for a while.' She knew this wasn't the right kind of advice, but it would break Laura's heart if Paul was sent to prison. And Len and Laura had been so very good to Kathleen.

'That's no good. They'd spit on a thousand.'

'Well, I'm afraid it's all I can manage. And I have to be in court in less than an hour. But I'll get your thousand first.'

'When can you get me the rest?'

'I'm sorry, Paul, but that's the best I can do.' She began to button her coat.

'What do you mean, the best you can do? You're loaded. That old biddy in Ireland left you her fortune. Everyone knows about it. And you're just offering me a measly thousand. What do you take me for?' He jumped to his feet.

His change from a gibbering, pathetic wreck to this hostile, threatening being was so instant and alarming that Kathleen stared up at him, speechless. Suddenly, he grabbed her shoulders and violently shook her backwards and forwards as though she was a rag-doll, shouting at the same time.

'Don't play games with me, Kathleen. I know you have the money.'

The more she tried to break free, the more fiercely he shook her. She had dealt with enough whiplash claims in her legal life to know that this was what it must feel like. At last he flung her back on to the settee.

'Now will you tell me when I can get the rest of the money?'

'I haven't got it,' she whispered, wondering if she could make a quick dash for the door, but doubting it.

'Of course you've got it. You couldn't have become a barrister without money. But you must have loads and loads left over.'

'Not any more, I'm afraid.'

'Don't give me that bullshit, Kathleen. You've a crummy little flat and a crummy little car. What have you spent it on?'

She knew he was going to be angry when she told him, but she had no choice.

'I've given most of it to the convent.'

For a moment, he stared at her in disbelief. Then he turned his anger on to his prized possessions. A glass ashtray smashed against the fireplace, an onyx lamp was knocked flying, glossy magazines were scattered across the room, and the marble horse hit the wall with a resounding thump and landed on the parquet floor in three pieces. Even his photographs were ripped from the wall and stamped upon. When there was nothing left to wreck, he began pacing up and down the room. The silence was almost more frightening but it didn't last long. Kathleen flinched when he swung around towards her.

'You've given it to those silly bloody nuns?' he yelled. There was no doubting he was losing every vestige of self-control. 'Why, for God's sake?'

'That's why, actually. For God's sake.' It was almost impossible to remain calm. 'The buildings were falling apart. They needed a new roof, damp-course, and pews. And Great-aunt Bernadette had promised them. It was my moral duty.'

His expression told her what he thought about moral duty, as he continued to pace the floor. 'When did all this moral argy bargy happen?' he asked.

'Last week.'

'Cancel the cheque.'

'It's been cleared.'

Again he paced the room like a tiger. Then a thought came to him.

'You've got trust funds, haven't you? What about the money you've got put by for the cripple boy?'

'Johnny is nearly twenty-one and will soon

be able to handle his own finances. I can't touch that.'

Now Paul began to walk faster, talking non-stop. 'I told them I was marrying a rich girl . . . a very rich girl . . . and I would pay it all back . . . but the stupid rich bitch has given it all away . . . to some bloody church in Ireland . . . so they'll kill me . . . ' He stopped suddenly and rounded on Kathleen, with the most horrifying expression. 'Do you want to know what that feels like? No? Well, it's all your fault, so I think you should.'

Kathleen's concern and unease at his behaviour had turned to worry, and then fear, but after this violent outburst, she felt terrified. He was obviously out of his mind, and she felt her life was in danger. Her only hope was to escape, but she was less than half-way to the door when he grabbed her arm, swung her around, and hurled her across the room with such force that her head cracked the corner of the glass coffee table.

'Thought you'd run away, did you? Well, at least I know who my friends are now — I haven't got any. And by the time I've finished with you, you won't have any, either. Not even that dopey nephew of mine will want to know you.'

Only half-conscious, Kathleen felt the blood trickling from her temple. Her arm felt

245

as though it had been pulled out of its socket, and she couldn't move a muscle without hurting. And all the time, Paul towered over her, watching her. His eyes, which she had once thought so soulful and romantic, were blazing with fury.

'And I'll tell you what I told that tart in Scotland,' he spat at her. 'No use screaming, darling. Nobody to hear.'

'But Eric . . . ' she gasped.

'He lied. I made it worth his while. And I can't be tried again for the same offence, so there's nothing you can do about it.'

Kathleen was too stunned to scream. She just stared back at him, the realization that she had helped a rapist escape justice flooding her mind with guilt.

Now a chill ran through her body. She knew what he intended to do. And she knew just how poor Gloria Benson had felt. Too terrified to move. Like a trapped animal, waiting for the snake to strike. Not since the bombs had rained down during the blitz had she felt so completely powerless to help herself.

'Take your coat off,' he ordered. 'If I can't have your money, I'll have you.'

'I can't move,' she moaned.

'Then I'll do it for you.'

It was as though everything was in slow

motion, but with strange sound effects. The buttons from her coat pinged against the floor as he wrenched the coat open, and she cried out in pain when he yanked her arms free. She heard the sound of tearing fabric as he ripped at her blouse and skirt. When there were no clothes left to remove, he threw her back on to the floor, the back of her head hitting the solid wood with a sickening thud.

Too frightened to open her eyes, Kathleen lay still, fighting waves of nausea, waiting for him to violate her body. She tried to pray, but the words wouldn't come. Then she heard his footsteps, across the room, into the bedroom, and back again. With all sense of time lost, she had no idea how long she lay there, and for one hopeful moment, she wondered whether he only wanted to look at her, not to rape her.

'Open your eyes, Kathleen.' His voice was quiet, but menacing.

She didn't want to look at him, but the click and whirr surprised her into opening her eyes. Through the haze she realized with horror that Paul was taking photographs of her.

'I'm the first man to see you naked, aren't I, Kathleen . . . aren't I . . . ?' He raised his voice.

'Yes,' she whispered.

'Thought so.' Click and whirr. Click and whirr. 'It's a long time since I had a virgin.' Click and whirr. 'Must have a souvenir.' Click and whirr. 'Might even send one to Desmond. Let him see what he missed, the stupid sod.'

'Please,' she pleaded. 'Don't do this to me. I'll try and get the money. Paul, I beg you. Please don't.'

His laughter was almost manic. 'Too late for money, now, my innocent little virgin.' Hurriedly he began to unzip his trousers. 'And you won't say a word to anyone. Because if you do, I'll tell everyone you enjoyed it.'

She cried out as he straddled her body, biting her neck and breasts, grunting like an animal. Struggling was useless. He was so much bigger and heavier, and she knew he would enjoy hurting her even more. Then he was inside her, thrusting again and again, until she felt her body would be ripped apart. Now the words of prayer came silently into her mind. *Holy Mother, give me courage. Help me through this agony.* And it was agony. So excruciating that she sank into a black oblivion.

When she regained consciousness, Paul was straightening his tie. His anger and lust seemed to be spent, but she was almost afraid to breathe, let alone move, in case he attacked her again.

'I'm taking your advice,' he said, not looking at her. 'Going into hiding, somewhere I can't be found. You can keep your thousand. I don't need it.' His breathing was still ragged and he ran his hand through his hair as he searched around the room. 'Car keys,' he muttered. 'Where are the bloody car keys? Must be in the bedroom.'

Eventually he left, with a final warning.

'Don't forget. If you go to the police, I'll ruin your reputation — and your career.' At the door, he turned and looked at her. No pity in his expression. No remorse. Just indifference. 'And if you know what's good for you, you'll get out of here before Ahmed comes back with his brothers.'

20

The door slammed. Kathleen lay still for a moment, her body filled with pain. Slowly, she sat up, looking around for her clothes. There was nothing she could wear. But she couldn't stay here. She needed help. Who? If only Auntie Nell and Jane would walk through that door. But they were in East Grinstead, with enough problems of their own. And Laura couldn't get here before those awful men arrived.

She needed someone nearby. But she couldn't telephone chambers. Nobody there to help. George would, but she couldn't let him see her like this.

Trying to think through the dizziness, she looked for her coat. Then she saw the blood. On the white fur rug in front of the fireplace. Her blood. So much blood.

Crawling on her hands and knees towards the bathroom, she knelt on the programme from the Talk of the Town. Cecilia's beautiful face smiled up at her. Of course. Her hotel wasn't far. Her friend would come straight-away.

It seemed to take for ever to find her

handbag and diary. Praying fervently that Cecilia would be in the hotel, she dialled the number. Her prayers were answered.

'I'll be there in five minutes.' Cecilia said. 'Don't open the door to anyone but me.'

The telephone receiver slipped from Kathleen's grasp and swung slowly backwards and forwards, eluding her reaching hand. Still on her knees, she tried to haul herself up by holding on to the half-circle glass shelf, but only succeeded in knocking the telephone to the floor. Exhausted by the effort, she leaned back against the wall.

During her years in law, she had witnessed rape victims weeping in court, and read statements that shocked her beyond belief. But nothing could have prepared her for Paul's savage attack. She wouldn't have though it possible that any man, however angry, could be so violent towards a woman. Even stronger than the feelings of revulsion and shame was the anguish that someone she had found very attractive, someone she trusted, considered a friend, could suddenly become such a monster.

The wall was icy cold at her back and she began to shiver. She must find something to cover her nakedness, but her coat was nowhere to be seen. It must have fallen down the back of the settee, but did she have enough energy to reach it? The rug? Perhaps.

As she reached the fireplace, the doorbell rang.

'Kathleen! It's me. Open the door,' Cecilia called.

Thank God. Cecilia would help her — if she could only get to the door.

'I'm coming, Cecilia.' Kathleen knew her voice was too weak to be heard, but she persevered. 'Please don't go away. I'm coming.'

Eventually, she slumped against the door and reached up to release the lock. 'It's open,' she gasped.

'I know, but there's something behind — oh, my God!'

Cecilia had managed to shove the door open, enough to slip through the gap. In an instant, she was down on her knees, holding Kathleen close.

'How could he do this to you?' she cried. 'The bastard.'

Kathleen's teeth were chattering so much, she couldn't speak, just clung to her friend, who eased Kathleen's hands away, slipped out of her mink coat and wrapped it around Kathleen's shivering body.

'Mind your coat,' Kathleen managed to whisper, trying to hold it away from her bloodstained legs.

When Cecilia spoke, her voice was tight. 'Sod the coat,' she said. 'Let's get you cleaned up.'

Somehow, she managed to drag Kathleen to her feet and half-carried her into the bathroom, where she wrapped her in two huge bath-sheets, grimacing as she noticed the marks on her breasts.

'Are those teeth marks?' She sounded horrified. 'I've met some animals in my time, but nothing like this. Here, sit on the stool.'

Gently, she washed Kathleen's face and body, wrapped her back in the towels, and draped the fur coat around her shoulders.

'Stay there, while I see if there's anything you can wear.'

Suddenly, Kathleen remembered.

'The camera!' she cried. 'Please look for the camera.'

'You're not telling me he . . . ?'

Cecilia found the camera and ripped the film out before she searched for a dress in Paul's wardrobe.

'I had a feeling he might have things for his models,' she said, slipping it over Kathleen's head. 'And that wasn't the only thing I found,' she went on. 'There's some white powder on the dressing-table and, if I'm not mistaken, it's cocaine.' She helped Kathleen back into the warm coat. 'No excuse, but it might account for this dreadful attack.'

Of course. Paul hadn't been drunk. He had been high on drugs. No wonder he had seemed demented . . . then realization hit Kathleen.

'They could be here any minute,' she gasped.

'Who?'

'The drug-dealers who were threatening him.' She grasped Cecilia's arm. 'We must get out of here. It's dangerous.'

For a moment, Cecilia stared at her. Then she went into action.

'As soon as I find your shoes I'll take you to Charing Cross Hospital. You can tell me all about it while we're waiting. Then we'll go to the police.'

'No!' The thought of sitting in casualty, with everyone staring at her, was too dreadful to contemplate. As for the police, and all their questions . . . 'No,' she repeated. 'I don't want to go to hospital, or the police.'

'But that gash on your head looks as if it needs stitching.'

Their argument was interrupted by a voice from the doorway. A man's voice.

'George!' Cecilia cried. 'What are you doing here?' Suddenly, she turned back to Kathleen. 'Surely he's not one of them?' she whispered.

Kathleen shook her head.

George stepped into the room. 'I got a bit worried when the phone was engaged for so long. Only Miss O'Connor's due in court, and . . . ' he surveyed the scattered debris.

'Bloody hell! What's been going on?'

As Cecilia tried to close the bathroom door, George looked beyond her to where Kathleen sat, still shivering, the blood again seeping from the wound on her forehead.

'Christ almighty, miss! What happened?'

Cecilia pulled the door to behind her, but Kathleen could still see through the gap and hear every word, even though Cecilia's voice was low.

'Paul West attacked her, that's what happened.'

George bent down behind the settee, retrieved Kathleen's coat and one of her shoes. The unspoken question in his eyes was answered by Cecilia's nod. For a brief moment, they just stared at each other. Then he turned and thumped the wall, very hard.

'If I get hold of him, I'll kill him,' he muttered.

'I know, George. It's unbelievable. But we have to get out of here as quickly as possible.'

'Why? Is he coming back? Just wait till I —'

'No,' Cecilia interrupted. 'There's some more nasty villains on their way. Don't know the details, but it's to do with drugs. Find the other shoe, will you, and help me get Kathleen downstairs.'

'I left my taxi ticking over outside, in case she needed it to get to court,' George said, finding the shoe beneath a chair. 'I'll ask the driver to take her straight to casualty.'

'She doesn't want to go to hospital.'

'But — '

'I know. But what she needs right now is family. Nip downstairs and ask the driver if he can take us to Upminster. Tell him I'll pay whatever he asks.' Cecilia picked up the telephone from the floor. 'I'll phone Laura and tell her why we're coming.'

'Isn't she his sister? Suppose the bastard turns up there?'

'Laura won't let him anywhere near Kathleen.'

'If you're sure.' He handed her the shoe.

'I'm sure. And her husband was Kathleen's guardian. They'll take good care of her.'

The only thing Kathleen could think of was getting out of this awful place. With Cecilia on one side and George on the other, reassuring her that he would explain to Mr Soames and send young Latham to the assizes in her place, she managed to get downstairs and into the taxi.

George handed a canvas holdall to Cecilia.

'It's what I could find of Miss O'Connor's things,' he said. 'You might need them for evidence.' He tucked Kathleen's topcoat around her knees like a blanket. 'If there's anything I can do, just let me know.'

Kathleen tried to smile her thanks, but the muscles wouldn't move. She knew she would never forget the expression on George's face as he closed the taxi door.

'Just in time,' Cecilia said, looking through the back window. 'Another taxi has just pulled up. They look like your villains — yes, that's the guy who was talking to Paul in the theatre.'

The journey was silent, and painful, particularly when they reached the cobbled stretch of Commercial Road. Kathleen was incapable of coherent thoughts and rested her head on her friend's shoulder, until the taxi slowed down outside the pub. Then she became concerned.

'Supposing she doesn't believe me,' she said. 'He's her brother. What shall I do, Cecilia?'

'I don't think you need worry about that.' Cecilia's expression was grim. 'Not from her reaction on the telephone.'

Len took one look at Kathleen, then reached inside the taxi and picked her up as though she were a child.

'Laura has got Lawrence's room ready for you, love,' he said, quietly.

Any fears Kathleen might have had about Laura were dispelled immediately. The older woman sat beside her on the bed and cradled Kathleen in her arms, her tears falling on both their cheeks. But even though she felt safe, and comforted, Kathleen could not release her own tears.

Eventually, Laura raised her head.

'Len, dear, will you get us both a brandy, please? I think we need it.'

'Me, too.' Len turned towards the doorway, where Cecilia stood, and raised his eyebrows.

'Yes, please. We've all had a terrible shock.'

As soon as Len left the bedroom, Cecilia and Laura gently helped Kathleen out of the fur coat.

'This dress is miles too big,' Laura commented, as she eased it over Kathleen's head.

'It was the only one I could find,' Cecilia said. 'I'm afraid her own things were . . . ' she stopped as Laura stared at the marks on Kathleen's body, already bruising.

'Oh, my God,' Laura cried. 'How could he be so cruel?'

Laura's nightdress swamped Kathleen, but it was warm. And there was a hot-water bottle in the bed.

'I know you don't want to go to hospital right now,' Laura said, taking Kathleen's hand. 'But I have asked my doctor to call in.'

'Oh, no.' Kathleen tried to sit up, but fell back against the pillows. 'The thought of a man touching me, even a doctor — '

'Dr Morgan is a woman, and she's very

compassionate. Here, drink this.' Laura took the glass from Len and held it to Kathleen's lips.

When Dr Morgan saw how distressed Kathleen became at the mention of going to hospital, she suggested leaving it for a day or two, until she felt a little stronger.

'I'll patch up your head injury as best as I can for now,' she said, 'and give you a mild sedative.' She handed a small bottle of tablets to Laura. 'But I do feel you need an X-ray, and you should see a gynaecologist as soon as possible.'

A sudden thought flashed into Kathleen's mind.

'I could be pregnant, couldn't I?' she asked.

'When is your next period due?'

'In about a week.'

'At least the timing is on your side.' Dr Morgan thought for a moment. 'However, if you are late, I can take a urine sample and have it tested at the hospital.' She smiled at Kathleen. 'You've had a dreadful experience. Your body and mind need recovery time.' The doctor clipped the lock of her bag and turned to Laura. 'Any signs of vomiting or blurred vision, phone me immediately. It could be concussion. Otherwise, I'll call back first thing tomorrow.'

After Dr Morgan and Laura had left,

Cecilia came into the room.

'I'm afraid I have to go, Kathleen,' she said.

'I'm so scared, Cecilia. What if I'm pregnant?'

'Don't think about it. Hang on to your faith.'

'I feel as though I'm drowning. I can't even remember how to pray.'

'You will, Kathleen. You will.'

Laura returned with a glass of water.

'I have to get to the theatre, Laura,' Cecilia said. 'But I'd like to phone after the show, if it's not too late.'

'Don't worry about that. We're always up late, clearing away downstairs.'

Laura pulled the curtains and refilled the hot-water bottle.

'Lawrence used to say this was the quietest room,' she commented, tucking Kathleen snugly into the bed. 'So try to sleep for a while. Later on, perhaps you'd like a nice warm bath.'

'Is Desmond . . . ?'

'No. School concert, so he said he would stay overnight with one of his colleagues. He'll be back tomorrow.'

Part of Kathleen was relieved; another part wanted him to be there.

Laura bent over and kissed her forehead. 'I can't tell you how deeply sorry I am, dearest child,' she murmured. 'To think that anyone could do this to you, let alone my brother. I feel as if I've betrayed your trust.'

'It's not your fault.'

'He swore he was cured. And I believed him.' Laura was weeping again. 'I shall never forgive myself.' She groped in her pocket for a handkerchief. 'I'm sorry, dear. You have enough tears of your own to shed.' Quietly, she closed the door.

But Kathleen couldn't shed any tears. It was as though her heart had frozen solid inside her body, refusing to allow any emotions to break through, apart from fear. Fear of pregnancy. Fear that Paul might suddenly appear. Fear of the drug-dealers. The man had seen her. Might they think that Paul had given her the drugs? Could they trace her?

Drifting in and out of sleep, Kathleen wasn't sure which was the most disturbing, her fearful waking thoughts, or the dreams when asleep. Dreams of being trapped, unable to move, unable to scream, while faceless men surrounded her, laughing at her shame.

Losing all sense of time, she awoke with a startled cry. The glow from the electric fire illuminated the figure sitting in a chair by the bed. It was Laura.

'You've been tossing and turning for ages,' she said 'Reliving it all?'

'Yes, I'm so afraid that he might . . . oh, no!'

'What is it, dear?'

'Bridie. I'd forgotten all about her.'

'So had I, but I'll phone Mrs Andrews. And don't be afraid. Paul probably guessed you would come here, as Nell is away. This is the last place he would come to . . . Len would willingly swing for him, and Paul knows it.'

'But he might have nowhere else to go. And his life is in danger from those men.'

'What men?'

'The drug-dealers.'

'Drug-dealers? Dear heavens! Are you saying that Paul is involved with drug-dealers?'

Kathleen realized that she had to tell the whole story, however painful. Laura didn't interrupt, just listened, tightly clasping Kathleen's hands. The anguish on her face as the story unfolded was almost unbearable.

When it was over, Laura leaned forward and switched on the bedside lamp. Laura, always so elegant and calm, now looked pale and shattered as she lit a cigarette with shaking hands.

Abruptly, she jumped to her feet.

'Len will know what to do,' she muttered,

almost to herself. 'This is even worse than I thought.'

'Is there anywhere else I can go?' Kathleen asked. 'Where they can't find me?'

Laura's anxious voice softened. 'We'll think of something,' she said. 'Now, how about that bath?'

★ ★ ★

The bath cleansed her skin, but Kathleen felt as though she would never feel truly clean again. She still found it difficult to walk, and needed Laura's help to get back to bed. A mug of hot milk and a sandwich were on the bedside table.

'I don't think I can . . . ' she began.

'Try a little, but don't force it.' Laura propped up the pillows behind Kathleen's head. 'Your clerk telephoned to ask how you are. He also said he would look after your shopping until you are better, and has hung the dresses in his wardrobe, so they don't get creased.'

'George has always been kind to me,' Kathleen said, nibbling at a quarter of the sandwich.

'And Len has suggested that I take you to Torquay tomorrow. I've spoken to Grace, and she said that's fine. They have no visitors

263

booked until the New Year.'

Torquay. The most peaceful place. And safe. Paul would never come there, Kathleen thought. And those men wouldn't find her.

'Thank you, Laura,' she said. 'But what about the restaurant? It's your busiest time.'

'Don't worry about that. Brenda has agreed to take over until I get back. And I have some more good news.'

Kathleen waited.

'Jane is there, with the children. Sandy drove them all down yesterday. A sort of convalescence for Jane and a chance for Nell and Fred to have a breather.'

'Jane,' Kathleen whispered. 'My nearly-sister, Jane.'

'Grace said she will make sure the children don't bother you too much. What you need is peace and quiet.'

'And Jane. I've missed her so much'

Laura didn't quite meet Kathleen's eyes.

'I think you'll find that Jane will be the perfect person to talk to.'

21

Dr Morgan thought it a splendid idea to take Kathleen to Torquay, especially when she learned that Aunt Peggy had been a nurse, and Grace an active member of the Red Cross during the war.

'I'll scribble a note, to put them in the picture,' she said. Repacking her stethoscope, she glanced out of the window. 'Who on earth is that?' she cried.

'Who is what?' Laura peered out of the window at her side.

'It just turned into your car park. The largest car I've ever seen.'

'I'm afraid I have no idea, but my husband will soon find out.'

As Dr Morgan handed the letter to Laura, Len knocked on the door.

'It's your friend, Kathleen,' he said. 'They are going to take you to Torquay in her Rolls. Much more comfortable than our old jalopy.'

A look of recognition came into Dr Morgan's eyes as Cecilia appeared.

'Of course,' she exclaimed. 'I thought your face was familiar when I saw you yesterday. Strange, I've just treated myself to your latest

LP for Christmas.'

'That's nice.' Cecilia smiled, then asked, 'Is Kathleen strong enough for the journey?'

'I think so. Just make sure she goes straight to bed when you get there. And don't be afraid to call in the local doctor. Some of the shock might come out later.'

'As it happens, there is a doctor in the house, if you'll pardon the pun. Her closest friend is staying there just now, and her husband is a doctor.'

'Really? Well, perhaps he can persuade Miss O'Connor to go to hospital.'

'We'll keep on at her. Thank you, Doctor.' Cecilia eased Kathleen's arms into the fur coat, over Laura's nightdress.

'I can't go like this,' Kathleen protested.

'Far more comfortable, and no one will see you.'

'But my clothes . . . '

'Mrs Andrews is packing a bag with everything she thinks you'll need.' Laura glanced at Cecilia. 'Can we pick it up on the way?'

'Of course. I have to be back for tonight's show, so we can bring you back here, if you like. Or come back for you another time?'

'It would be such a help if I can come back tonight. We're fully booked.'

'Thought you might be.'

Kathleen staggered to her feet.

'You'll never manage those narrow stairs,' Cecilia commented. 'Hold on a minute.' She opened the door.

Len was waiting on the landing, talking to Les, who came into the room instantly, wrapped Kathleen in a huge fur car-rug, and carried her downstairs, followed by Laura and Cecilia.

'Who . . . ?' Laura asked.

'That's Les. My bodyguard. He's very good. And Kathleen trusts him.'

It was true. Kathleen knew that whatever happened, whoever crossed their paths, Les would deal with it. She felt safe.

'James. Would you take the north circular, please?' Cecilia asked the driver. 'I can't stand those cobbles on the other route.'

There was no feeling of movement as the Rolls purred towards Kathleen's flat. She was able to lie along the back seat, cocooned by cushions and car rugs, while Laura and Cecilia sat facing her, their pulldown seats looking like small armchairs.

As the car slowed down, Laura glanced out of the tinted windows.

'Here's Mrs Andrews — and another passenger.' She glanced at Cecilia. 'I hope you don't mind.'

'Oh, she's adorable,' Cecilia exclaimed, as

the little dog scrambled into the car and up on to the seat.

'Bridie,' Kathleen murmured, as her beloved pet licked her face.

Mrs Andrews handed the suitcase to the driver.

'Have you got room for Bridie's basket and feeding things?' she asked.

'Plenty of room, madam.'

She shook her head. 'Silly question, wasn't it? With a car this size. But I've been so upset, ever since I heard . . . ' She leaned in towards Kathleen. 'At least you'll have a comfy journey now, dear,' she murmured, kissing her cheek. 'And you're in good hands.' She handed another small bag to Laura. 'Just a flask of coffee and some sandwiches, in case you get peckish, and . . . ' There were tears in her eyes. 'Will you let me know how things are?'

'Of course. And thank you, Mrs Andrews. You're very kind.'

Yes, very kind, Kathleen thought, as the car moved away. Everyone was so very kind. It brought a lump to her throat, but still the tears wouldn't come.

'That's right, Bridie.' Cecilia smiled as the dog found a nest in the rug and snuggled up against Kathleen. 'Make yourself at home.'

★ ★ ★

The Devon air felt crisp and clean after the London smog, and gulls whooped noisily across the downs as Les carried Kathleen into the guesthouse.

'Up the stairs, second door on the left, please,' Aunt Grace directed. 'And you must all have something warm to eat before you go back to London.' She took the suitcase from James.

'Oh, we wouldn't want to put you to any trouble,' Cecilia said.

'It's no trouble, my dear. Len phoned to say you were kindly bringing Kathleen down, and Peg has made a huge stew, with dumplings.'

Cecilia smiled. 'It sounds lovely. Thank you.'

Les and James grinned at each other.

'I'll bring you up a bowl of soup,' Aunt Grace said to Kathleen.

'I'm really not hungry, thank you.'

'I don't suppose you are, but Peg will be most upset if you don't try a little of her beef broth.'

After they had left, Kathleen sat by the window, still wrapped in the car rug. Uncle Joe managed to grow most of his own vegetables, in raised beds that he could tend from his wheelchair. The neat rows of cabbages and Brussels sprouts reminded her of Uncle Fred, and the garden and greenhouse that had long been his pride and joy. It seemed such a long time since she had seen him, and Auntie Nell.

A light tap at the door.

'Come in,' she called, expecting Aunt Grace with the soup. But it was Jane who carried the tray, set it down on a small table, and knelt by Kathleen's chair. They didn't speak, just clung together. Kathleen felt almost happy. Jane was here. The one person she needed above all others.

Eventually, Jane raised her head and looked at Kathleen, lightly touching the plaster on her forehead.

'We have much to say to each other, you and I.' Her voice was quiet and sad. 'But not now.' She moved the table closer to Kathleen's chair. 'You've had a long journey, and need to rest, but do try some of this first, if only to please me. It's delicious.' Another hug, and she was gone, with a promise to come back later.

Kathleen had thought she would never enjoy food again, but Jane was right. The broth was delicious. And after Aunt Grace had tucked her into bed, she realized she really was tired, and slept a dreamless sleep.

★ ★ ★

270

When Kathleen awoke, it was dark, the curtains were drawn, and a nightlight glowed on the dressing-table. She listened to the faint sounds from downstairs. Children laughing. A baby crying. For a moment, she was disorientated. Then she remembered where she was.

Aunt Grace quietly opened the door and peered in.

'Ah, you're awake,' she said. 'Feel better for your sleep, dear?'

'Yes, thank you.'

'Just what you needed.' Aunt Grace switched on the bedside lamp and blew out the nightlight.

'Have the others gone?'

'They should be well on their way by now. Didn't want to disturb you, but said they'll phone later. Fancy a cup of tea?'

'Yes, please.'

As Aunt Grace opened the door, a childish shriek of laughter made her smile.

'That will be Gillian,' she said. 'Peg's bathing them.'

'Do they know I'm here?'

'Oh, yes. They were very curious about the big posh car, so Jane told them you'd had an accident and weren't feeling very well.'

'Perhaps I could see them tomorrow?'

'Don't see why not, but I suggest one at a

time. *En masse* they can be rather lively, as you know.' A baby cried again. 'Jane's feeding the twins,' Aunt Grace explained, 'and the one still in the queue is rather impatient. I'll just pop up to my flat and make the tea.'

When she brought the tray of tea, the house was blissfully peaceful.

'I expect Joe is reading them a bedtime story,' Aunt Grace said. 'By the way, Peg can't manage the stairs too well now. She gets very wheezy. So I suggested you might be able to go downstairs for a little while, tomorrow.'

'Oh, yes. I do want to see them. And Uncle Nobby.'

'Poor Nobby. He doesn't quite know how to handle this kind of situation. Mind you, I don't think many men do.'

Kathleen sighed. 'Even Uncle Len was afraid to come near me. And I didn't know what to do, either. I don't think I shall ever be able to let any man touch me, not even those I love. Oh, Aunt Grace, what shall I do?'

'Give it time, my dear. Give it time. You are still very raw, physically and mentally. But time really is a great healer.'

'I hope you are right, Aunt Grace.'

'Actually, that reminds me. I showed that letter from Dr Morgan to Sandy, and he asked if he could have a word with you. He just wants to check that wound in your forehead. Jane will be with him.'

Kathleen knew the blood had been seeping through the dressing, and had dabbed at it with her handkerchief, hoping it would stop. She nodded.

Jane and Sandy were not alone. Each carried a sleepy baby. Two very tiny babies.

'Thought I would introduce you to the newest little Randalls while they are on their best behaviour,' Jane said.

'They are so beautiful. Can I hold them for a moment?'

First she held Julie, who had inherited her father's reddish-coloured hair. Then David, dark like his mother. He gripped Kathleen's finger tightly, and burped, quite loudly.

'Sorry about that,' Jane smiled. 'No table manners yet. Better let me take him before he really disgraces himself.' The instant she patted his back, there was an even noisier burp. 'See what I mean?' Jane pulled a face as she surveyed her blouse. 'Serves me right for not bringing a nappy for my shoulder.'

'We'll be back in a moment,' Sandy said as he followed Jane.

Jane was going to have her hands full, with five young children, Kathleen thought. But Jane had always been so calm, taking everything in her stride. She would cope.

Another thought crossed her mind as she

noticed the empty dog basket. Where was Bridie?

'Uncle Nobby has taken her for a walk,' Jane reassured Kathleen when she returned, wearing a clean blouse.

'Did you bring Esther with you?'

'No. Mum and Dad have taken her home. Sandy is going back tomorrow, and he'll bring them all here for Christmas, Midge as well. It's going to be quite a houseful, with Jack and Robert, and their families — not forgetting Miss Dawson.'

'Does she still do the clerical work here and help out in the garden?'

'Oh, yes. Trundles over two or three times a week on her trusty old bike, weather permitting. But not today.' Jane sighed. 'I'm afraid she had a break-in last night, and the police have been with her all morning.'

'That's awful. Is she all right?'

'Thankfully, yes, although she was very frightened when she heard the intruder breaking the glass in the back door. But she had the sense to stay in her room and wait until the burglar left before she went downstairs to phone the police.'

'Did they catch him?'

'Unfortunately, the local copper has a bike even older than Miss Dawson's and lives the other side of the village, so it was a good twenty minutes before he got there.'

'Did she lose much of value?'

'Only one thing, the most valuable of all.'

'Not the Turner?' Kathleen gasped.

'Afraid so. It's insured, of course, but it's worth so much more than that to her. It was the only thing undamaged when her home was bombed.'

'Poor Miss Dawson. She so loved that painting.'

Sandy joined them. 'Both sound asleep,' he said to Jane, then turned to Kathleen, and tried to ease the dressing away from her forehead. It was stuck fast with congealed blood.

'Sorry,' he said. 'I'll try not to hurt you too much. Ah, here it comes.' He examined the injury. 'As I thought, it needs a couple of stitches. I can do it now, if you like. Might sting a bit, but it will stop the bleeding.'

In no time at all the wound was stitched and dressed, and Sandy was peering into her eyes with a small torch.

'Hmm,' he said. 'I'd feel a lot happier if you'd have an X-ray. Actually, I'm taking Jane and the twins over to the hospital tomorrow morning to check their progress. Why don't you come with us? I can get you zapped in and out of X-ray in no time at all.' As Kathleen hesitated, he went on: 'Knocks on the head really shouldn't be ignored.'

Reluctantly, she agreed.

'Good.' He washed his hands at the vanity unit. 'There is something else, Kathleen. Dr Morgan is concerned that you may have internal injuries.'

'Oh, no!'

'Look, I know an excellent specialist at the Soho Hospital for Women. Why don't you let me arrange an appointment? Are you still in pain?'

She nodded.

'I can give you something to ease the pain for now, but it really is best to be on the safe side.'

'I'll think about it.'

'Please do.' Sandy found the painkillers in his bag, and then stood up. 'I'll leave you two alone, then. I know Jane wants to talk to you.'

At first, Jane seemed restless, wandering around the room, picking up a mirror here, an ornament there. At last, she pulled the chair close to the bed.

'This won't be easy, for either of us,' she began. 'I didn't even tell Sandy until last night.'

Kathleen waited.

'Ten years ago, Paul invited me to spend Christmas with a group of his friends in Paris. He said it would be all above board, and we would have separate rooms.'

Kathleen cast her mind back. 'Weren't you on an assignment for the magazine?'

'No. I knew Mum wouldn't understand, and I couldn't face another miserable Christmas at home. So I lied.' Gradually, the story unfolded. 'Christmas Eve was wonderful. My first flight. Watching the artists in Montparnasse. An evening at the Lido.' She paused. 'One of his friends did warn me not to allow Paul to drink cognac and champagne, but I was in heaven and so completely infatuated with Paul that I wasn't at all worried. In fact . . . ' she hesitated again, 'I felt there was more risk that I might allow myself to be seduced by Paul. But he was a perfect gentleman. At first.'

Jane poured herself a glass of water from the carafe before she continued with her story.

'On Christmas Day, while we were waiting to meet his friends for dinner, Paul asked if I would like to see the studio where he was working on some films. It was actually a run-down warehouse miles from anywhere. I still wasn't particularly anxious, until he produced a bottle of brandy, and one of champagne — and I remembered the warning. Then he started showing me the movies he was making. They were quite dreadful. Blue movies.' Jane sipped some more water. 'I begged him to take me back to the hotel, but he was beyond reason. All he wanted was sex, with or without my consent.'

Kathleen was horrified. 'He didn't rape you, too?'

Jane shook her head. 'He tried, but I'm much bigger than you, and I managed to stun him with a heavy canister and run for it. He tried to follow me and crashed headlong down the stairs. I thought he was dead. I really thought he was dead.'

'What on earth did you do?'

'I panicked. My French isn't that good and I was scared the police wouldn't believe me. So I found a telephone kiosk, rang for an ambulance and a taxi, waited all night in a seedy pension — and came home the next day.'

'I remember you had dreadful bruises all over your face. You said you'd fallen down the Metro steps. But it was Paul, wasn't it?'

'Yes.'

'Oh, Jane. You must have been so frightened.'

'I was terrified. Then Laura told me he was in hospital with a broken leg and concussion. It caused a terrible rift between us.'

'Didn't you tell her he'd attacked you?'

'No. I'd already told so many lies, and she was so defensive about him. It wasn't until he attacked the Italian actress that she realized he had a serious medical problem, caused by the alcohol mixture. She was full of remorse about me.'

'Was it Laura who paid the compensation?'

'Yes, and sent him off to an American clinic. They said he was cured. And, as far as I know, there was no further trouble until yesterday.'

'Earlier than that.' Kathleen's voice was flat. 'He admitted to me that he had raped Gloria Benson, and paid his assistant to give him an alibi.'

'Oh, my God.' Jane held Kathleen's hands. 'If I'd told you what happened to me all those years ago, would you have taken on his case?'

'I honestly don't know. We had no idea about the drugs, and he did tell me about the Italian girl. Said he wanted to be honest.'

'But he didn't tell you about me.'

'No.'

After a while, Jane said: 'If you go to the police, I'll tell them what happened to me.'

'I can't go to the police, Jane. I know the procedure, and I can't face it.'

'I do understand how you feel. My deepest regret is that I didn't tell you about my own experience. At least try to warn you. I didn't even know there was a trial, let alone that you were defending him.'

'You were so ill; Laura said it would worry you. I didn't realize why, of course.'

'And now poor Laura is consumed with guilt.'

'She meant well. It's not her fault. Like you, I was completely infatuated with Paul.'

Jane nodded.

'I'm so sorry you had to go through it all again, Jane, dear.'

'But this time I'm not alone. And neither are you.' Jane squeezed Kathleen's hands and then stood up.

'I'll tell Grace you might manage a light supper, shall I?'

22

The tablets numbed the pain a little, but it was still impossible to sleep. Kathleen lost all sense of time as she lay in bed, her mind whirling in circles, going through Jane's words, reliving her own experience. How could one man appear so charming to the outside world, and leave so many damaged women in his wake? Why hadn't she sensed that he was evil? Why hadn't Jane? And goodness knows how many others might be feeling like tarnished goods, but had kept the truth locked away inside. In less than two days her life had been turned upside down, and would never be the same again.

The grandfather clock in the hall struck twelve as Aunt Grace looked in to say goodnight.

'Still not asleep?' she asked. 'To tell the truth, I think it will take me a while to drop off tonight, so I'll probably read for a bit. Do you want a magazine?'

'No, thanks.' Kathleen winced as she tried to turn over. 'I can't get comfortable however I lie. My back feels as if it has been kicked by a mule.'

'Let's have a look.' Aunt Grace switched on the lamp. 'Oh, my goodness! You've a massive bruise coming out. Did he punch you?'

'No, but he threw me across the room.'

'He did what?' Aunt Grace shook her head in disbelief. 'Witch hazel will help bring the bruise out, and I'll get you a couple of sleeping tablets. How about a cup of Ovaltine while I'm up there?'

'That would be nice. Thank you.'

They both jumped as they heard someone knocking on the front door.

'Now who can that be, at this time of night?' Aunt Grace hurried downstairs, leaving the bedroom door open.

Kathleen listened. It was a man's voice, quietly spoken. She couldn't make out who it was. Aunt Grace talked to him in a low voice, as they both came upstairs.

'I'm not sure she'll want to see you tonight,' Aunt Grace was saying. 'Why don't we leave it until the morning?'

'If I could just see her for a moment. Please?'

It was Desmond.

Kathleen's heart began to thump, partly with anxiety, partly pleasure.

'What are you doing here?' she whispered.

He just stood in the doorway, looking at her, a pained expression in his eyes.

282

'I didn't get home until late, and as soon as Mum told me what had happened I jumped into the car.' He took a step inside the room. 'Don't be afraid. I won't touch you, or come near you. But I just had to see you. My dearest Kathleen. What can I say?'

'Do you feel up to another visitor, dear?' Aunt Grace asked.

Kathleen wasn't sure what she was, or wasn't, up to. But she didn't want him to go. Not just yet.

'It's all right,' she said, looking at Desmond. 'Thank you for coming.'

'You look so pale — and that bruising around the eye . . . God, I could kill him!'

'Join the queue.' Aunt Grace's voice was terse. 'Anyway, you might as well sit down. I was just about to make us a cup of Ovaltine. Would you like one, Desmond?'

'Yes, please.' His eyes never left Kathleen's face as he groped for the chair.

'You must be tired.' Kathleen couldn't think of anything else to say.

He shrugged. 'When Mum told me, I couldn't believe it. Even now, though I can see with my own eyes the pain he has caused you, I can't believe that my own uncle, of all people, could do such a terrible thing to you.'

'And I can't believe that I didn't sense the darkness within him. I'm usually a good judge of character, but now . . .'

'I imagine you feel you can't trust any man.'

Unhappily, she nodded.

'I understand. But I want you to know that I will never again allow anyone or anything to harm you. This is all my fault.' He removed his spectacles and fumbled for his handkerchief.

'Of course it isn't.'

'Yes, it is. If I had stopped dilly-dallying about and had asked you to marry me, you wouldn't have considered going out with him, would you?'

'I suppose not. But your mother feels guilty. And Jane. And now, you. Everyone wants to take the blame, even me. I keep wondering what I could have done to prevent it happening.'

'Nothing. You were the victim. The only person who is responsible for all this is Paul.' Still ferociously cleaning his spectacles, Desmond paced up and down, stopped by the window, pulled the curtain aside a little, and gazed out on to the garden, bathed in moonlight. 'All the way down here, I couldn't stop thinking about you.' His voice was low. 'And I realized how empty my life would be without you.' He turned to look back at her again. 'I know you probably don't want to hear this right now,' he went on, 'but I am going to spend the rest of my life protecting you from evil monsters like Paul, and loving you. However long it takes for you to recover your trust, I will always be there for you, my darling girl.'

Kathleen didn't realize she was holding her breath until Aunt Grace reappeared. They drank their Ovaltine silently, too drained for words.

'It's time I settled this young lady down for the night,' Aunt Grace said at last, as she collected the empty cups. 'And you must be travel weary, Desmond. You can have the room at the end of the landing. Have you eaten?'

He shook his head.

'Thought not,' she said. 'Come up to the flat and I'll make you a sandwich to keep you going until you're confronted by one of Peg's hearty breakfasts.'

Now Kathleen had something else to think about. Desmond's declaration of love. If only he'd spoken sooner. Would she ever be able to respond, she wondered? Then, feeling drowsy, she realized that she felt comforted by the knowledge that he was in the room at the end of the landing.

★ ★ ★

It was good to be able to wear her own clothes again. Mrs Andrews had chosen well, included everything that Kathleen needed, toothbrush and toothpaste, even her rosary.

She was staring at her best winter coat, hanging in the wardrobe, when Aunt Grace came back into the room.

'I don't think I can ever wear this coat again,' Kathleen commented softly. 'It will remind me too much.'

'I did wonder how you would feel about that, especially when I saw the buttons had been ripped off.' Aunt Grace slipped it off the hanger. 'What do you want me to do with it?'

'Anything. Jumble sale?' Kathleen couldn't bear to look at it.

'There's a young woman who helps out when we have guests. Her husband drinks every penny, and I'm sure she'd love a good coat like this. She's about your size, too.'

Kathleen nodded, and picked up her hairbrush.

'I'll go through Peg's button box while you're out,' Aunt Grace went on. 'By the way, your friend said not to worry about getting the fur coat back in a hurry. It's not her only coat.'

'I don't know what I would have done without Cecilia.'

'I remember when she used to come here

286

with you when you were both at college. Lovely girl.' Aunt Grace smiled. 'Ready to come downstairs, then?'

As Kathleen had expected, Aunt Peggy made sure she ate a bowl of creamy porridge, even if she couldn't manage bacon and eggs, but she beamed when Desmond and Sandy tucked into everything on offer.

'Jane has eaten earlier, with the children,' Sandy said. 'Right now she's seeing to the twins, and I suggested the others keep out of our way, or we'd never get out. You can see them later.'

'I'd like that.' Kathleen glanced around the table. 'Where's Uncle Joe and Nobby?' she asked.

'Joe didn't sleep too well last night,' Auntie Peg answered. 'So I made him have a lie-in. I think Nobby has gone up for the papers.'

'No, I'm just going.' Nobby Clark appeared in the doorway, tying his muffler. 'Hello, Kathleen. Are you feeling a bit better this morning?' He looked uncomfortable, shuffling from one foot to the other.

'Yes, thank you. And thank you for taking Bridie for a walk last night.'

'No trouble, dear. In fact, I'll be happy to take her out every day while you're here. She's a well-behaved little thing.' He looked at Sandy. 'I'm taking young Nicholas and

Gillian with me as well. Buy them a comic or something. Jane said it was OK.'

'That's very good of you. Sure it's not too much of a handful, with the dog as well?'

'They were as good as gold yesterday. Held my hands when we crossed the road. I might take them down to the beach. Let them run a bit. It's a nice bright day.' He pulled on his woollen gloves. 'I'll be off, then. Hope you get on all right at the hospital, Kathleen.'

He really is a dear man, she thought, as he snapped the lead on to Bridie's collar and followed the children. She wondered why he hadn't married and had a family of his own, but supposed it was because he had been away at sea so much. Still, he seemed contented enough, sharing the business with Grace, and too many people around to feel lonely.

Desmond insisted on coming with them, and sat in the waiting room while Kathleen was X-rayed.

'No serious damage, but probably a mild concussion,' the radiologist said, after she had examined the plates. 'You'll need to rest for at least a week. No knees-up for you on Christmas Day, I'm afraid.'

The last thing Kathleen felt like doing was a knees-up, but she nodded.

'Still got a headache?' the girl asked.

'Thumping.'

'Ask Dr Randall to get you some codeine tablets from the pharmacy, and make sure you see your own doctor when you get home.' She peered at the stitches. 'Must say he made a good job of that. I'll just ask nurse to put a clean dressing on it.'

It wasn't until she went into the ladies' room that Kathleen saw the notice. It gave an address where women could go if they suspected they might have a sexually transmitted disease, and it filled her with fear.

She remembered a divorce case where her leader was representing a businessman, whose wife accused him of passing on a venereal disease to her, claiming that a prostitute had infected him. The medical reports of both husband and wife were explicit, and appalling. How could she be certain that Paul hadn't contracted something similar from one of his trips abroad?

There was only one way, she realized, even though it was the last thing she wanted to do. She would have to ask Sandy to make that appointment for her in the New Year.

Back at the guesthouse, she was made comfortable in an armchair by the fire, while Auntie Peg fussed around her with a shawl for her shoulders, a blanket across her knees, and a cup of tea in her hand.

'Us'n can't have you catching cold after all you've been through, my pretty,' she said, as she moved Uncle Joe to the other side of the fire-place. He looked much older than when Kathleen had last seen him, but his faded blue eyes were filled with concern as he spoke to her.

'That young villain will get his come-uppance in time, don't you worry, girl,' he said. 'And my Peg will have you fit and well again in no time.'

Sandy waited for Nobby to come back with the children before he set off back to East Grinstead. Then, one at a time, the children were brought in to see Kathleen. They all had glowing cheeks.

Her godson held a pebble he had picked up on the beach.

'Would you like to have it, Auntie Kathleen?' he asked. 'It's got a hole in it, and that's supposed to be lucky.'

Gillian produced a shell. 'If you hold it to your ear, you can hear the waves,' she said.

Philip just stood, finger in mouth, and stared at Kathleen's bandage.

Nobby, last in the queue, clutched a box of Devon toffees.

'Hope you like them,' he said, nervously handing them to Kathleen.

'They're my favourites. Thank you.' She

longed to throw her arms around his neck, but couldn't. And she couldn't weep the tears she needed to shed, either.

When the telephone rang, Aunt Grace answered it.

'It's for you, Jane,' she called. 'Jack wants a chat with his sister.'

When Jane had gone out into the hall, Aunt Grace said:

'They are all coming over on Christmas Eve. You'll notice a difference in Johnny. Hardly any limp now, thanks to your generosity, Kathleen, and he talks as well as anyone else. As for his paintings — they are quite beautiful.'

Jane was gone for some time, and looked serious when she came back.

'Oh, I do hope I'm wrong,' she murmured.

'Wrong about what?' Aunt Grace asked.

'Well, Jack didn't know anything about Kathleen until I told him. Then he said that Paul had been in Brixham the day before yesterday. Arrived late, and went straight to Robert's house.'

'Oh, no!' Kathleen cried. 'You're not telling me he's coming here?'

'There's no reason at all why he should come here, and he certainly doesn't know that you're here.'

'Bet I know why he wanted to see Uncle

Robert,' Desmond said.

Jane nodded. 'To borrow money. Robert didn't have enough, so Paul drove off in a huff. Jack said he was in a very strange mood. And that's what's worrying me.'

'Probably the drugs,' Desmond suggested.

'More than likely. But there's something else.'

'What?'

'Well, that was the night Miss Dawson was burgled.'

They all looked at each other.

Kathleen broke the silence.

'It must have been Paul,' she said. 'He was the one who stole her lovely painting, to pay off his gambling debts. Oh, how could he!'

Aunt Grace looked troubled. 'We don't know for sure,' she said.

'Well, there's one way to find out,' Jane said. 'Laura has a key to his flat. I'll ask her to go over there. If he has stolen the painting, he'll need to find a private collector for something as rare as that, so he's probably not sold it yet.'

'It might be risky for Mum,' Desmond said. 'What if Paul is there, and turns nasty? She mustn't go on her own. Make sure Len goes with her.'

Kathleen had an idea. 'Ask her to phone Cecilia,' she said to Jane. 'If she and Les can meet Laura at the flat, he won't let any harm come to them. I'll give you the number.' She reached for her handbag.

Desmond looked puzzled. 'Who is Les?' he asked.

Aunt Peggy laughed. 'I think he's called her bodyguard,' she said. 'And he's big enough to take on anyone.'

'Is that the guy you were telling me about?' Desmond asked Kathleen.

She nodded.

'Then let's hope he's available. I'll feel much better if Mum and Len have got someone like him with them. There's no knowing what Paul might do if he's taken more drugs.'

The phone was constantly in use for a while. Eventually, Jane came back into the room and sat down. First she looked at Kathleen.

'They are all at the flat,' she said. 'And you were right. Laura found the painting hidden at the back of his wardrobe. So she phoned the police.'

'Was Paul there?' Kathleen whispered.

'Not exactly.' Jane's face was troubled as she looked at Desmond.

'What has happened?' he asked.

'He came back before the police arrived, but some of his villainous friends were also lying in wait for him. They dragged him into an alley and beat him up — quite badly.'

Kathleen felt sick. 'Have they killed him?' she asked, almost afraid to hear the answer.

'They might have done if Les hadn't heard a noise and gone down to investigate. As soon as they saw him, they ran off.'

'Sounds like he got his just deserts,' Uncle Nobby commented.

'Actually, he's in hospital,' Jane said. 'But there's a policeman sitting by his bedside.' She looked at Kathleen with a grim smile. 'I don't think he's going to wriggle out of this one quite so easily.'

23

'Hail Mary, full of grace . . . ' Kathleen murmured as she recited the rosary. One after the other, she said the words, but that was all they were. Just words. The Gloria completed, she sat silently in her bedroom, wondering why she still felt nothing.

Her period had started a few days ago. Never before had she welcomed it so. At least one of her fears had been laid to rest. She felt grateful. Of course she felt grateful. But her heart was still tightly locked in a wall of numbness. And she didn't know how to find the key.

It was Christmas Eve, for goodness sake. This morning Desmond had driven her down to Torquay, to buy one or two gifts to fill the gap in the pile that Sandy had brought down from her flat. After lunch, she had retired to her room to sort and wrap, and read the pile of Christmas cards that Mrs Andrews had given to Sandy. So many good wishes, mainly from friends at chambers. Some with letters — a beautiful one from Charles and Dory Henshaw, and flowers from the florist near her flat. George had sent her the largest card she had ever seen, and said the chambers seemed desolate without her radiant smile. She hadn't realized he could be so poetic, and knew she should be in floods of tears at so much affection — but nothing happened.

Downstairs, Aunt Grace and Aunt Peggy were busy stuffing an enormous turkey, while Nobby and Desmond peeled potatoes, trimmed Brussels sprouts, and filled two huge saucepans with carrots and parsnips. Kathleen had offered to help, and promptly been banned from the kitchen. In the lounge, Jane's children were adding a hopeful item on their letter to Santa, at the same time constantly reminding Aunt Grace not to forget to hang their stockings on the mantelpiece once the fire had died down, and when could they help prepare the tray with a glass of sherry and mince pie for Santa, and carrots for the reindeer?

It was the time of celebration for the birth of our Lord, goodwill towards all, and her favourite time of the year — usually. So why couldn't she feel the warmth of this very special day? She had been raped and injured, it was true, but she was alive, and Paul was in gaol, awaiting trial for the theft of the painting. So, hopefully, justice would be done. But it was as though he had killed something within her, created a rift between his nephew and Kathleen, and she was afraid it would never be healed, despite Desmond's assurances that he was prepared to give her all the time in the world.

Auntie Nell knocked on the door. She carried a tray with a cup of tea, two mince pies, fresh from the oven, and an envelope, addressed to Kathleen. It contained a Christmas card and note from Audrey Barnes, thanking Kathleen for the coat. She had never owned such a handsome coat before, she said, and would wear it on Christmas Day when they took the children to her mum's in Dawlish.

'It came through the letterbox just now,' Auntie Nell said, obviously curious.

Kathleen handed her the letter and card.

'At least there's been one good thing come out of this awful business,' Auntie Nell commented, after she had read them.

'Well, I hope it brings her luck. I asked Aunt Grace not to mention the attack, in case Mrs Barnes might be afraid the coat was jinxed.'

Auntie Nell shook her head. 'Grace told me that she'd made some excuse about you putting on a bit of weight, so it was too tight for you.' She put the letter back into the envelope, and sighed. 'I am so sorry I wasn't there to look after you. I'm sure Laura was wonderful, but a girl really needs her mother at a time like that.' She took Kathleen's hand. 'I know I'm not your real mother, Kathleen, but I always look on you as my daughter, and I like to think that you regard me as the next best thing to a proper mum.'

Kathleen gazed at the older woman with affection.

'You have always been a proper mum to me,' she said. 'I feel blessed to have had two mothers and two fathers to love me. And I hope you realize just how much I love you and Uncle Fred.' She frowned. 'Does it bother you that I don't call you Mam and Da'?'

'Oh, no, dear. Fred and I talked about it when you first came to live with us, and we agreed it wouldn't be fair to ask you to do that. If you'd been a toddler it might have been different, but you were old enough to have many happy memories of your parents.' She leaned forward and kissed Kathleen's cheek. 'You've given us years of happiness, and we're very proud of you. Our only regret is that we couldn't stop this terrible thing happening to you.' She wiped away a tear. 'Now, do you want to keep these cards around your bedroom, dear, or shall we take them downstairs and put them with the others?'

Kathleen thought for a moment, realizing what she had to do.

'Actually, Auntie Nell, I'm going out. Could you take them downstairs for me, please? I expect the children will enjoy doing them.'

'If you like — but it's almost dark, and the shops will be closing soon. Do you really have to go out?'

'I need to walk and think for a bit before I go to church.'

'But I thought the service wasn't until midnight?'

'It is, but I must go to confession first.'

'Oh, yes. I'd forgotten. You're not going on your own, are you?'

'Don't worry, I'll be fine. It's not far.'

'Good job you've got that lovely fur coat to wear. Don't know what I'd do without mine, this weather. Did you know Jane bought it for me in Torquay?'

'Yes, I remember.'

Five minutes later, Kathleen found Desmond waiting for her in the hall.

'I really will be all right on my own,' she protested.

'I know. But I want to be with you. We don't have to talk, but you may need a sounding board.'

'That's what the priest is for,' she said, gently.

'Oh, I thought he just sat and listened, and then told you what you had to do to redeem yourself.'

Kathleen would have preferred to be alone, but she hadn't the energy to argue. They walked in silence, past houses where the curtains were not yet drawn, revealing twinkling Christmas trees and colourful garlands strung across ceilings. Not many people about, just a few hurrying home with their last-minute purchases, calling 'Merry Christmas' to each other before they closed their front doors.

The notice on the church door gave details of various services, and times when the priest would be available for confession.

'Not for another half-hour,' Kathleen said.

'It's not really worth going home,' Desmond commented, looking around. 'Why don't we have a cup of tea in that little café on the corner? It's still open.'

The woman pouring from a huge enamel teapot looked at them curiously, probably wondering why they weren't at home this late on Christmas Eve, Kathleen thought. They were the only customers.

'Kathleen . . . ' Desmond sounded hesitant. 'I know I said I wouldn't talk unless you wanted me to, but something is bugging me.'

'Oh? What's that?'

'Well, you are the most innocent person I know. Why on earth do you need to go to confession? You can't possibly have any sins to forgive.'

For a long moment she stared at him, wondering if she would be able to explain. A priest heard many different sins all the time, but would Desmond understand what was troubling her? It was so complicated, and yet such an unforgivable sin.

'I think I am losing my faith,' she said, in a low voice. 'In fact, I think I have already lost it.'

He didn't answer at first, just sipped his tea, thoughtfully. Then he said, 'Is it because you prayed for help when Paul attacked you, and feel your prayers weren't answered?'

She nodded.

'Well, that's enough to shake anyone's faith.' He thought a little longer, and then said: 'Can you remember exactly how you prayed?'

Uncertain what he really meant, she shook her head.

'The words,' he prompted. 'Do you remember the words?'

It pained her to remember that day, but she tried.

'I was stunned by the blow to my head. But I think I asked the Holy Mother for courage, and to help me get through the . . . ' her words trailed off.

He reached across the table as though to take her hands, and then drew back. 'Kathleen,' he said slowly. 'I want you to listen very carefully to what I have to say.'

Curious, she waited.

'We had a wonderful chaplain at school,' Desmond went on. 'And he told us to think more carefully about the words when we prayed, as very often our prayers were being answered, although maybe not in the way we expected. But it would always be the right answer.' He frowned at the memory. 'After my father was killed, I used to pray that nothing would ever take my mother away from me. When she met Len, I was a right little so and so, trying to come between them.'

Kathleen remembered overhearing a row at Jane's twenty-first birthday party.

'Then I grew up,' Desmond continued, 'and realized that Len wasn't going to take Mum away from me. All he wanted was to make her happy, just as I did.'

Kathleen thought deeply for a long time.

'I think I do know what you mean,' she said. 'Immediately I had prayed, I lost consciousness. So I was spared a great deal of misery.'

'And you have been so courageous about it. You have no idea how proud I am of you.'

There were so many thoughts tumbling around her head that Kathleen could not speak. She looked at her watch.

'It's time to go to church,' she said.

'Even though you have nothing to confess?'

Her smile was weak. 'Even though you think I have nothing to confess.'

The church was peaceful, but with an air of anticipation of the very special Mass to come. Two women put final touches to the swags of holly and ivy entwined around the pillars, and an unseen organist practised an anthem.

While they waited, Kathleen studied the crib in front of the altar, and thought about Mary, and the many ordeals she had suffered. Kathleen's experience was nothing in comparison. Then it was her turn to go into the confessional.

The priest was compassionate, but she found herself thinking about Desmond's words, and those of his school chaplain. It was as though a great weight was being slowly lifted from her heart, and she knew she was taking deep breaths.

'What did he say?' Desmond asked, as they left the church.

'He said I hadn't lost my faith, just mislaid it, and to keep praying.'

Suddenly she knew what was going to happen, and began to run, faster and faster, with Desmond trying to catch up. She didn't stop until she reached the railings that edged the cliffs. Gasping for breath, she clung to the railings, feeling the key unlock her heart, and the tears escaping — slowly at first, and then an unstoppable torrent.

As Desmond reached her side, she held out her arms.

'Hold me,' she sobbed. 'Just hold me.'

Kathleen had no idea how long they stood there, alone on the cliff top, while she wept as she had never wept before, deep cleansing tears. Desmond made no attempt to stop her outburst, just held her close, wrapping his overcoat around her. It was as though the warmth of his love filled every part of her, body and soul. Now she knew, without a doubt, that she wanted to spend the rest of her life with this wonderful man.

Eventually, she raised her head and groped in her pocket for a handkerchief.

'You might need a bigger one,' Desmond said, producing a clean handkerchief from his overcoat pocket. 'Let's sit in that shelter for a moment, shall we? It's out of the wind.'

She didn't mind where she went, as long as Desmond was next to her, holding her in his arms. Idly, she looked out to sea, watching the lights of a ship break the darkness, and wondered if it would be in a home port for Christmas.

'Warmer now?' Desmond asked.

'I didn't think I would ever feel this warm again.' She lifted her head from his shoulder and gazed into his face. 'It was a terrifying thought, and I didn't know what to do.'

'Did the priest help?'

'Partly, but mainly it was you.' In the dim light from a nearby street-lamp she could see he was smiling. 'I don't know how long I would have gone on like that if it hadn't been for you.'

'I think the tears helped.'

'Oh, yes. I feel drained, but I also feel I shall recover from this.'

'Of course you will. It will take time, but we'll work at it together.' He pulled up the collar of her coat. 'And I meant what I said, about giving you all the time in the world. The last thing I would ever want is to cause you any more pain.'

'You could never do that.'

'Not intentionally, but let's put it this way. I want to marry you more than anything in the world, but it must be when you are ready, my darling.' He hugged her closer, looking up at a brightly shining star. 'And I will always have a dream, that one day perhaps we'll be filling stockings on Christmas Eve.'

She drew back. Children. Of course he wanted children. It had been her dream, too. But what if . . . ?

'What's wrong?' He looked concerned.

'It's just that too much has happened in such a short time. I can't take it all in, and I can't think beyond tonight,' she said.

'Of course you can't. You've been on a roller-coaster. So if I ever seem to be rushing you, I want you to promise you'll haul my lead in.'

'Thank you.' She knew he would keep to his word.

Desmond broke the silence. 'Did anyone tell you that Mum rang while we were out shopping?' he asked.

'No. How is she?'

'Not too good It's been a tough week, one way and another. And Paul is still making life difficult for everyone.'

'What do you mean?'

'He's denying all involvement in the theft of the painting. Said the other guys must have stolen it and planted it in his flat to frame him because he owed them money.'

Kathleen was angry.

'If he pleads not guilty, poor Miss Dawson will have to give evidence. As if she hasn't suffered enough. What about the drug-dealers?'

'They seem to have disappeared from the face of the earth.'

Kathleen's legal training helped her realize the implication of this.

'Then they can only charge him with possession,' she said. 'I doubt whether there was enough cocaine in the flat to warrant a charge of dealing.'

'Unless the cameras turn up, complete with drugs. But that would be too much to hope for.'

'So he will get away with it — again.'

'Not if you take him to court.' Desmond's voice was quiet.

'No!' Kathleen jumped to her feet. 'I can't. I really can't.' She began to weep again. 'I know the way the prosecution works. It would feel as though I was in the dock, not him. Every sordid detail would be read out and questioned. Please, Desmond, don't tell me it's the right thing to do. I know that, but I can't do it.' Kathleen was trembling from head to foot.

Desmond was on his feet, holding her close. 'Shush, my darling,' he soothed. 'I do understand, honestly.'

'I don't think many people will understand. Everyone expects me to go to the police.'

'Because they want to see him punished for

what he did to you. No one wants to cause you more pain.'

'But the pain would be more than I can bear. I just want to put it all behind me, and get on with my life.'

'If that's what you want, I'll back you up. OK?'

As she shuddered a small sigh of relief, Desmond took the handkerchief from her hand and gently dabbed at her cheeks.

'I think we ought to go home now,' he said. 'You'll want to clean up a bit before we go back to church, I expect.'

She nodded. 'What shall I tell the others?' she sniffed.

'Would you like me to explain that you're feeling much better now? And if Sandy or Nobby want to wish you a happy christmas with a friendly hug, that's all right. Will that do?'

'Oh, yes please. What is it about you?' she wondered. 'You always seem to know exactly the right thing to say.'

'It's easy when I love someone as much as I love you, Kathleen O'Connor.' He smiled down into her face. 'Would you consider it rushing things too much if we pretend that there is a bunch of mistletoe hanging from the roof of this shelter?' he asked, a little breathlessly.

'Do you mean that mistletoe just above your head?' she murmured, as she stood on tiptoe.

She had forgotten how warm and loving Desmond's kisses were. It was a gentle kiss, but she felt sure that one day she would not mind at all if his kisses were more urgent.

All they needed was time.

24

The courtroom was hot, stuffy, and crowded. The theft of a painting by J.M.W. Turner had attracted a great deal of interest, from art collectors as well as the media.

Kathleen hadn't attended the earlier days of the trial, partly because she had been so busy with a complicated fraud case in another court, and partly because she couldn't bring herself to be in the same room as Paul. But today was the closing day, and she knew she had to be there, to see and hear for herself.

The Hon. Julian Mountford still applying unsuccessfully for silk, was acting for Paul, and Merrick Soames for the prosecution, aided by the increasingly competent Michael Latham. Charles Henshaw QC sat on the Bench, resplendent in his new scarlet robes and full wig.

Kathleen knew that Miss Dawson had already given her evidence, and a friend from the Women's Institute had travelled to London with Miss Dawson to add some weight to her testimony. Mrs Lovelace lived on the road to Exeter, a mile or so from Miss Dawson's cottage, and she suffered from insomnia. Thus it was that she was heating some milk when she heard a car roaring up the hill out of the village. Curious as to who might be travelling at this hour of the night, 2.45 by her kitchen clock, she drew back the curtains, just in time to see one of those sporty little cars racing by. No, she didn't recognize the driver and no, she hadn't been able to read the number plate from that angle. But the Coach and Horses inn along the road had all their security lights full on, and she was sure it was red, probably an MG. Oh yes, there was something wrong with the gearbox. How did she know? Because she had driven and maintained all manner of army vehicles throughout the war, and knew that when a car made that awful noise changing gear, it was usually the gearbox.

Mr Merrick Soames produced a mechanic's report that Mr West's car did, indeed, have a faulty gearbox, but the counsel for defence argued that there was insufficient evidence that the defendant had been driving the car, or that it was his car, or that it had come from Miss Dawson's cottage.

Kathleen was unsure which way the jury might go, given the evidence, until a surprise witness appeared. An art dealer, he recognized the defendant as a man who had brought a photograph of a Turner painting to his gallery, asking if he might know a private collector who could be interested. The art dealer thought it must be a forgery, particularly when Mr West said an elderly aunt, who had lost the provenance, had bequeathed it to him. The reason he had not reported the facts to the police was because he was leaving that day to tour Europe for several months, collecting paintings, and it was not until he returned that he learned of the trial. No, there was no reason why he should have suspected it was stolen. Word usually got around pretty quickly on the grapevine when a painting as valuable as this went missing, but he had heard nothing until be began to set up the exhibition for his latest protégé, one of the new school and an artist of outstanding merit who — yes, I understand, your honour — not entirely relevant.

The summing up by Merrick Soames had been the best she had ever heard him give. By contrast, Julian's was pathetic, and when Mr Justice Henshaw addressed the jury, although he warned them of the risks of confusing circumstantial with factual evidence, he also pointed out that there was considerable factual evidence in this case, which must be taken into account.

Kathleen knew what he meant. Paul's fingerprints were all over the frame; he hadn't told the police of the mysterious appearance of the painting in his flat; he knew the layout of the cottage; he was heavily in debt; a photograph of the painting was found in his brief case — which he claimed he took as a souvenir; and the evidence of the art dealer could not have been more damning.

When the jury retired, Kathleen sat still for a moment, reflecting on the events of the last few months. The hospital tests had been unpleasant but, thank goodness, negative. There had been severe internal bruising, which would heal in time, but nothing critical, and no reason why she should not be able to conceive a child.

Jane was also back to her normal state of health, constantly chasing the twins, who were determined to crawl in different directions at the same time.

Laura had been very ill, on the verge of a nervous breakdown. Although she was recovering, she and Len had decided to sell the pub and restaurant, and would soon be moving to a small bungalow in Maiden-combe, not far from the guesthouse, so they could ease the workload of Peggy and Joe in the busy season. Laura hadn't attended any of the days of Paul's trial.

As for Desmond, he had at last achieved his ambition to be a headmaster, and in

September he would be taking up his new post in Middlesex.

Everyone had tried to persuade Kathleen to charge Paul with rape, but she remained adamant. Looking down on him from the back of the visitors' gallery, she felt nothing. And that was how she wanted it to be. A bad dream that she never wanted to think about.

'Shall we try to get a coffee?' Desmond stood up.

'I don't think they'll be out for very long, but yes, let's try.'

'Well, if anyone can take us through the crush, it will be Les. Just look at him.'

They watched the burly figure hustling Cecilia through the crowd, glancing over his shoulder, signalling to Kathleen and Desmond to follow him. And he was successful.

'It looks pretty cut and dried to me,' Cecilia commented, as they found a quiet corner. 'Do you think he saw us?'

'No,' Kathleen said. 'We're too far back and partly screened by a pillar.' Suddenly, she saw a familiar figure searching the faces in the crowd.

'George,' she called. 'Are you looking for me?'

'Yes, Miss O'Connor.' He nodded a greeting to her companions, and then went on, gleefully: 'Got some news I thought you'd like to hear. Two of those cameras have turned up.'

'Where?'

'There's a known fence out Kilburn way. The police were after some stolen jewellery, and turned his place over. What should they find but two cameras with a nice little cache of the white stuff tucked away. I'll lay evens that fingerprints belonging to you know who are all over it.'

'That's great news,' enthused Desmond. 'Do you know what happened to the other things stolen from Paul?'

'Already sold. But they wouldn't be workable, if they were stuffed. Whoever bought them would probably have been scared stiff, and dumped the lot. They might come to light eventually.'

Les grinned. 'So, whatever happens today, they can nail that bastard on the drugs charge as well? Begging your pardon, ladies.'

'Oh, yes.' George's grin equalled that of the bodyguard. 'Talk about made my day.' He looked at Kathleen. 'You all right, miss? It must have been a bit of an ordeal for you, seeing him again.'

'Not quite as bad as I expected, but thank you, George, especially for coming to tell me about the cameras. Are you going back to chambers now?'

'Reckon I'll hang about a bit longer, just to see how long that scumbag gets. I'll make a couple of phone calls, then slip into court when the jury is back.'

As soon as it was announced that the jury was returning, Kathleen and her friends went back to the gallery. This time, they sat in the centre of the row and, as the court rose for the entrance of Mr Justice Henshaw, Paul glanced around. He seemed very much in control, almost like an actor on centre stage. Then he looked up at the gallery, and noticed Kathleen. He bowed slightly, with a sardonic grin, and his expression was so arrogant that she gasped.

Desmond had dropped something and was bending over, but he realized something was wrong as he stood up.

'What is it, darling? You're terribly pale,' he asked.

'Look at him. He's taunting me.' She clutched her throat. 'He really thinks I'm still afraid of him.' Suddenly, Kathleen made up her mind. 'I'll do it,' she said. 'He shouldn't have smirked.'

Desmond knew what she meant, and squeezed her hand.

Paul was still staring at her, with a look of utter contempt, which faltered as the light flashed from the diamond ring on the third finger of Kathleen's left hand. The person in front of Desmond sat down, and Paul frowned as he realized it was his nephew with Kathleen.

For a brief moment, there seemed to be only the three of them in court, Paul in the dock, Desmond and Kathleen standing together, defying him ever to hurt them again.

After the shuffling of a courtroom of people sitting down, came the hush that always precedes a verdict. As the clerk repeated the words of the jury foreman, some of the reporters rushed out of court to phone the news to their papers. The others waited to hear what the sentence would be.

Mr Justice Henshaw made a note, and then sat back in his chair, staring at Paul. Kathleen had never seen him look so stern.

At last he spoke.

'You have been found guilty of a dreadful crime, Mr West,' he said. 'And I agree totally with the unanimous verdict of the jury. You caused terror to the heart of an innocent lady, merely to satisfy your own needs. You have lied profoundly, causing her even more anguish. In my opinion, someone as ruthless and heartless as you should be prevented from causing any more harm for as long as possible.' He looked down at his notes and he sentenced Paul to seven years in prison.

The colour drained from Paul's face, and his knees appeared to buckle as the two officers led him back down to the cell.

Cecilia grinned. 'I was hoping he might put on the black cap,' she said. 'Must go, dears. I've got a show tonight. I'll phone you.' With a kiss, she was gone, together with the ever-loyal Les.

Desmond held Kathleen's hands. 'Did you mean what you said?' he asked.

'If he hadn't gloated, I might have felt differently, but not now.' Her voice held conviction. 'Yes, my darling, I meant what I said.'

'It won't be easy.'

'I know. But I have to be strong, not only for myself, but for Jane, and Gloria Benson, and the Italian girl.'

'And goodness knows how many others.'

'Exactly. You were right, and it took that horrible expression on his face to make me realize he mustn't ever do it again to someone else.'

'And we'll all be there for you, you know that, don't you.'

Her smile was a little wobbly. 'With you there, I know I can do it.'

The judge's clerk was waiting with a message for Kathleen.

'Mr Justice Henshaw asked if you and your fiancé would care to have tea in his chambers, Miss O'Connor.'

'Thank you. Please tell the judge that we are delighted to accept.'

She slipped her arm through Desmond's. 'You know, when he made that speech just now, it was as though he was thinking of me.'

'That thought occurred to me as well. And I'm sure he'll be cock-a-hoop that another judge will be able to add a few years on to his sentence. I can't tell you how relieved I am that my brute of an uncle is going to be unable to hurt any more innocent victims for quite a long time.'

Kathleen shuddered at a brief memory of Paul's violence when he attacked her.

'Oh, yes.' Breathing a sigh of her own relief, she smiled at Desmond. 'Come on,' she said. 'Mr Justice Henshaw likes his tea very hot and not brewed for too long.'

Linking arms, they followed the clerk to the judge's chambers.

We do hope that you have enjoyed reading this large print book.

Did you know that all of our titles are available for purchase?

We publish a wide range of high quality large print books including:
Romances, Mysteries, Classics
General Fiction
Non Fiction and Westerns

Special interest titles available in large print are:
The Little Oxford Dictionary
Music Book
Song Book
Hymn Book
Service Book

Also available from us courtesy of Oxford University Press:
Young Readers' Dictionary
(large print edition)
Young Readers' Thesaurus
(large print edition)

For further information or a free brochure, please contact us at:
Ulverscroft Large Print Books Ltd.,
The Green, Bradgate Road, Anstey,
Leicester, LE7 7FU, England.
Tel: (00 44) 0116 236 4325
Fax: (00 44) 0116 234 0205

A GIFT OF TIME

Barbara Murphy

After the death of her daughter and her husband's desertion, Beth feels as though everything has been taken from her. But her life changes drastically when she moves to a smaller house on a new development. Firstly, suspecting that her new home is haunted, she uncovers a disturbing story. She feels the only way to exorcise this ghost is to write about it . . . Then there is Dr Tom Masterson, who has moved nearby with his two daughters and an invalid wife. Beth and Tom grow closer each day and Tom reveals that his marriage is in name only. But Beth is not going to find a relationship with him easy . . .

OLIVIA'S GARDEN

Patricia Fawcett

Olivia, Anna and Rosie form an unlikely schoolgirl friendship. Olivia is the beauty and the dreamer; plain Anna's future career as a doctor is already mapped out; whilst bubbly, flame-haired Rosie simply wants to marry a millionaire. Leaving school, they lose touch with each other until, years later, Olivia meets Rosie once more. Then Anna's brother Ben, himself a doctor, seeks Olivia's help with a family crisis. The happy result is that she and Ben are drawn together. However, she is shocked by Anna's stubbornness, dismayed by Rosie's refusal to speak to her again after a bitter row and rocked by a personal tragedy.

LIARS AND SAINTS

Maile Meloy

Yvette Santerre met the photographer on the beach as her children played, and he offered to take their picture for her husband, away at war. When he arrived at her house with his camera, the last thing she expected was that he would try to kiss her. But that kiss will haunt her family for generations . . .

OF SILENCE AND SLOW TIME

Catherine Bruton

August 1914, German Occupied France. When twelve-year-old Amelie stumbles across an injured British soldier in the woods, her family keeps him hidden from the enemy. But the presence of Captain James Winter starts to create suspicion and resentment in the village when he embarks upon an affair with Amelie's sister and attracts the attention of another local girl. As James's activities come under close scrutiny, Amelie becomes an unwitting accomplice. In early 1915, James disappears. Seventeen years later his son comes to the village to find out what happened to his father. Now the secrets of the past look certain to come out . . .

SAFE HARBOUR

Janice Graham

As Canon of the Parisian cathedral of St John's, Crispin Wakefield has attracted a devoted following, but also the jealousy of his Dean. And the expensive indulgences of his wife and daughters are threatening financial ruin. Into this turmoil steps Julia Kramer, international actress and childhood friend from Crispin's family home back in Kansas. With her partner Jona frequently away, Julia is drawn into the cocoon of Crispin's family and his beloved cathedral. Deeply indebted, Julia uses her celebrity and wealth to promote Crispin's career. When Jona's business dealings lead him into deadly waters, Julia turns to Crispin for support, igniting vicious gossip . . .

A ROPE OF SAND

Elsie Burch Donald

A chance encounter in a French town brings dark memories flooding back to fifty-five-year-old Kate. As a student in the 1950s, she'd been one of five girls from Sweet Briar College, Virginia, to take a life-changing grand tour of Europe. Flung headlong into the dangerous freedom of the old world, Kate and her friends giddily soak up all that's on offer. When, one by one, three intriguing but very different young men latch on to the party, what seems to be a privileged and sophisticated clique is formed. But nobody is quite as they appear, and as facades crumble, the grand tour will prove eye-opening in ways the girls couldn't possibly have imagined.